HOMESPUN HOLIDAY

PATCHWORK MYSTERIES

HOMESPUN HOLIDAY

KELLY ANN RILEY

Guideposts
New York, New York

www.guideposts.com
(800) 932-2145
Guideposts Books & Inspirational Media

Cover design by Wendy Bass
Cover illustration by Joyce Patti
Interior design by Lorie Pagnozzi
Typeset by Aptara

Printed and bound in the United States of America
10 9 8 7 6 5 4 3 2 1

DEDICATION

To Rick,

who makes my holiday dreams come true,

again and again.

HOMESPUN
HOLIDAY

CHAPTER ONE

Sarah Hart scooped more golden brown cookies onto the waiting cooling racks. The granite countertops in her daughter-in-law's kitchen were laden with pinwheels, pecan tarts, gingersnaps, and oatmeal spice cookies. The afternoon baking session with her twin granddaughters Amy and Audrey had been more than productive.

Sarah glanced out the window. An icy wind gently rattled the windowpane as it whipped down Bristol Street, swirling the few remaining leaves off the ground. Temperatures were supposed to drop into the teens, but the twins and Sarah had been snug indoors baking all afternoon. After a break for a quick soup supper, they were finishing up the sugar cookies while Sarah's son Jason strung up Christmas lights outside on the 120-year-old Victorian, and his wife Maggie worked on bookkeeping for her antique store in the dining room.

Sarah's cell phone rang, tearing Sarah's gaze from the window.

"Hello?"

"Oh, I'm so relieved you answered." It was Martha Maplethorpe, Sarah's best friend. "Something's happened, and I need to talk. Where are you? You didn't pick up your house phone."

Sarah paused, spatula poised over the cookie sheet. The stress in her usually cheerful friend's voice tripped her heart into overdrive. "What's wrong? Did something happen with Ernie?"

"No, no, everyone's fine, although I may be developing an ulcer. Where are you?"

"I'm over at Jason and Maggie's."

"Perfect! I need to talk to Maggie too. I'll be there in fifteen minutes."

"Okay, but—" the line went dead, and Sarah stared at the phone with dismay. What could be so urgent to make Martha venture out on such a cold winter evening?

"Who was that?" Amy asked. Sarah's granddaughter sat at the kitchen table surrounded by small bowls of colored frosting. Lime green stained the tip of one of her blonde braids, and the blue frosting smudged on her cheek matched her eyes.

"Mrs. Maplethorpe. She'll be coming over in a few minutes."

Sarah surveyed the kitchen. Despite the growing disaster area around what the girls had designated the decorating station, the scene warmed Sarah's heart. No amount of dirty dishes could deter her from cherishing this evening with her granddaughters. If only her daughter Jenna and her boys were here too.

"One more batch to go. You girls are doing great," Sarah said, then turned at a loud sound behind her.

"I hate Christmas!" Audrey said, staring at the yellow mass oozing from the overturned egg carton on the pine flooring.

"Are you upset because you broke a few eggs?" Sarah asked. "Don't worry about it. We'll get it cleaned up."

"You don't hate Christmas," Amy said with a roll of her eyes.

"I can hate Christmas if I want to." Audrey snatched a wad of paper towels. Angry tears glazed her eyes before she turned away.

"Can I have your presents then?" Amy flashed a big grin.

"Amy," Sarah cautioned with a slight shake of her head. What had gotten into everyone tonight? Maggie and Jason had seemed tense during supper. Martha, who was perpetually sunny, had sounded ominous on the phone. And now, the twins were getting at each other.

"Can you check to see if that batch on the counter is cool enough to frost?" Sarah asked Amy.

"Okay." Amy set her paintbrush down and skirted around the mess Audrey was trying to clean up.

Sarah grabbed a mixing bowl and squatted down by Audrey. The twelve-year-old's miserable expression tugged at her heart. She wanted to pull the girl in for a close hug, but she wasn't sure Audrey would welcome it right now.

"What's the matter, dear?" she asked in a gentle tone.

Audrey shrugged, her focus on picking up the broken egg shells.

"It might help to talk about it."

Audrey shook her head. She tossed the shells in the bin under the sink, and after a few moments blurted out, "It's so boring here!"

Sarah paused in her cleanup efforts. Boring? The last two weeks had been frantic with activities as the twins finished up their school semester, attended practices and the school Christmas program, caroled with the youth group, shopped for their family, decorated the Christmas tree, and now baked dozens of cookies.

"Okay, I think it's time for a break and to sample some of your hard work. Why don't you girls sit at the table, and I'll get the milk." Sarah straightened and dumped the paper towels into the garbage can. She grabbed a milk carton from the refrigerator and poured two glasses.

Amy bit the top off a Christmas tree. "Yum. These sugar cookies are the best."

Sarah sat next to Audrey after the girl devoured a couple of cookies and asked, "Is there anything I can do to make things better?"

Audrey took a long swallow of milk and grimaced. "Nobody can. Everything's changed. Christmas doesn't feel like Christmas anymore. We used to have so much fun. We'd go down to Grandma and Grandpa's house near Newport and watch the boat parade with all the lights and sing Christmas songs. And I miss shopping at the Galleria with my friends and visiting the reindeer at the zoo—"

"Every time Audrey gets a text from Madison, she gets grumpy," Amy said.

"I do not!" Audrey narrowed her eyes at her sister. "Were you looking at my phone again?"

Amy shrugged and licked a drop of orange frosting off her fingertip. "I thought it was mine."

Sarah slid her arm around Audrey's shoulder before the quarrel escalated. "I'm sorry you're feeling bad, honey. I've lived in Maple Hill all my life, so I don't know exactly how you feel, but I imagine missing your friends and grandparents is really hard, especially at Christmas."

"Like you miss Grandpa Gerry?" Amy asked.

"Yes, something like that," Sarah answered, surprised at Amy's perceptiveness. Although Sarah still carried the ache of her husband's passing, she didn't discuss her pain with the twins. She only wanted to share happy memories of Gerry.

She gave Audrey's shoulders a squeeze. "I just want you to have a wonderful Christmas. We're going to have fun. You'll see."

Audrey nodded but didn't appear convinced.

Amy picked up a knife and spread soft yellow frosting on a star. "I just wish it'd snow so I can build a snowman and learn to ski. Our first Christmas in New England and no snow. How lame is that?"

Sarah playfully tugged Amy's braid. "Be careful what you wish for. There are some huge storms heading our way. After a month, you'll be so tired of having cold toes, frozen ears, and a red nose, you might be wishing for spring."

"No, I won't." Amy giggled. "I'll wear a hat and scarf. I got new boots too. Did you play in the snow a lot when you were a kid?"

Sarah nodded. "When I was your age, I used to spend hours playing outside. We made snow angels in the park and giant snowmen. But the most fun was sledding. Mrs. Maplethorpe's parents lived at the top of this big hill, and all the neighborhood children used to race down it on our sleds."

"That sounds so cool."

"It was," Sarah said, grinning at the memory of Martha hollering with glee as her sled bounced over the ruts, her long braids flying out behind her. Which reminded her, Martha was on her way over.

"You girls keep frosting. I'm going to tell your mother that Mrs. Maplethorpe is coming for a visit." Sarah pushed open the swinging door to the dining room where Maggie sat at an antique mahogany table. Piles of invoices and receipts surrounded her laptop. She leaned toward the screen, her head propped on one hand as she studied a spreadsheet.

Sarah cleared her throat. "How's it going?"

Maggie straightened in the spindle-backed chair and rubbed her lower back. "Six more days, and the Christmas craziness will be over. I can hardly wait."

"Have sales been going well?"

"Yes. Much better than expected. And I know I shouldn't be complaining. The holidays are terrific for business, but

I feel so behind in *everything*, including the bookkeeping. Maybe next year I'll be able to afford a part-time accountant." She glanced toward the kitchen. "How's the baking marathon progressing?"

"Pretty good. We're almost done. I don't think the girls will want to bake another cookie for months."

"Was that Audrey I heard complaining?"

"Yes, but not about the baking. She said she hated Christmas. Everything is boring."

"Boring?" Maggie let out a short laugh. Her green eyes twinkled. "How can she be bored? They've only been on Christmas break for three days. I thought they'd enjoy some quiet time at home after the big rush of finishing tests and all that work with the Christmas play."

"Apparently not," Sarah said with a small smile. "I think Audrey's missing her friends and the fun you had in California."

"Well, that's understandable. We used to do a lot of things at Christmas. Running here and there. Fun, but it got pretty hectic. Personally, *I'm* looking forward to an old-fashioned, small town Christmas. Jason has some great memories of the holidays here."

Sarah's smile widened. "And I'm so glad you're here to make new memories with me. I just hope the girls will enjoy the change."

"They will," Maggie said confidently. "And if they're bored, they can put their energy to good use and help me down at the store. There are people popping in all the time.

Besides, I'd like to spend more time with them during the break...."

Sarah chuckled. Over the years, she'd watched Martha interacting with her nine grandchildren who all lived in town, and wished her own lived closer. Now that her wish had come true, she planned on enjoying every rambunctious second of their time together, especially their first Christmas in Maple Hill.

"I was going to tell you Martha called a minute ago and said she needed to talk to us about something. I'm sorry. I should've mentioned it right away. She's on her way over," Sarah said as the doorbell rang. "Sounds like she's here. If you're not up to seeing visitors tonight, I can invite her into the kitchen and see what it's all about."

"Oh, no, that's fine. I'm finished working for tonight. Jason should be done with the lights soon too."

Audrey charged past them to the foyer and looked through the peephole. "It's Mrs. Maplethorpe." She flung the door open, letting in a blast of frigid air.

"Hello, hello. Merry almost-Christmas! I hope I'm not intruding," Martha said, clouds puffing out of her mouth with every word.

"Of course not." Maggie smiled. "We're always glad to see you. Come in by the fire. You look frozen." She shut the door behind Martha. "How's your husband doing?"

"Ernie's doing as well as can be expected. Thank you for asking." Martha unwound her orange scarf and unbuttoned her heavy wool overcoat.

"Would you like some cookies? I decorated a whole bunch of them," Amy asked.

"I can see that." Martha laughed. "You have frosting on your ear. It must've been fun."

Amy nodded and grinned as she rubbed her ear.

"There's also hot cocoa if you'd like some." Maggie took Martha's coat and scarf, and hooked them on the stand by the door. "Or I can make fresh coffee."

"Grandma put her secret ingredient in the cocoa," Audrey said. "It's good."

"Well in that case, I'd love to try the cocoa and the cookies." Martha smiled as the girls headed back to the kitchen and then raised her eyebrows at Sarah. "Secret ingredient?"

"If I told people, it wouldn't be a secret, now would it?" Sarah teased as they headed into the parlor.

Martha paused by the heat of the fire before settling on the pale blue camelback sofa by Maggie. "It feels good to sit down. I'm getting plum worn out. I should've been suspicious when Marlene Hobber said organizing the Old Town Holiday Home Tour would be as easy as baking a cake. Have you ever seen Marlene's cakes? They look like those elaborate creations you see on the Food Network." She took a deep breath. "I have a problem."

"Oh?" Sarah raised an eyebrow. "I thought everything was going well with the tour." Martha was this year's director for Maple Hill's annual Old Town Holiday Home Tour. She had convinced Sarah to open her snug, three-bedroom Queen Anne for the occasion, and already had most of the details of the tour planned.

"It was until today, which brings me to why I'm here." Martha leaned forward, rubbing her hands on her navy slacks. "The pipes in the Nelsons' laundry room burst while they were at church this morning, and flooded the entire downstairs. They're going to have to rip up all the carpets and move the furniture into storage."

"How awful. Is there anything we can do to help them?" Sarah asked.

Martha waved a dismissive hand. "I'm sure the offer will be appreciated, but they've already hired a company to do the work. Meanwhile, they've decided to visit relatives in Florida for Christmas, which is why I need to ask a huge favor, Maggie."

Sarah sensed what was coming. She tried to catch her friend's attention, but Martha's gaze was focused on Maggie.

"We have five homes participating in the tour already, and the Nelson house was going to be number six. I know this is short notice, but would you and Jason consider taking the Nelsons' place and opening your home for the tour?"

"Cool!" Amy said, coming into the room carrying a plate of cookies. Audrey trailed with a steaming mug. "Our house will be famous."

"Whoa, wait just a moment." Maggie clasped her hands together. She blew out a deep breath. "Mrs. Maplethorpe, I'm so flattered you asked to include us, and I'd love to help, but as you can see my house isn't ready for anything... extravagant."

"But you have such a lovely home. Great lines and structure. A classic Victorian. And your house is in the perfect location so I won't have to fiddle with the order of the homes on the tour."

"But we're in the process of remodeling." Maggie gestured toward the hall where paint cans and drop cloths partially covered the scratched hardwood floors. "And the mess is worse in other parts of the house. We're still replacing tile in the downstairs bathroom."

Sarah said quietly to Martha, "Maybe we should let Maggie think about it for a while."

"Nobody will mind a work in progress," Martha went on, oblivious to Sarah's hint. "People will just be thrilled to get a glimpse inside this lovely home. Besides, you can limit the tour to only the rooms you want to be seen. I've been in your kitchen before, and it's delightful. You have wonderful taste. With some minor decorations through the rest of the downstairs, it'll be fine."

Maggie paused. "Well...I suppose that's possible. But people will still need to come in here, and there isn't anything I can do about this wall." Maggie pointed behind her to the wall above the couch. A dark, rusty water stain ran down the plaster, which was riddled with holes and deep scratches. "We're waiting for the contractor to come give us an estimate on replastering before we decide how to fix it."

The front door swung open, and Jason walked in with several strands of Christmas lights wound over one arm. "These aren't any good. I think one of the sockets is broken. Luckily the previous owner left behind a box of lights in the attic, but they still only covered two-thirds of the house. I didn't realize how much bigger this house is compared to the one in California."

Audrey wrinkled her freckled nose at the old-fashioned colored bulbs. "We had white twinkly lights in California. They looked like icicles. I liked them better."

"Well, it doesn't hurt to try something different, Audrey. These are nice too." Jason said in a merry tone. He looked up from examining a bulb and noticed Martha on the couch. He pulled the wool cap off his dark hair. "Hello, Mrs. Maplethorpe. I'm sorry, I didn't mean to be rude. How are you?"

"I'm fine, thank you, and you're not being rude, just a busy husband and father." She smiled at him. "I'm afraid I've been badgering your wife into helping us with the home tour." Martha repeated her sales pitch to Jason. "It's really a lot of fun and a great way to widen your social circle. The exposure will be good for both your businesses."

Jason's face settled into what Maggie called his "court face." Over the last couple of months, Sarah had worried about the couple, with Maggie's heavy workload and Jason's law practice's slow growth, but things had been going well lately. She hoped Martha hadn't tweaked a nerve with her request.

"And remember, it's for a worthy cause," Martha added. "Half the profits from the tour and all of the other little fund-raisers we're having will go to the Children's Home. I know this is an imposition, but I'm in a bind. Sarah and I already have our homes in the tour, otherwise I'd use one of us."

Jason grinned. "If you were arguing a case in a court-room, I'd sure hate to be on the opposing side."

"So, you'll do it?" Martha asked.

Jason shrugged. "It's up to Maggie. Whatever she wants is fine by me."

"We'll help, Mom. We can do this as a family," Amy said, elbowing Audrey who nodded. "You'll see, it'll be so much fun."

"Well I suppose we could clean up most of the remodel-ing mess," Maggie said, her resistance obviously weakening. "But what about this wall? We won't be able to fix that, will we, Jason?"

"Not before the tour," he answered. "And we really shouldn't spend any more money on decorations."

Since Maggie seemed okay with the direction they were moving, Sarah piped in. "I still have lots of old decorations in my cellar. You're welcome to them. This morning I lent our manger to the church for their nativity scene, since theirs broke, but there's still the old Santa's sleigh you and your father built. There might be extra lights too."

She turned to her daughter-in-law, giving her a supportive smile. "And Maggie, don't worry about the wall. I have an idea."

"Are you sure you want to do this?" Martha asked as she trudged up the stairs to Sarah's second floor. "I can't imagine your living room at Christmas without that beautiful quilt hanging on the wall."

"I wouldn't have thought to lend it to Maggie if you hadn't tried to convince her to be in the home tour." Sarah grinned over her shoulder. "The store has been so swamped with customers lately, I'm amazed Maggie accepted."

Martha froze, a hand over her heart. "I'm so sorry. I guess I might have been a little too pushy. Why didn't you stop me?"

Sarah chuckled. "I tried, but you were like a force of nature. Unstoppable. But I agree with you. I think they'll have fun doing the tour. It'll give them a chance to meet more of the community." And she hoped it would help Audrey over her holiday blues too. "As for the quilt? The colors will look wonderful in her parlor, and it's the perfect size to cover the stains and holes in the wall."

Martha huffed a little up the last few stairs. "Thanks for helping me out tonight. We could've gone forward with just five homes, but the advertising says six. Someone might have fussed about not getting her money's worth. Now all I have to do is get the Copy Shop to remove the Nelson house from the tour map and add Maggie's address. I'm glad you were finally able to convince her. It was the quilt that did it."

"I think it might have been," Sarah said with a smile at the memory, "which is why I'm going to give it to her for a Christmas gift. I think it's time I passed the quilt on to the next generation. This will be Maggie's first Christmas away from her folks. I hope the quilt will help her feel closer to the Hart side of the family."

"I'm sure she'll love it," Martha said as they reached the sitting area Sarah had put in for her boarders. "The Star of Bethlehem pattern is one of my favorites. It's so unusual and pretty."

"I agree, and this one is special." This quilt had been modified from the traditional star pattern. Gerry's great-great grandmother had added an expanded border so a different design could be embroidered on it each Christmas. "There are a lot of fond memories sewn into that quilt. Now it'll be Maggie's turn to enjoy it." Sarah opened the door to the attic stairs.

"Brr," Martha shivered, wrapping her arms around herself. "Do you feel a draft?"

"It looks like the door at the top of the stairs is cracked open." Strange. Had she left the door ajar when she'd gotten down her tree decorations last week? But surely, she would have noticed the draft before now. "Belle might've been poking around up there. She needed a few extra items for that treasure hunt you're planning for the tour."

"She's been a jewel. I'm glad you recommended her." Martha had decided to try something new with the tour this year, and had included a special game that people could play as they stopped at the different houses. Belle loved puzzles, and had volunteered to organize the game as soon as she heard about it. "She took right over and planned the whole thing. Although now that I think about it, I haven't heard from her recently."

"And now that you mention it, I haven't seen her for a couple of days." Sarah glanced at Belle's door. No light shone on the threshold. "Maybe she's been working extra hours for the holidays."

Sarah glanced up the stairway again, and pulled her sweater tighter around her. "It's going to be freezing up there. You can wait here where it's warmer, if you'd like. I'll try to hurry and find those lanterns you need so you can go on home to bed."

"I'll help you look. It's the least I can do after disrupting your evening with your family." Martha followed Sarah up the narrow passageway. "I could've gotten the lanterns later too."

"It's no problem. I want to get the quilt for Maggie anyway. Normally I would've brought it downstairs by now, but the twins' activities kept me hopping all week."

"At least your tree is decorated. I've been so busy taking care of the tour details, mine's still bare. I'd hoped Ernie would see to all the decorations and the house lights, but he's been dragging his feet. All he's gotten out so far is his nutcracker collection." Ernie's Parkinson's disease was still in its early stages, but it was hard for the once-coordinated athlete to be hit with the gradually debilitating illness. "And he dropped one of my snow globes and it broke. Since then he's been moping around the house, not wanting to touch anything breakable."

"This must be so difficult for him. And you. Has he seen the doctor recently?"

"He has an appointment next week. We'll see what he says."

"If there's anything I can do to help, just ask."

"Thank you. It helps to be able to talk to someone." Martha swiped at her eyes and smiled. "But you know what? I could've waited until after we got those lanterns and were someplace warm."

"Anytime you want to talk is fine with me. Even in a cold, drafty attic."

Sarah flipped the switch inside the attic. Dim light filled the spacious storage room. Boxes and trunks lined the walls under the eaves, each neatly labeled. Furniture, too dilapidated to be used but rich in family history, huddled in the middle of the room. Sarah planned to have the pieces repaired someday. Maybe Maggie would have some ideas on the best way to refurbish them.

"Watch your step," Sarah said as they maneuvered around an ancient rocker. "If the lanterns aren't up here, they'll be in the cellar." Sarah led the way to a row of cardboard boxes all labeled "Christmas." "How about you start searching at this end, and I'll begin at the other?"

They pulled dusty lids off boxes and dug into the contents until Sarah finally said, "Here they are." She extracted one of a dozen small brass lanterns and rubbed the dust off the glass dome.

"Those are perfect," Martha exclaimed. "I'll get them polished up and buy some fresh oil. Mr. Olsteen has iron holders that we can stick in the ground in front of each of the tour homes. I also made some plaques with the tour numbers to help people identify the houses."

"You've put a lot of work into this project. The tour is going to be superb this year." Sarah rewrapped the lantern in newspaper and placed it with the others.

"I hope so." Martha sighed. "I appreciate your lending these to me. I'll take good care of them."

"Oh, don't worry about it. They haven't been out since the church Christmas reception six years ago. I'm just glad they found a use again." Sarah shivered and turned to one of the three travel trunks stored in the corner. "Just let me get the quilt, and if you'd like, we can have a cup of tea before you go. Take away some of the chill."

"That sounds wonderful." Martha hefted the box of lanterns in her sturdy arms and started toward the stairs.

Sarah flipped the trunk latch and lifted the lid. "I found a special Christmas tea blend and—"

Sarah pushed her hand through the pile of white tissue paper, not believing what her eyes were telling her.

"What's wrong?" Martha asked, turning in the doorway.

"The quilt's gone."

CHAPTER TWO

G one?" Martha set her box down and hurried to where Sarah knelt by the trunk. "Are you sure you didn't pack it somewhere else?"

"Positive. I always store the quilt in this trunk because it's cedar lined." Sarah stood, hands on hips, staring at the pile of tissue paper. This couldn't be happening. Of all the family treasures stored in the attic, the quilt was the most precious to her. How could it just vanish?

"Okay, let's think about this," Martha said. "When was the last time you saw it?"

"Last Christmas."

"Oh dear."

Exactly what Sarah was thinking. *Oh dear*. How long had the quilt been missing? Her stomach knotted.

"Who else has been in the attic?"

"The door doesn't have a lock, so anyone can get in." Sarah rubbed her temples, trying to think. "Jason drops by to borrow tools, but those are in the cellar. He might've come to the attic for something else though. The termite man inspected last October, and the twins were up here playing at Thanksgiving. Then, of course, there were my previous boarders, and now Belle."

"You mentioned that Belle might've been up here looking for things for the treasure hunt. Do you think she might have borrowed the quilt?"

"It's a possibility, but she's usually so polite. I had a hard time getting her not to ask my permission to use the kitchen every time she wanted to cook. Besides, I mentioned the quilt when we were discussing Christmas decorations a week or so ago. She knows it's supposed to go on the wall downstairs. But I can ask her when I see her."

"What about the twins? My grandkids love to make forts out of chairs and blankets," Martha said. "Maybe they took it out to play and put it away somewhere else."

"The twins are almost teenagers. They probably haven't made a fort in years. But I did give them permission to explore." Hope bubbled. "I even suggested playing dress up. Maybe they stuck the quilt in one of the other trunks."

They searched the clothing trunks and then the storage bins full of miscellaneous collections of craft supplies, fabric, holiday dishes, and some of Jason's and Jenna's old toys and trophies. They found more Christmas decorations and other infrequently used items until they had worked their way around the perimeter of the attic. Dust rose from their efforts and danced around the bare bulb hanging from the ceiling. By the time Sarah reached the area near the attic door, her lungs puffed from exertion, and the cold air no longer bothered her.

"Do you smell something?" Martha asked, leaning on an old dresser. "Nice, whatever it is. Like pie."

Sarah sniffed. A familiar fruity scent hung lightly in the air. "There might still be some candles stored up here. I thought I moved all of them to the basement after a bunch melted last summer."

Martha turned back to her search as Sarah spied a blue plastic crate wedged in the corner behind the door. She yanked it out. "This wasn't here before."

"What wasn't?" Martha asked, popping up from behind a sheet-covered sofa.

"Looks like a crate of books."

Martha lifted out a few and read the titles: "*Beginning Spelunking, Survival in the Wilderness*, and *Advanced Outdoor Photography*."

"They must belong to Belle. She's interested in those kinds of things." Sarah dug deeper and pulled out a framed picture of a couple with two young children on a beach. All were sandy haired with tanned, freckled faces.

Sarah leaned closer to the light. "The girl looks like Belle. You can tell by the smile. The boy is probably her brother. She mentioned that she had a brother who'd recently moved back to Pittsfield," Sarah said, referring to the small city about twenty miles from Maple Hill. She set the photo in the crate and tugged out a chess board. "The rest of this stuff is games and puzzle books."

"But why did she leave all this in the attic?"

"I have no idea. She never asked to store anything up here, but I don't mind. There's plenty of room."

Martha helped pile the books back in the crate. "At least now you know that she's been up here."

Sarah nodded. "This whole thing is odd. I still can't imagine her taking the quilt without permission." She stood, slapping the dust off her slacks.

"When was the last time you talked to Belle?" Martha asked.

Sarah thought. "She paid her rent last Thursday, and I invited her to the twin's Christmas program, but she had to work. I don't think I've seen her since."

"She's probably working overtime. They're extra busy at the Copy Shop. I was in there several times last week going over the tour material. Belle did the layout of the tour map for me."

"I don't typically see my boarders every day. When Belle's not at the Copy Shop, she's usually outside somewhere. I'm used to not hearing her around the house," Sarah added. "With all the holiday craziness I probably just missed running into her."

Martha glanced at her watch. "The Copy Shop closed at eight. Maybe she's home now."

"Well, let's see if she's in her room." Sarah pushed Belle's crate against the wall. Martha grabbed her box, and they descended one level.

"Belle?" Sarah called and knocked on the door. She waited and then knocked again. "Belle, it's Sarah."

"Is the door locked?" Martha asked, leaning against the hall wall.

Sarah rattled the doorknob. "I don't feel right invading her privacy."

"You just said you haven't seen her for days. Just take a quick peek. Maybe she's unconscious or something."

"Unconscious?"

"It can happen," Martha said. "Besides, wouldn't it be better to know for sure if she's in there or not?"

Sarah sighed. Martha was right. She'd worry about Belle if she didn't at least check. She turned the doorknob and peeked through the crack. Shadows hung over the room lit by the streetlight outside. No lump lay under the bed covers to indicate a sleeping person.

"Belle?" Sarah pushed the door open further into the spacious, high-ceilinged room. The light she flipped on usually sparkled off framed photos and assorted trinkets, but tonight it shone from the polished surfaces of bare furniture. Only Sarah's white peacock quilt on the twin bed and mulberry curtains remained.

"How strange." Sarah crossed the hardwood floor and checked the small closet. Two wire hangers swung from the bar. "Her clothes are gone."

Martha tugged open the dresser drawers. "Empty here too."

Sarah hurried into the small bathroom. Not even a toothbrush remained. She returned to the middle of the bedroom, spinning slowly. "I don't understand. . . ."

Martha sat on the bed. "I hate to say this, but it looks to me like Belle's moved out."

"We shouldn't jump to conclusions," Sarah said, checking the spot on the refrigerator where Belle usually left a note if she planned to be gone overnight. Nothing.

Martha sank onto a kitchen chair as Sarah turned on the burner under the kettle. "I didn't know Belle well, but it seems strange for her just to leave. She was so enthusiastic about organizing the treasure hunt, and put so much time into it, surely she's not going to miss the tour."

"I can't imagine her doing that. There has to be a reasonable explanation for her not being here," Sarah said, although the sick, hollow feeling that had started in her chest continued to swell. Something was very wrong.

Belle, an excellent tenant, always paid her rent on time. The young woman had a friendly, outgoing personality, and Sarah enjoyed her company. How could she have left without even telling her?

Martha sighed. "I just hope she's okay."

"I'll try calling her." Sarah flipped open her address book to where she'd stored Belle's cell phone number and dialed. The connection went straight to voice mail. She left a message for Belle to call back.

"The Copy Shop will be open at eight tomorrow. We can check there in the morning," Martha said. "Someone must know where she went."

The kettle whistled, and Sarah poured hot water into her red Christmas teapot. The wonderful aroma of cinnamon and orange infused the air, a scent Sarah always associated with the holidays.

Martha toyed with the fringe on the tablecloth. She looked at Sarah with a worried wrinkle on her forehead. "Had Belle mentioned any problems? Family issues? Financial trouble?"

Sarah mulled that over as she checked the steeping tea. "I don't know. I don't think so. She said she took the graphic design job at the Copy Shop because it paid better than her last job in Pittsfield. The only reason she's boarding here is to save money to pay off her college loans and buy a house."

"Oh that's good. The thought crossed my mind that . . . "

"That maybe she stole the quilt to sell?"

Martha frowned. "I hate to suggest it. She seems like such a nice person."

"Well, I'd be lying if I said the same thought hadn't crossed my mind. But I agree with you. It doesn't seem like something she'd do. Besides, the quilt wouldn't bring much. Its value is in its sentimentality and family history. There are more expensive things to steal around here if she was desperate."

Sarah poured the tea, and Martha took a sip. "This is just what I needed, and this tea blend is wonderful."

Sarah brought over the cookie jar. They savored their tea and nibbled on lemon cookies, lost in their thoughts for a while.

Martha reached for a second cookie and asked. "Did Belle tell you what she had planned for your house for the treasure hunt?"

"She didn't specify, although she asked how I was going to decorate the living room so she could figure out the clue to plant." Belle had decided that each house on the tour would have a clue to the treasure hunt hidden in its decorations. "I showed her a photo from Christmas several years ago and left it on the mantle in case she wanted to refer to it again. I'll show you."

Sarah retrieved the photo of her decorated living room and handed it to Martha. The tree stood in the window as it did now, decorated with white lights and colorful, antique ornaments. Around the room, she'd placed bright poinsettias. Strands of holly graced the mantel and banister. The Star of Bethlehem quilt hung on the wall, its rich green and red fabrics drawing in the vibrant holiday colors of the room. Gold threading around the border gave the quilt a royal air.

"I told Belle I'd decorate the living room the same way this year."

Martha examined the snapshot. "Your house always looks so lovely for Christmas. And this quilt would've looked wonderful at Maggie's place. I hope you find it." She sighed and laid the photo on the table.

"Me too. I'll check with Jason and the girls tomorrow just in case they know anything," Sarah said, although she dreaded bringing Jason into this before she knew what had happened to the quilt. After someone broke into Maggie's shop a few months before, he'd been talking about how unsafe Maple Hill had become over the years. She didn't want to worry him more.

She glanced out the window at the dark, frigid night, worry for her boarder rising even higher. "Maybe Belle had a family emergency and was in such a rush to leave, she forgot to tell me. She could've taken her clothes because she didn't know when she'd be back."

"That's plausible," Martha said, rubbing the back of her neck. "I guess I need to figure out what to do about the treasure hunt, just in case she doesn't make it back in time. She never gave me the answer key or told me where she planned to hide the prizes. Oh!" She dropped her hand, her face brightening with a smile. "Did I ever show you what I ordered for the prizes?"

"You talked about it, but I never saw them."

"I have a sample in my purse. I have to show you." She moved down the hall to the entryway and returned dangling a small gold photo frame.

"Aren't these cute?" she said. "This was Belle's idea. We had the frames engraved with *Treasures of the Past*, which is our theme this year. They come with a magnet so they can be put up on a refrigerator, and they also have a string so they can be hung like an ornament." She handed the frame to Sarah.

Sarah turned it over in her hands, examining the details. "This makes a great souvenir. How do they win one?"

"That was Belle's department again, but the way she explained it to me was that everyone will get a treasure map. Each house will have some Christmassy object or 'treasure' that the participants have to count and note on their map. When they finish at the last house, which will be here, they'll use the numbers they collected to fill in the blanks of the last clue. It's supposed to be easy, and to tell you the truth, anyone who even tries to finish the hunt will get a prize. Belle was also going to offer to take a photo of each participant."

"It sounds like fun." Sarah grinned. "I almost wish I wasn't going to be stuck at the house hosting."

"Me too." Martha laughed. "Anyway it's not like the game is critical, but we advertised the treasure hunt on the flyers as a fund-raiser for the Children's Home. We're asking for a donation from those who want to participate, and we're hoping to raise a couple hundred dollars. I just hope we can pull it off if Belle's not here."

Sarah took a deep breath. "Don't worry. We'll figure everything out."

"Thanks. I know it will be fine, but I'm glad to know I can always count on you."

Sarah studied Martha over the rim of her teacup. The lines around her eyes had deepened, and her mouth drooped a bit with fatigue. During the last two weeks of frantic Christmas preparation and dashing around with the twins, Sarah hadn't noticed how frazzled and worn her best friend looked. Guilt weighed on Sarah—she was the one who had suggested Martha recruit Belle to take charge of the treasure hunt. If Belle let Martha down, then Sarah would feel she'd also failed her friend.

"Want to meet for coffee after breakfast at The Spotted Dog? If we don't hear from Belle by then, we can make some plans."

Martha's lips lifted in a smile. "That sounds like fun. We can meet earlier and eat if you'd like. Ernie has a men's breakfast tomorrow, so I'm free until my afternoon meeting with the tour committee."

"Eight-thirty all right?" Sarah asked as Martha pulled herself to her feet.

"Perfect." Martha bundled into her coat, gloves, and scarf. She picked up the lantern box by the front door. "Thanks again for the loan. See you in the morning."

"You're welcome, and give my best to Ernie."

"I will." Martha stepped outside and turned. "I'll be praying about Belle. Try not to worry. I know if anyone can figure out what happened, you can."

Sarah said good-bye and headed back to the kitchen. She just hoped she could live up to Martha's confidence in her. She tried Belle's cell phone again with no luck. Where was the girl? Had they missed something obvious?

She trotted up the stairs to Belle's room. People who left on vacation typically did not take everything with them, unless they planned on being gone a long time. Nor did they leave belongings in the attic without notice.

But Belle didn't have a lot of possessions in the first place. She'd arrived with just a suitcase, her laptop, and a couple of boxes. Belle told Sarah she didn't need much at this point in her life and could live out of a backpack for weeks while hiking.

Sarah looked beneath the bed and unearthed a lone sock. She checked under the mattress and found nothing. On the windowsill sat a row of potted African violets that Sarah had placed there because of the great morning light. She stuck her finger inside a pot. The soil was still damp.

She couldn't see any clues to where Belle might have gone, and she returned to the attic to survey the disorder she and Martha had created in their quest to find the missing quilt. They'd made a mess of Belle's box, too, and she'd have to repack it. She shoved boxes back into place and tidied the attic. The lid to the quilt trunk was still open. She folded the tissue paper the quilt had been wrapped in and spotted something glinting at the trunk bottom.

Two Christmas tree ornaments lay on top of a book. She carefully lifted the items out. The ornaments, a glass angel with gold-tipped wings and a ceramic Christmas tree, were a common design and resembled some of the ornaments on her own tree. The book was one of the beginner's quilting guides she kept on her sewing room bookshelf downstairs.

She shut the trunk lid and noticed a couple of dark drops on the wooden flooring. She touched the dried substance. Her finger came away sticky and smelled like fruit. It was the same scent Martha had commented on earlier in the evening.

Something must have spilled. Sarah didn't think the twins had been eating or drinking anything up here last month, plus the stain seemed too fresh to have been there that long.

A gust of wind hit the roof and the rafters creaked. Sarah placed the book and ornaments in Belle's box and took everything downstairs to her sewing room, which doubled as her office. Pushing aside scraps from her last quilt project, she emptied the box, one item at time, onto the table.

She leafed through Belle's books, searching for any stray pieces of paper that might give a clue to her normal hangouts. The book on photography appeared heavily used, with its cracked spine and frayed corners. Belle had written notes in the margins. She'd once confided in Sarah that someday she'd love to be a professional photographer, but right now a steady job in graphic design paid her college loans and built a nest egg.

The crosswords, sudoku, and other puzzle books were partially filled in. Belle always seemed to have one with her in her spare time. Sarah replaced a rook and pawn that'd been jostled out of the chess box. Nothing seemed out of the ordinary, other than the mystery of why Belle had stashed this stuff in the attic.

At the bottom of the crate were a few leaflets with descriptions and maps of natural attractions around the area. Some depicted caves, others trails and camping sites near Mount Greylock. Belle had probably picked them up at the ranger station or one of the visitor centers in the area.

Sarah neatly repacked the box, and placed it at the bottom of the stairs to return to the attic later. She hoped Belle would forgive her for snooping through her things.

She picked up the ornaments and book that she'd found in the trunk and carried them to the living room. The angel and Christmas tree were slightly different from the ornaments on her tree, and judging from the dark dust in their crevices, they hadn't been used for years. How they'd ended up in the quilt trunk, Sarah didn't know.

Her cold feet and the crick in her neck made her aware time had passed. She glanced at the clock. Almost midnight. She had to meet Martha in eight and a half hours. She set the ornaments and book on her chair, turned off the lights, and checked the door locks. The house seemed eerily quiet now that she knew Belle was gone.

Sarah returned to her sewing room and dug into the drawer where she kept the rental applications. For references, Belle had listed her Pittsfield roommate, a previous boss, and her pastor. The emergency contact number was for her roommate also. Interesting. No family was listed. It was too late to call now, but if she didn't hear from Belle tomorrow, she'd try the roommate.

A twinge rose in her chest. She might be overreacting, but the whole situation didn't feel right. Sarah had learned long ago to trust her intuition about people, and she wasn't going to let the matter drop until she was sure Belle was safe. Sarah whispered a brief prayer for Belle and stood.

She turned off the light; and as she passed through the kitchen, she picked up the Christmas photo of her living room, carrying it with her upstairs. After washing up and changing into a long, flannel nightgown, she climbed into her mahogany sleigh bed. She plumped the pillows behind her, leaned against the headboard, and studied the Hart family quilt in the picture.

A smile tugged at her lips as she remembered the Christmas Gerry's mother, Elizabeth Hart, entrusted the quilt to Sarah. It'd been a beautiful holiday season. Christmas lights glowed in the town square, casting red, green, and blue shadows on the fresh, thick blanket of snow. Snowplows had created giant dunes along the sides and at the ends of streets, which meant extra shoveling for some folks, but great fun for children to climb and slide down. The air nipped at her nose and cheeks as they trudged up the freshly shoveled walkway to Gerry's parents' house.

As was the tradition, the Harts gathered on Christmas Eve for a delicious supper and to exchange family gifts. Sarah had been so full of holiday joy. She and Gerry had been married for eight years, their children were young, and the future bright with anticipation of wonderful things to come.

Happy holiday sounds filled the house. While Sarah chatted and helped Elizabeth and her sister-in-law Anne prepare a Christmas Eve buffet, Gerry, his younger brother, and their father talked politics and football in the living room. Jason and Jenna raced through the three floors of the sprawling old farmhouse, playing hide-and-seek with their four cousins.

Every holiday season, Elizabeth baked the most scrumptious cranberry-orange bread and cinnamon rolls, giving them away to family and friends. She always added a generous amount of pecans, Gerry's favorite, to both recipes. Sarah had continued the tradition of baking those treats every Christmas after Gerry's mother passed away.

After dining, the family gathered in the living room to exchange gifts. Sarah had settled on the overstuffed love seat with Gerry, across from his parents on the couch. Jason and Jenna and the cousins sprawled on the rug as close to the Christmas tree as they could get.

Gerry's father always got the biggest tree that would fit in the high-ceilinged room, and this one towered over them, covered with beautiful ornaments and wound with strands of cranberries and popcorn.

A fire crackled and snapped in the stone hearth, heating the room and melting the frost on the windows. Sarah snuggled against Gerry and had a clear view of the Hart quilt hanging on the wall in a place of honor above the piano. She'd been in awe of the beautiful Star of Bethlehem design from the first time she saw it and remained intrigued by the history the embroidered symbols represented. Every year, Elizabeth would initiate a discussion of what that year's Christmas symbol should be, and then she'd carefully embroider it on the quilt's dark green border.

After most of the gifts had been opened, Elizabeth handed Sarah a small, exquisitely wrapped gift box. Inside Sarah found a spool of gold thread and a needle. The significance of the gift caused her heart to swell. She glanced up at the quilt and then met her mother-in-law's gaze.

Elizabeth smiled and nodded. "It's time."

"Are you sure?" Sarah asked, her eyes tearing with emotion. Gerry slid his arm around her shoulders. The first Christmas they'd visited his family, he'd told Sarah that, traditionally, the quilt was passed down to the eldest son's family, but Sarah hadn't expected it yet.

Elizabeth smiled. "It's time to pass the quilt on. You'll know when it's your turn. I could tell you loved our family quilt from the first moment you saw it. I know you and Gerry will give it a good home, and pass the history down to your children."

Sarah crossed the room to give Elizabeth a hug. "Thank you so much. I'll treasure the quilt, and I'll keep the tradition going." She looked around at the smiling faces of Gerry's family and asked. "So what should the Christmas symbol be this year?"

Sarah's eyes misted as she set the photograph on her nightstand. She tugged her bed quilt—a blue and green log cabin pattern—up to her chest and turned off the lamp.

The symbol she'd sewn on that year, 1982, was a tiny snowman, because of the year's record snowfall. She didn't need the quilt to remember that special Christmas. Elizabeth had passed away only two years later, making the memory and the gift of the quilt all the more cherished.

A lump rose in her throat. Now the precious quilt was missing, and it felt like a piece of Sarah's heart was too.

CHAPTER THREE

G ood morning, Sarah," Liam Connolly said in his
rich Irish brogue as she entered The Spotted Dog
Bookstore and Café.

"Hello, Liam. I see you've added another dog to your
collection."

"I have?" Liam asked, his green eyes twinkling. "How can
you even tell?" Dog decorations were scattered throughout
the store.

"I'm referring to the one at your feet."

He glanced down. A small, stuffed Dalmatian puppy lay
on its side. "Oh that's one of Murphy's new toys. You can tell
it's new because the nose isn't completely chewed off." He
let out a short whistle. "Murphy, come."

An adorable scruffy white Corgi dashed out from under the counter, his black ears flapping out behind him.
He skidded to a stop in front of Liam. The black spot on
Murphy's back wiggled in rhythm with the wagging of his
tail.

"Take your toy, Murphy, before someone steps on it." Liam tapped his shoe on the stuffed dog. Murphy snatched the Dalmatian up, raced back under the counter, and curled up by his cookie bowl.

"Martha's already here and waiting for you." Liam gestured toward the café. "Can I bring you a gingerbread latte?"

"Oh yes, that'd hit the spot. It's so cold out. The temperature must've dropped at least ten degrees since yesterday." Sarah's boot heels clicked on the black-and-white checkered tiles as she followed Liam into the little eating area. Martha sat at one of the tables, her head bowed over a clipboard.

"A good, hot breakfast will warm you up." Liam pulled out the other chair for Sarah. "What I can get for you?"

"I'll have the special," she said, referring to the pecan pancakes and scrambled eggs she'd seen on the menu board in the entrance.

"Excellent choice. We'll have a batch of pancakes coming hot off the griddle before you know it. Be back in a few minutes." Liam strode toward the kitchen.

"Hi!" Martha gave Sarah a bright smile. "How are you?"

"Good, considering I had trouble falling asleep last night."

"Me too. I keep thinking about Belle. Any news?"

"None, I'm afraid." Sarah shrugged out of her coat. "I called her cell again and still no answer. Then I tried the emergency number she'd put on her rental application, but her old roommate wasn't home, so I left a message. Maybe she'll know something."

"I hope so. Are you still planning to stop by the Copy Shop this morning?"

When Sarah nodded, Martha said, "Good. I'll go with you. I need to make those changes to the map since Maggie and Jason's house is replacing the Nelsons.'" Martha set her clipboard on the floor next to her purse and leaned forward, elbows on the table. "So. Did you find anything else in the attic last night?"

Sarah smiled. Of course Martha assumed she'd gone back to the attic. They'd been friends for decades, and Martha shared Sarah's overwhelming curiosity and slight stubbornness.

"Nothing significant. I looked in Belle's room first and checked the soil in one of the African violets' pots. It was still moist, which means she probably hasn't been gone more than a few days. When I repacked Belle's crate I found some brochures for local natural attractions at the bottom. I'm not sure if any of them will prove helpful, but you never know."

"Right. You never know."

"One other odd thing. In the quilt trunk I found a book and two Christmas ornaments."

"What's odd about that? Don't you have lots of stuff up there?"

"Well, I'm pretty sure they aren't my ornaments. Mine are stored in their own special box, which I took downstairs when I decorated the tree. The quilting book is a guide for beginners, and I haven't touched one of those in years. The last place I saw it was on the bookshelf in my sewing room."

"Do you think whoever took the quilt left the ornaments and the books in the trunk?"

Sarah nodded. "I'm going to talk to the twins, and see if they know anything. I just hope this doesn't cause any more stress for Maggie."

"Yeah, she seemed relieved after you talked her into using the quilt. Do you have another one that would work?"

"Of course. But it's not a Christmas quilt. I guess Maggie could always hang a painting."

"Or rearrange the room and move the Christmas tree over there." Martha suggested. "It's big enough to cover a lot of wall."

"That'd work too." Sarah said. "Maggie's so creative, I know she can come up with something. I just hope the quilt isn't lost forever."

"Oh, honey, I'm sure it'll turn up."

"Meanwhile, finding Belle is more important than the quilt," Sarah said. "I don't even know how to contact her family. I'm hoping her old roommate may know," Sarah said. "Do you need any help with the treasure hunt today? Was there something Belle was supposed to handle?"

"Well, nothing urgent. There's still time before I panic. I just keep hoping Belle will check in. Meanwhile, I can call the home tour participants and see if Belle told them what she'd planned. And remember, now that the Nelsons are out of the tour, I need to get Maggie set up too. I just wish we could find the answer key. I don't want to have to start from scratch."

"I was thinking about the treasure hunt this morning, trying to imagine what Belle had planned." Sarah pulled the snapshot out of her coat pocket and held it up. "In my living room alone, I counted at least eighteen different Christmassy things she could've used."

"Here are your lattes," Liam said, setting them down on the table. "Enjoy!" He glanced at the photograph in Sarah's hand. "That's a handsome quilt on the wall. Did you make it?"

"Actually, it's an antique. My late husband's great-great grandmother quilted it in 1910," Sarah said, surprised Liam had noticed the quilt. Liam was so kind and friendly to his customers.

"Tell him the unique part about it," Martha said.

"It's also a memory quilt. If you look closely you can see there are symbols with dates embroidered in gold around the border." She handed him the photo.

He held it up and squinted. "Oh yes, there's a dove, a candle, and is that a cradle?"

"Yes, it is. Every year, someone in the family embroiders a symbol that captures the essence of that Christmas or something special that happened during the year," Sarah said. "The cradle was embroidered in 1915, after Gerry's great-uncle was born on Christmas day. The candle was the blizzard of 1924. Gerry's grandmother's grandmother kept candles burning in their farmhouse window, hoping it would help people find their way home. The dove represents peace and was sewn in 1945—"

"When the war ended." Liam returned the photo.

"Right." Sarah beamed. "The Hart men came home from war that year. There are a lot stories in that quilt. There are ninety-nine symbols. This year's will be the hundredth."

"Remarkable." Liam said. "The history is grand. I'd love to see the quilt someday. Maybe I could drop by."

Sarah's uneasiness about the quilt's disappearance returned. "That'd be fine but . . . I don't have it displayed right now. I'll let you know."

Martha sent her a sympathetic smile and Sarah's heart squeezed painfully. She couldn't bear to discuss the possibility that she might have lost the family heirloom forever.

"Ah, here's your breakfast." He stepped back as Karen Bancroft carried a tray out of the kitchen.

"Morning, ladies. Two breakfast specials." The dark-haired, blue-eyed college student set the plates in front of them.

"Karen, do you know Belle Silver?" Sarah asked, hoping maybe the twenty-somethings might have hung out at the same places.

Karen paused. "I'm not sure."

"She came in here once or twice with me. She has short, curly blonde hair, blue eyes. Lots of freckles."

"Oh, the Smoothie Girl."

"Smoothie Girl?"

Karen smiled. "That's what I nicknamed her because she pops in here three to four times a week during the lunch hour and always orders a blueberry smoothie. She doesn't want any sugar added and specifically asked if our yogurt contains acidophilus," Karen said. "She seems real nice and friendly. A couple of times she hung around and worked on the crossword in the newspaper and browsed the bookstore, right, Liam?" she said over her shoulder.

"If I remember correctly, the young lady was very interested in the travel book section," Liam said. "Bought a couple of books."

"Has she been in here lately?" Sarah asked.

"I haven't seen her this week," Karen answered. "But between work and finishing finals at the university, I've been so rushed, I may not have noticed."

"I don't recall either," Liam said as he refilled their water glasses. "Doesn't she board with you, Sarah?"

"She does." Sarah exchanged a glance with Martha, caught between wanting to sound an alarm and not wanting to violate Belle's privacy. "But I haven't seen her in a couple of days and usually she lets me know her plans. It's probably just an oversight, but I can't help worrying. It's the mother hen in me."

"She's very lucky to have such a thoughtful landlady who cares about her," Liam said with a reassuring smile. The bell on the door jangled, drawing his attention away as Karen returned to the kitchen.

"That was a nice thing for him to say." Martha tucked her fork into her scrambled eggs.

"Yes, it was. Makes me feel less like a busybody." Sarah took a bite of pancakes, and sighed as the toasty sweetness hit her tongue. Liam was right. This breakfast was just the right thing to warm her up.

Martha started in with a story about her youngest granddaughter Sylvie and they spent the rest of breakfast chatting about Martha's family until Karen brought them their checks.

Sarah pulled bills out of her wallet and left a generous tip. She knew the money went to help Karen pay for college. "Ready to head to the Copy Shop?"

"I'll meet you over there. I need to stop by the post office and mail some packages. If I get there now, with luck there won't be a long line. Were you able to get your presents mailed to Jenna?" Martha asked, digging in her purse and extracting her wallet.

Sarah nodded. "Got to the post office just before they closed on Friday. The packages should get to Texas before Christmas." She wished Jenna, David, and her two grandsons could be here for Christmas, but she'd been blessed by a surprise visit at Thanksgiving. Her daughter had promised to call on Christmas and e-mail photos of Thomas and Jonathan opening their presents.

"I'll see you in a bit." Martha paid for her meal and bundled up before heading out the door.

Sarah looked around for Liam and eyed him talking to customers in the bookstore. Murphy spotted her and bounded over with his new toy. He dropped the stuffed Dalmatian at her feet.

"You want to play?" Sarah asked.

The Corgi wagged his tail. Sarah chuckled and tossed the toy into an empty corner of the room.

Murphy bounded after it and brought the toy back. Sarah praised him and played with the dog until Liam finished with his customer. She gave Murphy a final pat and turned to Liam. "I know I'm being nosy, but do you happen to remember what travel books Belle bought? Might give me a clue to where she is."

"I think one was for Europe, and the other somewhere in the U.S. I can look up the receipt for you."

"Only if you have time later. I know you're busy." Several customers crowded up behind her, their arms loaded with books and other items.

"Anything for one of Murphy's favorite people." He smiled as the dog returned to his spot under the counter.

"Thank you, Liam." Sarah leaned down to peek at the dog. "You too, Murphy. Hope you both have a great day."

She stepped outside, and a gust of frigid wind met her, sending icy chills down the back of her neck and along her spine. She tugged up her coat collar. "Oh! Of all days to forget my scarf."

"You can borrow one of mine."

Sarah jumped. She hadn't realized Liam had followed her to the door, holding it open after she stepped out. "Be right back," he said and turned inside before she could protest.

She waited, shivering, under the spotted awning until Liam returned a few seconds later, holding a black scarf. "This is so nice of you," she said, trying to keep her teeth from chattering, "but I don't want you to be cold just because I was dumb enough to leave home without mine."

Liam smiled. "I have another. Go on, I insist. No sense in catching cold."

"Thank you." Sarah wrapped the soft, thick wool around her neck, the width covering her ears. "I'll get it back to you later today."

"No rush."

Sarah gasped as another arctic blast hit her. She gave Liam a little wave and dashed to her car. Martha was right. What a nice man Liam was. She fished her keys out of her pocket and scrambled into her car.

As she waited for the engine to warm, her mind scrolled through the long list of things she needed to do before this weekend and the home tour, but right at the top of the list was to find out what had happened to Belle.

"I haven't seen Belle since…last Friday," the tall brunette with square glasses said from behind the counter of the Copy Shop. The tag on her uniform indicated her name was Julia. She flipped open a fat, black notebook, and her finger ran down what appeared to be the employee schedule. "She's not due back in until after Christmas. Perhaps I can help you with your copying needs?"

"Actually, this is a personal matter. Did Belle say she was going on vacation?"

Julia peered over the top of her glasses at Sarah. "I'm sorry, I'm not at liberty to discuss an employee's personal information."

"I realize your position, but I'm concerned." She raised her voice as an industrial-size copier kicked into motion and spat out colored copies. "I'm Sarah Hart, and Belle is a boarder in my home. I haven't seen her for a couple of days, and I'm worried."

"Is she in some kind of trouble?"

Sarah sighed. "I don't know."

The door swung open, and Martha darted inside. The wind had tousled her brown hair and painted her face pink. She sidled up next to Sarah, her hazel eyes sparkling. "Only four people ahead of me at the post office and all my Christmas packages are mailed."

Julia's thin lips broke into a smile. "Good morning, Mrs. Maplethorpe. I pulled up your order. I'll be with you shortly."

She turned back to Sarah. "I'm sorry. My hands are tied. All I can tell you is that Belle is expected back on December twenty-sixth . . . ." She shrugged. "Now, is there anything else I can do to assist you?"

"No. Thank you." Sarah respected the woman for protecting Belle's privacy, but that wouldn't deter her. She'd just have to change tactics. Maybe she should go down to the police station and talk to Chief Webber. If this were a police matter, maybe they could get more information faster. But, really, she didn't have much to tell the police at this point.

Sarah didn't have any proof of wrongdoing, simply a feeling that Belle might be in trouble. To all appearances, the girl had merely moved out. According to her rental agreement, Belle should have given two weeks' notice, but Belle didn't owe her money. It wasn't a crime to store things in the attic. Sarah wasn't even inclined to believe Belle took the Christmas quilt. She needed to dig a little more before sounding an alarm with the police.

Julia spread the contents of a large folder out on the counter for Martha. As the two ladies discussed details, Sarah took a quick peek at the schedule book that'd been left open. Beside Belle's name, the boxes for the week were blank; and although she'd been scheduled over the previous weekend, someone had scratched an X over both days with red pen.

Sarah wondered if Belle had asked for the days off or just didn't show. At least Julia expected Belle back after the holiday, which meant Belle hadn't given notice of quitting. Maybe she planned to move someplace else in Maple Hill when she returned. That would account for her packing up her things.

"Mrs. Hart?" a high-pitched voice asked. Sarah jumped, her heart thumping. She turned to find a teenager clad in a brown Copy Shop uniform.

"Sorry. I didn't mean to startle you." The girl let out a nervous giggle. "You probably don't know me, but I'm Wendy Tollson. You once came to my art class at the high school and talked about restoring quilts."

Sarah studied the round face surrounded by a mass of tight cocoa-colored curls. "You look familiar. Don't you have a sister a grade or so ahead of you in school?"

Wendy smiled, her braces glinting in the fluorescent light. "Yeah, that's Jessica. She's at Boston University now. I plan on going next year, which is why I'm working here to earn money. I overheard you talking to Julia about Belle." She lowered her voice. "She's been cranky ever since Belle left because she has to cover for her."

Sarah sucked in a quick breath. "Do you know where Belle went?"

Wendy motioned for Sarah to follow her to the far end of the counter, away from the two women. "Okay, truth is, I don't actually know where she is, but . . ."

She glanced around them and then whispered, "I think Belle eloped."

CHAPTER FOUR

E loped?" Sarah asked. "Belle told me she was engaged last year, but that it ended before she moved here. She's never mentioned being serious with anyone else."

Wendy's brown eyes narrowed. "All I know is she's been talking to some guy for the last couple of weeks. Julia doesn't approve of personal phone calls on the company phone, so Belle would go outside and call him back on her cell."

"Did he leave his name?"

"No, he'd always hang up if Belle wasn't here. But once I heard her say on the phone it was time for a fresh start. Then these flowers arrived last Thursday. Isn't it romantic?" Wendy pointed to a dozen fading roses on the counter. "That afternoon she got another call and left. She seemed excited and in a big hurry. I haven't seen her since."

"This was last Friday afternoon?" Sarah asked. "About what time did she leave?"

"Must've been in the middle of the afternoon, probably around one because I'd just come over here after school. It was a half day because of Christmas vacation. Belle left right afterward. Didn't even take the flowers. Probably too excited to remember."

Last Friday afternoon Sarah had been at the gymnasium with the twins helping tear down the stage after the previous evening's Christmas program. Belle would've had the house to herself. Plenty of time to pack up, put the box in the attic, and leave unnoticed.

But elope? Surely Sarah would've sensed some hint of love in the air. When Jason had come home for a visit soon after meeting Maggie, he'd walked around with a huge grin on his face. And when the phone rang, he'd race from anywhere he was in the house to answer it. The last few times Sarah had seen Belle at home, she had seemed her normal, easygoing self.

The door flew open, and a gust of cold air heralded another customer. "Do you have any flash drives?" a young man stuffed in a bloated orange parka asked as he approached the counter.

"Yes, we do." Julia smiled at the customer. "Wendy will help you find them." She shot a pointed glare at the immobile girl.

"Right over here, sir." Wendy led the way down an aisle, leaving Sarah alone with the flowers. She noticed an envelope stuck on a plastic pick in the vase.

Sarah glanced over to see Julia and Martha deep in discussion. "Maybe Belle left a copy of the treasure hunt key at her desk or maybe on her computer," Martha said with an encouraging smile. "Would you take a look for me? It would save me a lot of time."

Julia gave a half smile. "Sure. I'd be happy to check for you." She headed toward the row of desks and computers. With Julia's back turned, Sarah lifted the flap on the envelope and tugged up the card.

Looking forward to a renewed future. Yours always, Andrew.

"Oh here's a file labeled Treasure Hunt," Julia said.

Sarah tapped the card back into the envelope. Renewed future? Could Andrew be Belle's ex-fiancé?

"But all that's in here is the same draft of the map I just gave you, and what appears to be an invoice for some sort of small trinkets. Photo frames." Julia held up a printed pink sheet. "We sell something like these, but this looks like a custom order."

"Those are the photo frames Belle ordered for the treasure hunt prizes," Martha said.

"Do you want a copy?"

"Please. The committee treasurer will need the receipt to reimburse Belle." Martha glanced over at Sarah by the roses and mouthed, "What are you doing?"

Sarah offered a quick smile as Julia's manicured fingernails flashed like pink petals over the keyboard on Belle's desk.

"I don't see any files in the main system, which isn't unusual if it's not a work order." Julia clicked the mouse twice. "And I don't see anything in any of her personal folders.

Perhaps it's on her laptop computer. She sometimes works from home on miscellaneous design jobs. She uses a flash drive like those that customer over there is looking at."

"Thank you so much for trying," Martha pulled her gloves on. "I appreciate your help."

"Anytime. We're here to serve," Julia said in a pleasant tone. She lifted the lid of a copier and placed the pink invoice for the frames on the screen. "I'll be sure to input the change on the tour map from the Nelson house to the Hart home on Bristol Street. The draft should be ready tomorrow for your approval."

Martha smiled. "That'll be wonderful." Julia handed Martha the copy the machine had spit out.

"Excuse me, Julia?" Sarah asked. "Would you happen to know who Belle got the flowers from?"

Julia turned to her, her smile fading. "No, and it's none of my business or anyone else's," she said with a prim set to her lips. "It's a shame Belle didn't take them with her. I'm going to have to throw them out before she even gets back. They're getting old and beginning to droop."

"I think I know how they feel," Martha whispered to Sarah.

Sarah smiled. "Thank you for your help, Julia. Would you please call me if you hear from Belle before the twenty-sixth? Here's my number." Sarah wrote it down on a scrap piece of paper sitting on the counter. "Thank you so much!"

Sarah didn't give Julia a chance to answer as she headed out the door arm-in-arm with Martha.

Sarah watched the fog recede up the windshield of her silver Grand Prix, away from the blasting defrost as she finished giving Martha a recap of her conversation with Wendy. Martha waited a beat, then asked, "Why don't you think Belle eloped?"

"Just a feeling. Wendy is young and the idea of eloping is romantic, so of course she'd jump to that conclusion. But Belle certainly didn't act like a love struck young woman these past few weeks." Sarah rubbed her hands together, willing the car to warm up faster. "And think about it, if you suddenly decided to elope, would you take the time to pack all your things and store some in the attic? Her room was paid up until the New Year. There was no rush to move, even if she was getting married."

"You have a point, although people in love sometimes do strange things." A tiny smile lurked at the corners of Martha's lips. "Ernie and I almost eloped. We even started driving to Maryland in that old wreck of a Buick he had."

"What?" Sarah's eyes grew wide. "But you had that huge church wedding. We'd been planning it since we were what? Ten?"

"I know. I know. Sounds insane, doesn't it?"

Sarah held up a hand. "Wait, really? You never told me this. What happened? Did your parents find out?"

"Nope. They never knew."

"Then what stopped you?"

"Flat tire."

Sarah stared at her friend for a few seconds and then burst out laughing. "You're kidding!"

Martha chuckled. "No, seriously, it was the flat tire. My parents wanted us to wait another year and a half for Ernie to get his business established and for me to finish college."

"I remember. You were fit to be tied, but you never even mentioned eloping. It was only a couple months later and we were collecting bridal magazines, talking gowns and flowers."

"Those are some of my favorite memories," Martha said.

Sarah laughed. "So tell me the truth. Are you glad you waited and didn't elope?"

"Yes. Eloping sounded romantic at the time. We figured our parents would just have to accept the idea once we were married."

Sarah snorted.

"Okay, so we were a little naive. At twenty-one, we thought we knew everything," Martha said with a twinkle in her eyes.

"Was eloping Ernie's idea or yours?" Sarah asked.

"Truthfully, I think eloping was more my idea than his. He just wanted me to be happy. I packed a bag with a few clothes and snuck out of the house. We were only about twenty miles out of town when the tire blew. You know, that turnout near Tillman's Corner?"

Sarah nodded.

"Well, while Ernie was out there fixing it, I started thinking about all the hours my mother had spent in the car, driving me places like school, music lessons, church, and the shopping mall. My dad would spend weekends working on the engine to keep it running well. They both had put so much effort into my upbringing. Funny what things go through your head. I suddenly felt really guilty about running away and depriving them of being a part of one the biggest moments in my life."

"Well, I'm not surprised. You were always a good daughter."

"Yeah, I guess, and although it sticks in my throat to say it sometimes, my mother was right. Turns out Ernie had second thoughts too. We loved each other so much, but things were much easier once we'd grown up another year. Besides, if I'd eloped I'd never have seen you in that purple bridesmaid's dress."

"Do you have to bring that up again?"

"Hey, you picked the color."

Sarah giggled. "So? You should have told me I looked like a giant grape. The worst thing was how much the petticoats itched."

"I know. You made me wear them at your wedding too!"

They both laughed. Sarah wiped her eyes. "I'm just glad I got to be there at your wedding."

Martha nodded. "That's why I didn't tell you about eloping."

Sarah placed her hand on Martha's shoulder. "I would've been disappointed if you had eloped, but I would have understood."

"It was just a brief couple of hours of craziness, but you know what? It's actually been fun having it as Ernie's and my secret. Whenever we have a flat tire, we look at each other and smile."

"Thanks for telling me now. I needed a good laugh. Those were great times," Sarah said with wistful longing. Gerry had been at the wedding too, so handsome in his tux. Every time she had looked at him, her heart fluttered. He'd been away at college for a couple of months and came home for the wedding. The saying "absence makes the heart grow fonder" was true, at least in Sarah's case.

"I miss Gerry too." Martha's voice broke into her thoughts.

Sarah gave her head a little shake. "Sorry, I didn't mean to spoil the mood."

"You didn't. We still have good times ahead of us, don't we? Different, but still fun." Martha's grin turned mischievous. "Heard from Chester Winslow lately? It's been awhile since your last dinner date."

Sarah rolled her eyes at Martha's teasing tone. "Not since he called me about my next article for *Country Cottage* about a week ago. Besides, our dates, if you can call them that, consisted of talking business," she insisted, but Martha continued to grin.

Sarah tried to will the blush from her cheeks. "You just reminded me. I need to come up with another idea for my next article. I told Chester about the Hart family Christmas quilt, and he suggested I write about its history. With it missing right now, I don't know if I'm in the mood to write on that particular topic."

"Don't worry. He'll understand," Martha said and then they lapsed into silence, watching the shoppers bustle in and out of the stores, basking in the warm, secure quietness only two old friends could share.

"Remember my boarder Katie?" Sarah asked.

"The one running from a bad relationship?"

Sarah nodded. "What if Belle's situation is similar? She said she moved here for the job at the Copy Shop, but the breakup must have played some role too. What if this guy forced her to go off with him? I'd hate to think that Belle's in trouble and I've done nothing to help."

"Me too. Do you think we should talk to Chief Webber?"

"I want to, but what can I say?" Sarah held up her hands, empty palms open. "There's no evidence of foul play. No crime, unless you count the missing quilt. I can just hear Chief Webber saying 'she's over eighteen.' And if there isn't any evidence she's in trouble or committed a crime, there's nothing he can do right now. I can still file a missing person report if forty-eight hours pass, but they won't do much."

Martha tapped her fingers on the dash. "I think we need to find this Andrew person who sent her the flowers."

"I was thinking the same thing," Sarah said. "I'm still waiting for Belle's roommate to get back to me. She may know where Belle is, or at least can tell us if Andrew is Belle's ex-fiancé. If not, we can check at the florist, and maybe they'll tell us who paid the bill."

"Someone on the tour might know something too. She was popping in and out of their homes last week." Martha pulled a tour map out of the folder Julia had given her. "Here, I'll give you a copy in case you want to visit them. I better get going. I have a lunch meeting with the tour committee, and then I'll give you a call." Martha shoved the door open and they both gasped at the icy rush of wind.

Sarah waited until Martha dove into her own car before she motored away and circled the town square. As she passed Maggie's store, she spotted one of the twins inside the window. So Maggie had brought them in to work after all. Maybe she could ask them if they knew anything about the quilt. She parked and hurried into the cozy shop, the chimes hanging on the door announcing her arrival.

Maggie stood behind the antique steel cash register, busy chatting with two customers. She sent Sarah a bright smile.

"Back here, Grandma," Audrey called from the depths of the packed store.

Sarah sidled by the display case full of pocket watches and ladies trinkets of a bygone elegant era. For the holiday season, Maggie had arranged a seating area with couches and chairs. She'd set a gleaming mahogany table with an elaborate silver tea set and china platters with assorted cookies.

The twins stood by the table like soldiers manning their station. Audrey was dressed in her usual jeans and a stylish lime green top. Amy wore black jeans and a red sweater with a stylized Christmas tree on the front. The ornaments, made of shiny buttons, twinkled as she moved about.

Pastor John Peabody lounged in one of the plush high-backed chairs, a plate of cookies on his lap and a china cup in his hand. "Why hello, Sarah. Your granddaughters were just telling me how they helped bake these delicious cookies yesterday." His easy smile reached all the way to his green eyes. "They are blessed to have such an accomplished baker to teach them."

Sarah slid off her coat. "Thank you, but the girls should take all the credit. They're both quick learners, and their mother is a marvelous cook."

Amy stepped forward with a silver tray. "Would you like some more?" she asked with a shy smile.

"Thank you, I think I will." Pastor John helped himself to the assortment. "And I must say, I like your Christmas sweater."

"Thanks. Grandma Jo sent it from California. She bought it, but sewed on all the buttons herself. Audrey has one too, but she wouldn't wear it." She glanced at her sister, who rolled her eyes.

"Your grandmother did a great job. Betty used to knit sweaters for all the youngsters in our family." His smile faltered for a second.

"I remember one blue and white sweater Betty knitted. It had a cute sailboat pattern," Sarah said, as Audrey took a plate of cookies from Amy and walked over to the ladies by the cash register.

"Oh yes, that was for my nephew Jeremy. Can you believe he's in the Navy now? He's still obsessed with boats." He chuckled. Sarah perched on the velvet couch facing the pastor and tried to relax. She really wanted to ask the girls about the quilt, but didn't want to bring it up in front of Pastor John.

Amy slid behind the couch, her braid tickling Sarah's neck. "Grandma, would you like something to drink? We have cocoa, tea, or coffee."

"I'll have some tea, thank you," Sarah said with a smile. "Do you need a refill, Pastor John?"

"I'm fine, thanks. I'm just waiting for something to be gift wrapped. Maggie found a lovely cameo that reminded me of one my mother had. After she passed away, we couldn't find it. I bought this one to send to my sister in Florida."

"What a thoughtful gift. Your sister is a lucky lady."

"Here you go, Grandma." Amy handed Sarah a delicate teacup on a saucer.

"You girls are good hostesses," Sarah said.

"Thanks. Mom hired us to serve refreshments and clean up around the store for the rest of the week. I like the cookie part, but the cleaning isn't as fun," she said as Audrey returned with the cookie tray.

"Yeah, Mom said if we were going to be bored at home, we might as well be useful and keep her company," Audrey added in a glum tone. The door chime rang, and she glanced over her shoulder. "Amy, it's Brita and Pam."

Amy took off toward the front of the store, which quickly filled with chatter and giggles.

Audrey sighed and plunked the cookie platter down on a foot stool, then slowly followed the same path her sister had just run down.

Pastor John exchanged a smile with Sarah. He leaned forward, asking in his friendly pastoral tone that inspired confidences, "How are you doing, Sarah? Things have been so busy the last couple of weeks, I haven't had a chance to talk to you. Everything going okay?"

"Oh, I'm fine. I mean, of course I miss Gerry more over the holidays, but it's better this year with Jason and his family here. They keep me hopping. Gerry would've loved it too," Sarah said, meeting the pastor's gaze. Pastor John had lost his wife ten years before and had a deep understanding of how difficult going through the holidays without your spouse could sometimes be.

"Gerry's manger looks wonderful in front of the church," he said. "Thanks for coming to our rescue. They still haven't fixed the church's yet. I hope your yard isn't bare without it."

"Oh it's fine. The church needs the manger more than I do. I can go one year without some of my traditional decorations." Sarah usually set the small nativity scene up in a corner of the porch to protect it from the weather. When the pastor had called, she'd given him the manger and carted the rest back to the cellar.

"Did Gerry make your entire nativity scene?"

"Yes. It started with the manger. Jenna's fifth-grade class needed one for the Christmas pageant. Later he and Jason made the Mary and Joseph and then eventually the wise men and shepherds. He wanted to carve a donkey or a lamb, but he never got around to it."

"As I've said before, your husband was a talented man. He's truly missed."

"Thank you." Sarah replied. "So, do you have any plans for the holidays?"

"After the Christmas service, I'm taking my sister's gift to her down south and enjoying the Florida sunshine."

"That sounds wonderful, as long as you don't get too attached to that sun. We need you here."

Pastor John chuckled again. "Don't worry. I'm a Maple Hill man through and through. Someday I might get a part-time home down there, and travel in between and become...what do they call them?"

"Snowbirds?"

He grimaced and rubbed his tummy. "That's the term. But if I keep eating these cookies, I'll get so big and round, I won't be able to fly south for the winter."

Sarah laughed with him, and then they fell silent for a moment. "I was wondering if you'd keep my boarder Belle Silver in your prayers," Sarah finally said. "I'm worried about her. She left abruptly, without word of where she was going."

"Is this the young lady you brought with you to church a few weeks back?"

"Yes, that's Belle. She's gone most weekends, but I'm trying to get her involved in the young-adult group when she has time." Sarah looked up as Maggie approached.

"I'll certainly keep her in my prayers," the pastor said as he got to his feet. Maggie handed him a gift bag tied with holiday ribbon. "Thank you, my dear. Arlene is going to love this."

"I'm always happy when one of my treasures finds a good home. I hope she enjoys it," Maggie said, sweeping a shiny auburn lock behind her ear. She waited until the pastor bid them good-bye and strode out of the shop, before asking. "Keep who in prayer? Is someone sick?"

"No, it's Belle. I haven't seen her for a couple of days."

"Are you sure she's not off on one of her adventures?" Maggie asked. She'd met Belle a couple of times when she'd been at Sarah's house and was well acquainted with Belle's interest in the outdoors.

"I'm not sure of anything. It's just strange this time." Sarah summarized the details, or lack thereof, for Maggie as the door chimes rang again. More adolescent chatter filled the air. Three of Martha's granddaughters, Lexie, Pru, and Trina, scampered in the door, followed by Pru's mother Mandy, who waved and headed for the cookie table in the back, careful not to bump into anything with her rounded belly. Martha would have another grandchild this spring.

"I hope Belle's okay," Maggie said, keeping watch over two elderly ladies browsing the lamp section of the store. "Jason isn't going to be happy if Belle flew the coop without notice. It'll give him ammunition to try to convince you to stop taking in boarders."

"Belle may be back tomorrow. Who knows?" Sarah said with a small smile. "Jason inherited his dad's protective streak."

"That's for sure," Maggie said. "I pity the boys when Amy and Audrey start dating."

Sarah looked over at the group of seven girls trying on old hats, scarves, and gloves. Audrey, apparently the judge, stood off to the side and would point her thumb up or down. Mostly down.

It was hard to imagine any of them being anything but mischievous twelve-year-olds; but before too long, they'd be planning each other's weddings like she and Martha had, which was all the more reason Sarah wanted to focus on the present and make this the best Christmas possible. And she needed to begin by fixing the problem she'd created by helping to convince Maggie to participate in the home tour.

She took a deep breath. "Maggie, I have some bad news about the quilt."

CHAPTER FIVE

Maggie took Sarah's hand in hers. "Oh, Sarah, I'm so sorry. I loved that quilt. The first Christmas I visited at your home, Jason told me all kinds of stories about the symbols embroidered on it."

"He did?" Sarah asked with pleasant surprise. "I used to tell the stories to him and Jenna, but he never seemed to show much interest. Jenna was always the one to ask for more."

"Trust me, he remembers." Maggie said.

"I'm glad you told me," Sarah replied, happy some of her efforts to instill a sense of family history in her children had paid off.

"I hope you find the quilt soon."

"Thanks. Chances are it will turn up. I just wanted you to know in case we have to find something else to put on that wall. I have another quilt that might work, although the pattern isn't very Christmassy. Or maybe you have a picture you could hang temporarily."

"I might have something around here that could work," Maggie said as an elderly couple approaching the counter snagged her attention. "I'll have to think about it, but don't you worry. Everything will work out fine."

"Thanks for understanding, Maggie. I feel like we railroaded you into doing the home tour."

"Actually, after I got over the surprise of being asked, I realized Martha was right. It'll be good for us to get to know more of the community. I see lots of people in the store, but Jason's more isolated in his office. This will be a great opportunity to mingle."

"Glad to hear it. I feel better then."

"Let me know if Belle shows up. I'll keep her in my prayers. Excuse me, I better see to these customers." A big smile stretched across her face as she hurried over to the couple waiting for assistance.

Sarah took her teacup and saucer to a sink in the back room and washed them. Somewhere in the store a grandfather clock chimed twelve. She'd been in the store far longer than she'd planned. She slung her coat over her arm and grabbed her purse.

The twins and their friends were still switching hats and scarves around, snapping photos with each other's cell phones. Sarah couldn't help but grin as she waded into their group. Audrey was dressed like a flapper, with a green cloche hat and long beaded scarf.

"I don't want to interrupt your fun, but I'm on my way," Sarah said. "Could I talk to Amy and Audrey for a moment?"

"Sure. We have to go anyway," a girl with curly, black hair said. Sarah thought it was Pam, though it could have been Brita. "My mom's going to take us to Pittsfield to go Christmas shopping at the mall." She poked Audrey in the arm. "You two want to come? Pru's mom said they could go too."

"Yeah!" Audrey exclaimed, pulling off the hat. "That'd be so cool."

"We have to ask our mom," Amy said in a soft voice.

Maggie, only a few feet away, looked over and shook her head at Audrey without interrupting her sales pitch. The elderly couple was very interested in a Tiffany lamp.

"Bummer. Maybe next time," the girl said as she and the others grabbed their coats and headed out the door. "See ya."

"I wish you could go," Trina said with a backward look as she followed the girls out the door. Mandy waved to Maggie and departed also. The store suddenly seemed too quiet.

Audrey scowled and slumped down on a round piano stool, arms crossed over chest. "Mom never lets me have any fun. She thinks we're babies. Pam's mother would've watched us. How come the other girls can go to the mall with their friends?"

"Audrey, we'll discuss it later," Maggie said with a look that meant business. Audrey's scowl deepened, but she refrained from complaining further as Maggie led her customers to the back of the store where more lamps were displayed.

Sarah sighed. At age twelve, life sometimes seemed unfair. They'd understand when they had kids of their own. She remembered her mother saying that very thing, and eventually it turned out to be true.

Amy picked up the hats and returned them to the coat rack. "What's up, Grandma? Did you want to tell us something?"

"Listen, girls, remember when you were over at my house last Thanksgiving weekend and were playing in the attic?"

"Yeah. We tried on some of those old clothes and looked through the boxes," Audrey said with a shrug.

"Did you happen to open the trunk that sits under the lamp? It had the Christmas quilt in it."

"You mean the quilt with the sparkly thread?" Amy asked. She'd finished with hats and was now making neat rolls with the scarves.

Sarah nodded. "That's the one. Did you take it out of the trunk?"

The twins glanced at each other, and Amy said, "You said we could explore."

Sarah nodded. "You're right. I did. You're not in trouble. I'm just trying to figure something out."

Audrey blew out a breath that ruffled her blond bangs. "We got the quilt out, but we only looked at it and put it back."

"In the same trunk?" Sarah asked, relieved the quilt had at least been in the attic after Thanksgiving.

Audrey and Amy nodded.

"When you took the quilt out, did you see anything else at the bottom of the trunk?"

"Like what?" Amy asked. She stopped straightening the accessories and looked straight at Sarah.

Sarah smiled. Amy took after Sarah and loved mysteries. "Christmas ornaments and one of my quilting books."

Audrey shook her head. "There was nothing in it but the quilt and some paper. We took everything out so Amy could hide."

"You tried to lock me in." Amy stuck out her tongue at her sister.

"You didn't have to get in."

"You dared me to!"

"Girls. Concentrate," Sarah said with an amused smile. "And you didn't put anything else back in the trunk with the quilt?"

They shook their heads.

"What's up?" Amy asked. "Did something happen to the quilt? We were extra careful."

"You didn't do anything wrong. I'm just trying to figure out where I might have misplaced some things." Sarah set her purse on the counter and pulled her coat on. "I hope you have fun this afternoon. Looks like your mom is staying really busy." She glanced at Maggie, who now held a lamp in each hand and was heading to the counter.

"She's going to show me how the cash register works later today. That'll be fun." Amy grinned as she lined up the last scarf in the wooden box.

Audrey hopped off the stool and followed Sarah to the door. "Grandma, can you do something for us?"

"What is it, honey?"

"Can you come and pick us up early on Friday and take us home? We want to clean the house for the home tour and surprise Mom and Dad."

"I think that's a wonderful idea." Sarah beamed. She'd half expected Audrey to ask her to take them to the mall. "What time?"

Audrey thought for a moment. "Well, we probably should work here in the morning, but we can tell Mom you're taking us shopping. Then we can stop by a store so we're not lying."

"Ah, I should've known shopping would sneak in there somewhere."

Amy walked up behind them. "We don't have to go to the store if you don't want to."

Audrey's mouth dropped open. "Yes we do!"

Sarah laughed. "We'll work out the details later." She glanced toward the door and whispered, "Here come Mrs. Rosenthal and Mrs. Cole. I bet they're coming in here. Better get back to your cookie station."

The girls wandered back to the table as Sarah paused by the Christmas tree near the door. Antique ornaments glistened and glittered, reminding her of the ones on her tree. Her finger brushed a glass snowflake, and she marveled at the glass etching. The date on the tag said 1930s and the price was forty dollars. She reluctantly let go of it. She owned too many already.

She waved at Maggie and the girls and nodded a hello to Mrs. Rosenthal and Mrs. Cole before hurrying to the cold car. A flicker of anticipation tickled her spine as she gripped the steering wheel. Time to hunt for more clues about Belle.

"Hello, Mrs. Hart? This is Kelsey Manning, Belle's friend. I had a message you called. Sorry I couldn't get back to you sooner. I had to wait until my lunch break."

Sarah set down the grilled cheese sandwich she'd fixed for lunch and shifted her cell phone to a better position on her ear. "Oh that's okay, Kelsey, I'm sorry to bother you. I was wondering if you'd heard from Belle lately."

"Not since Thanksgiving, although we were planning on getting together sometime over the holidays. Why? Is something wrong?"

"I'm not sure," Sarah said, hesitating. "Your number was on her rental application as an emergency contact. Belle apparently left a couple of days ago and neglected to tell me when she'd be back. I was wondering if you knew where she might've gone."

"She didn't mention anything to me, but you know Belle, she's a free spirit. She's probably off taking photographs somewhere, or caving, or skiing, or all three," Kelsey said with a laugh. "When she lived with me, she was always on the go. I couldn't keep up with the girl. She'll probably be back any time now."

"She packed most of her things, and her room's empty. Someone at her work suggested she might've eloped."

"You're kidding?" she asked. "Really? With whom?"

"Andrew something."

Kelsey snorted. "No way. Andrew? That relationship was so over. I'm still mad at him about that. He was one of the reasons she moved out of Pittsfield."

"That's what I thought too, but he sent Belle roses and a card implying he wanted them to get back together."

"Really? He's such a cheapskate that surprises me."

"A cheapskate?"

"Yeah. Belle used to mention how they went Dutch on a lot of their dates, and far as I know, he never gave her flowers."

"Is that why they broke up?" Sarah asked as she made notes on a pad of paper. "I know I'm being nosy, but it might give me a clue."

"I don't know all the details, but they were such opposites. He's a real geek, although he doesn't look like one. Always with his nose in a computer, and I don't mean in a creative way like Belle. He had a weird obsession with spreadsheets. Didn't like sports. The only activity he seemed to like was going caving. He likes bats. To me that's just creepy." A shudder wobbled her voice.

"In your opinion, was he...er...unkind to Belle in any way?" Sarah asked, tightly clutching her pencil.

"You mean did he ever hurt her physically? No." Kelsey snorted again. "If they had hand-to-hand combat, it'd be an even match. Belle took some martial arts in college."

"That's a relief."

"But he did do a number on her emotionally. She cried for about a week, and then told me she'd gotten a new job over in Maple Hill and was moving. I was surprised since her brother had just relocated here."

"That is surprising. She had to have strong reasons to move. I'd like to talk to her ex-fiancé. What's his last name?"

"Oh man," Kelsey said with a moan, "I don't remember. It was a common name like Smith or Wilson. All I remember is that the name sounded boring. He works for an accounting firm, but I don't know which one."

"That gives me a place to start looking." Sarah jotted a note. "What do you know about Belle's brother Ben?"

"Belle moved away before I got a chance to meet him, but I know she's been back in Pittsfield off and on to help him get settled. If he hadn't gotten a job, I bet she would've convinced him to move over to Maple Hill. She worries about him. He has a tendency to get into trouble."

"What kind of trouble?"

"She didn't really say, and I quit trying to pry. She just talked about the fun they had as kids. She used to make up games or puzzles to help her brother learn to focus and get through his homework."

"Belle's good at puzzles," Sarah agreed. "She helped me figure out the pieces of a quilt awhile back and, more recently, she's been organizing a game for the home tour, which is taking place this weekend."

"How cool! I bet she loves that."

"Yes, but it makes me even more concerned. She kind of left us hanging and she doesn't seem like a person who'd go off and drop such a big responsibility without a word."

"Oh I agree. She wouldn't do that." Kelsey paused. "Belle may be spontaneous, but she's always been reliable."

"Do you know how I might get in contact with Ben or where he works?"

"Unfortunately not. Belle implied she was helping him make a fresh start in Pittsfield. He'd lost his job at a gas station, and she mentioned she needed to help him find an apartment close to his new job, so he could walk. His car was an old clunker and about to die. I never did hear where he ended up."

Sarah thought about the photo of Belle and her happy family. "What about Belle's parents? Can I get in touch with them? Maybe Belle went to visit them for the holidays."

"Her mother passed away years ago. Her father's an archaeologist and spends most of his time now in the Middle East. It's sad, but it explains why Belle is always taking care of Ben."

"Do they ever see their dad?"

"Every couple of years. Belle used to e-mail him a lot. I think I have a contact number for the research firm that employs him. You can get a message to him through them. Just a sec."

Sarah could hear the sound of drawers being opened.

"Here it is. Dr. Anthony Silver. Glazier Research." Kelsey rattled off the number. "And now that I think about it, Belle's Aunt Lisa called here awhile back and got our answering machine. I don't know if Belle ever called back. I got the impression they'd had some kind of falling out."

"Do you know where she lives?"

"Nope, but I think it was long distance. Probably Boston since Belle and Ben lived there for a while." Kelsey blew out a deep, noisy breath. "I'm sorry. I wish I knew more. I'm afraid I haven't helped much."

Sarah gazed at her page of notes. "Oh no, you've been very helpful. Thank you, Kelsey."

"No problem. I'll ask around with some of our other friends. If I find anything out, I'll let you know. But I really think she's fine. Have Belle call me when she gets back from wherever she's gone."

"I will. Thanks again." Sarah clicked her phone off and hauled out her copy of the extended yellow pages covering Pittsfield businesses. She found three accounting firms listed in Pittsfield. She called the first number, which turned out to be a husband and wife partnership by the name of Brahms. The second was for the Berkshire Heights Accounting firm.

"Berkshire Heights, how may I help you?" a man's voice asked.

"I'm hoping you can help me find one of your accountants. I've lost his card, but remembered he worked here."

"Name, please."

"Dear me. His name is Andrew … Andrew …," Sarah let her voice trail away.

"You must mean Andrew Blake," the man said helpfully. "Mr. Blake won't be back until tomorrow morning. Can I take a message?"

"Would you know where I could reach him today?"

"I'm sorry, ma'am, he didn't leave a forwarding number."

"Was he in earlier today?"

"No, ma'am."

"Is he on vacation?" Sarah persisted.

"I'm sorry, I don't know." The cheerful voice started to fade. "I just answer the phones and take messages."

"Is there anyone else—"

"Mr. Blake doesn't have a personal secretary."

"All right, thank you. Please have Mr. Blake call Sarah Hart as soon as possible." She left her number, hoping the man wouldn't just throw her message away.

Sarah called customer information, and asked for Andrew's home number. She wrote it down and dialed. Getting no answer, she hung up and twirled the pencil in her fingers. The fact that Andrew Blake wasn't at work or at home could be good news. Maybe Wendy was right, and the two had reconciled and eloped.

"Hey, Mom!" Jason knocked on the kitchen door, startling her. Sarah got up and let him in.

"Hi, Jason. I didn't expect to see you in the middle of the day. Is something wrong?"

"I saw your car in the driveway and decided to pick up that old sleigh, if that's okay. I want to get it cleaned up and decorated before the tour."

"Of course. It's in the cellar behind the yard tools. It's really dusty down there. You might get your clothes dirty."

He glanced down at his navy slacks and open-collared white dress shirt. "Doesn't matter, I don't have any more appointments this afternoon. In fact, I don't have any more this week." He looked at the half-eaten sandwich and peeled orange sections on her plate. "I'm sorry. I didn't mean to interrupt your lunch."

Sarah shrugged, always glad to see her son. "Not a problem. I always love to see my favorite son. Did you eat?"

"Not yet."

"Would you like a grilled cheese sandwich?"

He hesitated, rubbing his chin. "If you don't mind making more."

Sarah smiled and headed for the counter. "I like cooking for you. Reminds me of when you were little."

"Well, in that case, I'd love one. Thanks." He settled into the other chair, his attention caught by the yellow pages she'd left open. "Do you need an accountant, Mom?"

"No, I'm just trying to locate someone."

"Who do you know in Pittsfield?"

Sarah held up the bread bag. "Do you want one or two sandwiches?"

"Two, please."

"Do you want tomato on it?" Sarah asked, getting the cutting board down at his nod. "I saw Maggie and the girls this morning. Amy and Audrey seem happy to be helping out in the store. I think it's the social aspect that appeals to them. Some of their friends stopped by. They were trying on hats. I'm sure they'll want to show you the photos later."

"They already e-mailed me one of them," Jason said, the first sign of a smile touching his lips since he arrived. "Goofy, but I'm glad they're having some fun instead of moping around the house. I just hope they don't drive Maggie too crazy."

Sarah flipped the browning sandwiches in the frying pan. "They seemed to be doing pretty well when I left."

"That's good. I'll run by there later." Jason leaned back in his chair, his gaze roaming from the cranberry-colored walls where Sarah had hung some framed Christmas cross-stitch to the cream-colored cabinets draped with green garland.

She cut the grilled cheese sandwiches in half and set the plate and a bag of chips on the table. "Grilled cheese for your thoughts?"

Jason grinned. "Guess that's a fair trade. A penny doesn't buy much these days."

Sarah sat opposite him as he bit into his sandwich.

He ate nearly half of one in two bites. "I was just thinking how familiar everything is, even with the changes you've made. Different. Part of me still expects Dad to come in any moment and head for the cookie jar."

Sarah patted his hand. "I do, too, sometimes."

"Being back in Maple Hill, especially at Christmas, brings back so many memories I'd almost forgotten. Like how Grandpa William taught us how to build the best snow forts in the neighborhood, and how we'd almost always win the snowball battles. And then when we got tired out, Grandma Ruth would boil molasses and pour it on bowls of snow to make candy."

His blue eyes crinkled with mirth. "Remember the year Dad bought us that old-fashioned red toboggan?"

Sarah nodded. How could she forget? Jason had been five and Jenna three. The old-fashioned toboggan had been six feet of wood planking with cushions to sit on and a curled front end. Gerry said the whole family could fit on it. Her heart still pitter-pattered at the memory, but she smiled, encouraging Jason to continue.

"I watched Dad wax the bottom in the workshop until it was shiny, and then we all climbed Mercer Hill. I sat in the front, Jenna got on behind me, and Dad was going to take the rear and show us how to steer. Only I must've been too excited and lifted my feet or something because next thing I knew, the toboggan was flying down the hill. And Dad was running behind us, yelling, 'Lean! Lean!' I didn't know what he meant. I kept looking for the steering handles like on my little sled, and then—poof—we were inside a snowdrift with Dad still yelling and digging us out."

He laughed, small wrinkles appearing around his eyes. "I love that memory."

Sarah chuckled more at her son's reaction than at the story. "I have photos of you both covered with snow and grinning from ear to ear." She'd been at the bottom with the camera, helpless to do anything but pray they didn't hit a tree or overturn. Miraculously the snowdrift they hit was fresh and soft.

"Poor Dad. It took some convincing for us to try the hill again. I didn't realize it then, but the whole incident must've shaken him up some. I guess I would have been too if Amy and Audrey had been on that toboggan."

"Amy would've loved it though, just like you did."

Jason smiled. "That she would. Is that toboggan still in the cellar too?"

"Yes it is, probably near the sleigh you wanted," she said. "You want to see if you can do a repeat performance?"

"I think we'll start with sleds you can steer a little more easily. The toboggan is fun but you need a long straight area. Besides, the twins are old enough to set their eyes on something more exciting and expensive, like snowboarding. I hope we have time to go at least once this year."

Sarah hoped so too. How quickly time flew. The day Jason and Jenna had their adventure on the toboggan seemed like only yesterday. The kids, on their Christmas break, would've been playing about this time of the afternoon while she finished her household chores, like making sure the cookie jar stayed full of Christmas cookies in anticipation of Gerry coming home. He'd come in the back door and always give her a kiss even before taking his coat off. She'd give anything for another moment like that.

"Thanks, Mom, for lunch." Jason had wolfed down the rest of his sandwiches and chips. "I'll get the sleigh and be on my way. I'll take it out the bulkhead."

"Don't forget, there are extra holiday lights in the boxes on the top shelf," Sarah said, clearing the plates and putting them in the dishwasher. "Take whatever you need."

She wiped off the table and glanced at the kitchen clock. Martha should be done with her committee meeting by now. "Let me know if you need help." She called as Jason's footsteps receded, and there was a loud thumping sound.

"Mom?"

She rushed to the cellar staircase. "Jason, are you okay? Did you fall?"

"I'm fine, but one of your suitcases tumbled down the stairs."

"It can't be my suitcase." Sarah descended the stairs. "Mine are in the attic."

Jason stood, gazing at the overturned case and clothes strewn across the floor. "The suitcase was halfway down the stairs, and I didn't even see it until I accidently kicked it."

"I have no idea how it got there." Sarah picked up a T-shirt with a wild tiger print. "And these obviously aren't my clothes."

"Uh-oh. There's something solid in here." Jason unearthed a lime green laptop computer.

Sarah gasped. "That's Belle's computer!"

"I hope I didn't break it." He carried the laptop over to Gerry's old workbench and flipped on the hanging work lamp.

He opened the lid. "The screen's not cracked, but it's not turning on. Battery might be dead. Is there a cord anywhere?"

Sarah dug through the mess and discovered an electrical cord. "Here, try this."

Jason plugged the computer in and pushed the power button, but the screen flickered as if struggling to come back to life. Jason shifted the computer gently and the boot up process began. "Something must've shaken loose inside. I'd just leave it here until Belle gets home, so she has a chance to back everything up, if she hasn't already. If we move it, the computer may not start up again."

He stepped back, his hands planted on his hips. "What's her computer doing down here anyway?"

Sarah's heart thudded. "I'm not sure what's going on, but I think it's time to call the police."

CHAPTER SIX

So you think something has happened to Miss Silver?" Chief Nate Webber leaned back in Sarah's kitchen chair and sipped his coffee, but his brown-eyed gaze remained alert and attentive.

"At first I thought she moved out without informing me or maybe even eloped, but Belle wouldn't leave her laptop. She sometimes brings work home. She even joked once about it being her boss," Sarah said, relieved the chief of police had responded to her call. Since they'd worked on several mysteries together in the past, Sarah felt he might take her intuition more seriously than some of the other officers.

"But most of all, Chief, I really don't believe she'd disappear for this long without contacting me or Martha. She's always been so responsible, and people are depending on her for the treasure hunt."

"I agree the circumstances are odd. Is anything of yours missing? Do you keep cash in the house? Have you checked your jewelry box?"

Sarah glanced at Jason, who leaned against the counter, arms crossed over his chest. She hadn't wanted to mention the quilt in front of him, especially after what Maggie had revealed back at the store. "I don't know if this is related to Belle's disappearance, but a quilt I stored in the attic is gone."

"Which one?" Jason asked.

Sarah sighed, turning toward him. "The Christmas one, honey."

"You've got to be kidding!" A flush crept up Jason's neck. "You mean your boarder stole our family quilt and skipped town?"

"We don't know that for sure," Sarah said, placing a hand on Jason's stiff arm. "The attic is never locked. Anyone could've gone up there. You were up there not long ago. Did you notice anything unusual?"

"No, I was looking for an old trophy of mine to show Amy. I don't even know which trunk the quilt is in. Was in."

Chief Webber cleared his throat, drawing their attention back to him. "Was this quilt valuable?"

"I suppose it could be worth a couple hundred dollars, maybe five hundred or more if auctioned off as a historical heirloom. But the quilt's real worth is its history and sentimental value."

"It's irreplaceable," Jason said flatly. "The quilt has been in the family for a hundred years. You have to find it."

Jason's words stung because Sarah knew they were true. She'd mourned over the quilt last night, but sentimentality shouldn't be a reason to jump to conclusions. She squared her shoulders. "There is no reason to accuse Belle yet. At this point we don't know what happened to the quilt. My granddaughters saw it last Thanksgiving, so sometime between then and now, it was taken out of the attic. Belle could've borrowed it, I suppose, but she knew I was going to hang it on the wall for the home tour. She was involved in preparations for the treasure hunt during the tour too. I seriously doubt she would steal the quilt with the intention of selling it. I could be wrong, but right now that's how I feel. I'm more concerned that she may be in serious trouble."

Chief Webber ran his hand over his gray-salted hair and rubbed the back of his neck. "Well, I'll say again that Miss Silver's actions have been rather unusual, but leaving behind a suitcase and computer and other items is still no indication of foul play. She took the time to clear out her room. She doesn't seem a threat to herself or others. And if you think she didn't take the quilt, then there's no crime here."

"Isn't there anything we can do?" Sarah asked, the sick dread she'd felt last night returning.

"You can file a missing person report at the station, and I'll see that we run a routine check at hospitals and morgues.

If we get evidence of foul play we can go further. I suggest you file a report on your quilt too. Take another look around the house to see if anything else is missing."

Jason slid his arm around Sarah's shoulders. "We'll take care of it, Chief." Sarah sighed. "I appreciate your coming over."

"You're welcome. Thanks for the coffee," Chief Webber stretched his long frame upward. "Come into the station tomorrow and we'll get the paperwork started."

Sarah ripped the page off her notepad where she'd copied the phone numbers from Belle's references and the two for Andrew Blake. She handed it to Chief Webber. "These are all the contact numbers I have. Her brother Ben lives in Pittsfield, but I haven't found a number or address for him yet."

"Thanks. These may be useful." He folded the sheet carefully and pocketed it. His assessing gaze swept the room and landed on Sarah and his stern face softened. "I know you're worried. Hopefully this will get straightened out soon. Call me if you think of anything else that may assist us in finding Miss Silver."

After Chief Webber left, Jason let out a long, troubled sigh. "Mom...maybe it's time to think about not having boarders. It's a security risk. You don't need the income. The house is paid for, and Dad had good life insurance."

"Sweetheart, I wish you'd stop worrying about me. As for boarders, I like having the extra income and the company. I check their references carefully. Belle has been an excellent tenant, other than—"

"She skipped out on you and stole the family quilt."

"*Borrowed*, if anything, and I'm not even sure about that. You're a lawyer. What happened to being innocent until proven guilty?"

He held his breath this time, then finally let it out evenly. "So what progress have you made so far?"

Sarah struggled not to smile at her son's attempt to resist lecturing her on sleuthing. He'd been trying lately to be supportive rather than critical of her attempts to help solve mysteries—though he still struggled at times.

"I've talked to her former roommate and have a lead on her ex-fiancé. There's a chance they reconciled and eloped, but after finding Belle's suitcase I'm doubtful. I also have a contact number for her father and there may be an aunt living in Boston."

"If you're trying to locate addresses and phone numbers, the online white pages can be helpful. I also have access to some databases at the office, if you don't have any luck with that."

Sarah smiled. "Thanks for the suggestion and offer, Jason."

"You're welcome, but this still doesn't mean I'm totally comfortable with you poking around. Please be careful. Regardless of how much you like Belle, you haven't known her that long. Everyone has secrets."

"Honey, I do try to be careful. But I can't just sit by and do nothing."

"I know. And I try not to nag," Jason said, a grin playing at the corners of his mouth. "I better get the sleigh and get home."

Sarah followed her son to the cellar. As Jason dug the sleigh out from behind the yard tools, she climbed on her stepladder to get the boxes of lights down.

"Mom, did you unlock the bulkhead earlier?" Jason asked, standing on the stairs by the metal doors that led to the yard. He had pushed one panel of the door open and light poured in from outside.

Sarah stepped down the ladder with a box in her arms. "No, I always keep it locked unless I'm taking tools in or out. I haven't opened it since I raked leaves in November."

Her gaze locked with Jason's, realizing they were thinking the same thing. "Why would Belle go out through the cellar?" she asked.

"Beats me. I'm still trying to figure out why she'd leave her suitcase on the stairs." Jason grunted as he dragged the five-foot Santa's sleigh up the stairs. "You probably should mention this to the chief."

"I will when I file the report." After her son left, she returned to the cellar and locked the bulkhead doors. The glowing screen on Belle's computer beckoned from the workbench. Photos rotated on the screen saver. She watched the different scenes evolve. Some were nature shots and others showed Belle with people dressed in a variety of sporty clothing. Which one of the young men was Andrew?

The phone trilled from the kitchen, and she hurried up the stairs. It was Martha.

"How did the meeting go?" Sarah asked.

"As expected, and no, Belle didn't show," Martha said with a sigh. "No one's seen her since the last meeting, which was over a week and a half ago. Any luck on your end?"

"I wouldn't necessarily call it luck, but things have been happening. Chief Webber was here. We found more of Belle's things."

"I'm about five minutes away," Martha replied.

"The front door's unlocked, so just come on in." Sarah set the phone back in its holder and returned to the cellar. Chief Webber had taken a brief look at Belle's suitcase and the laptop, but Sarah wanted to be sure she hadn't missed anything.

The suitcase lay empty, the clothes piled beside it. Mostly shorts and T-shirts. Maybe Belle used the suitcase to store her summer items, but that didn't explain why the laptop was in there. Belle always traveled with her computer in its special red and black backpack.

Belle also owned another large green backpack she took on her camping excursions. It hadn't been in her room or the attic, so she must've taken it with her.

Sarah dug her fingers into every crevice of the suitcase and any pockets in the clothing, but found nothing but a couple of supermarket receipts and a nickel.

"Sarah?" Martha's voice called from the stairs.

"Down here."

Martha's footsteps echoed down the staircase. "What are you doing in the cellar?"

"Trying to figure out why Belle left all this behind. Jason found it on the basement steps." Sarah filled Martha in on the recent developments.

Martha eyed Belle's computer. "You don't suppose there's a clue on there to where she went, do you?"

"Maybe, but I've been resisting snooping on it. I feel like I'm invading her privacy. I still expect her to walk in any moment and be annoyed at all the fuss."

Martha headed over to the workbench with a purposeful stride. "If you suddenly disappeared, even if you had a logical reason, wouldn't you understand and appreciate that people worried?"

She had a point. Sarah followed her. "Just be careful. Chief Webber said if facts surface that Belle may be in danger, they'll want to take a look at her computer files. But when the computer fell, we think something broke inside, so we decided not to move it."

Martha studied the screen saver still rotating Belle's photos. "Do you know any of these people?"

"I think the guy with the sandy hair is Ben, but I don't recognize anyone else. She never brought friends by the house."

"Okay, we'll take a quick look inside. Maybe we can find something that will help."

"Good idea. Oh, and Liam left a message on my answering machine while I was out. Remember he'd mentioned

Belle had purchased travel books? He said one was for Turkey and the other for the Colorado Rockies. I'm guessing she might be interested in Turkey since her father works in the Middle East."

Martha touched the mouse pad with the tip of her index finger. The photos stopped revolving, and the screen blinked to life, revealing rows of application icons. Martha moved the cursor to the documents file. All those years helping Ernie at his office had made Martha computer savvy.

"Oh look, there's one labeled Tour. Let me check that one and see if the answer key for the treasure hunt is in there." Martha opened the file. "Rats. There are only two documents. One labeled tour map and the other the advertising brochure."

She opened each and scanned them. "These are just older versions of what I already have." She closed the file and scrolled quickly through Documents.

"Try the one labeled Blog." Sarah said, pointing to the screen.

"Blog?" Martha asked. "I don't know why they named them that. Sounds like a swamp."

Sarah grinned. "Vanessa once suggested I do a blog about my quilts. Maybe Belle has one and she talked about her travels."

"That would help us so much if she did." Martha clicked the icon and a word processing program popped up. "Looks like an article she was writing."

A remarkable photo of stalagmites and stalactites was positioned above the text. Sarah read the caption: "Pirate Treasure Found in Gideon's Cave." She scanned the rough draft of the article.

"There's nothing else in the folder, so maybe she's still in the planning stage," Martha suggested as she clicked on an e-mail file. A few e-mails with ads and messages from the Copy Shop popped up, but there wasn't anything in New Mail or Old Mail to indicate where Belle could've gone. "She keeps her files very clean. I must have a thousand e-mails stored on my computer."

They searched a bit longer. Sarah sighed. It was as if Belle didn't want to be found.

"Thanks for trying," Sarah said. "Julia at the Copy Shop mentioned Belle used a flash drive. I went through the suitcase and didn't see one there. I'll look through her room and crate again later, but chances are it's in her purse or car."

"I suppose there's a chance she could have made plane or hotel reservations from her work computer and stored the information on the flash drive." Martha scrolled through a photo file, labeled with different locations, most in the Berkshires.

"I should take a closer look at her photos again later. Maybe there's some clue that she went back to one of those places."

"Good idea. I know you'll figure this out."

Much as she loved solving mysteries, Sarah wished she shared Martha's confidence. She felt like a car spinning its wheels in the snow, going nowhere fast.

Sarah sat in front of her laptop in her cozy kitchen studying Belle's photos on the screen. Outside the window, moonlight danced across the lawn as scattered clouds rolled swiftly in from the west. She made herself a simple supper of chicken noodle soup and crusty sourdough bread before returning to her search for Belle.

After Martha left to run errands for the home tour, Sarah had searched through Belle's computer one more time and then copied several of the photos on Belle's screen saver to her own flash drive. Several contained the sandy-haired young man who could be Belle's brother or possibly her ex-fiancé.

She checked the notes she'd been compiling about Belle. Kelsey had mentioned the girl had an aunt. Sarah brought up the Internet, accessed the online phone directory as Jason had suggested, and typed in *Lisa Silver* for the Boston area and then the state of Massachusetts. She groaned at the number of names that popped up on the screen. It would take a couple of hours to call them all. And it was possible the aunt was a sister who had married and changed her name. She needed more information.

Belle's father would know, but she hadn't been able to reach him earlier in the evening. Sarah had put in a call to Glazier Research. They said it might be a day or two for him to return the call since phone service could be sketchy in the desert. The scientists usually checked in via satellite phone every day depending on their location. The woman took Sarah's e-mail address too, explaining that sometimes the archaeologists could connect by Internet. She also asked if this was a life-and-death emergency. They could send a helicopter out to retrieve him. If not, they would relay the message.

Sarah had pondered what to say. No, it wasn't an emergency. At least she couldn't prove it. How did one explain that Dr. Silver's daughter had behaved weirdly, and Sarah had only a strong hunch that Belle might be in trouble? It would be cruel to frighten someone so far away if Sarah turned out to be wrong. So she explained who she was and that she was trying to locate Belle who might be traveling. At least that seemed vague enough. It shouldn't give a father a heart attack. Best to explain in a phone conversation. Sarah hoped she could get his son's contact information from him too.

She grew tired of looking at photos and decided to search Belle's crate again. She retrieved the book, the two ornaments, and the box of Belle's things from the bottom step. She'd meant to put the box back upstairs that morning, but got rushed when she'd gone out to meet Martha at The Spotted Dog.

Fortunately, her absentmindedness saved her a trip to the attic. She doubted Belle would've left a flash drive in there, but she'd told Martha she'd check.

She plunked the box down on her desk and turned on the gooseneck lamp. A fresh cup of orange-cinnamon tea sat beside her. The cheerful, Christmassy scent lifted her spirits as she settled in a chair and methodically went through the items in the box again. She held each book up by its binding and shook gently. No paper fell out. No flash drive and no new clues to why Belle had left these things in the attic.

Sarah leafed through the quilting book. The guide had been one of her favorites when she'd first started quilting. The simplified instructions detailed hand quilting techniques, as well as machine sewing, and offered simple, fun patterns for a beginner to try. Photographs gave the reader stunning examples of a broad array of common quilt blocks. Sarah hadn't referred to it in years. The most recent book she'd read on quilting was one Liam had ordered for her about unusual patterns.

Someone had penciled notes about fabric in the margins, and it wasn't her handwriting, she noted with surprise. She turned to her bookshelf. Her copy of the same book still sat wedged on the shelf.

She flipped open the book's cover and found a tiny goose logo from the Wild Goose Chase store. So the book wasn't even hers. It belonged to Vanessa Sawyer, who owned the local fabric shop.

A lump rose in Sarah's throat. She desperately wanted to believe that Belle would never have taken the quilt. But things didn't look good. It was possible Sarah would never see the quilt again.

"I'm sorry, Gerry," she whispered, although the quilt disappearance wasn't her fault. Elizabeth had entrusted the quilt to her care and she felt as though she'd let the family down. Would the centerpiece of a family tradition disappear forever?

She set the photo of the quilt on the table in front of her. She couldn't just sit around and worry about Belle. Her fingers itched to do something. To feel fabric beneath her fingers. To create something new out of her sadness.

Sarah pulled a spiral notebook from her desk, the kind she used when starting a new quilting project. She stared at a blank page as the excitement of a new quilt rose. How hard would it be to re-create the Star of Bethlehem quilt? Even if the family quilt was eventually recovered, a duplicate would be a fun project. Although she enjoyed the challenges of her work as a quilt restorer, it was refreshing and stimulating to create something from scratch.

She clipped special magnifying lenses on top of her glasses and studied the photo. The fine details were still tiny. She'd go cross-eyed if she worked from the snapshot. Remembering how she'd once copied a family photo, Sarah grabbed her digital camera and centered the LCD screen over the photo. Zooming in on the quilt, she snapped the image and then transferred it to her computer. The program expanded the quilt image, filling the screen. The results were slightly blurred, but now she could make out the individual diamond pieces and the embroidered symbols.

She picked up her pencil and jotted notes. The Hart quilt consisted of a large eight-point star, each point constructed from many small diamonds to form a starburst medallion. She counted eight different fabrics in the star and listed the colors in her notebook.

She punched in measurements on her calculator. For a king-size quilt, she'd need a total of ten yards of a variety of fabrics for the front, and eight and a quarter yards of a solid fabric for the back. The Hart quilt had an extra wide border that had been added onto over the years, as families continued to embroider it. So Sarah would have to consider fabric for that too.

She tapped the pencil eraser on the table. Gerry's great-great grandmother and her daughters had hand-sewn the original quilt, but Sarah would use her sewing machine. The reproduction quilt wouldn't be as authentic as the one sewn in 1910, but the machine stitching would make strong, lasting seams, so the quilt could last for the next hundred years. Besides, with all the hand quilting that needed to be done, plus the embroidery, Sarah had plenty to sew by hand.

She closed her eyes and imagined a circle of women sitting around a table. Sewing needles flashing as they talked and laughed, sharing their lives and stories with each other as they created the beautiful keepsake. She prayed she'd be able to recover their handiwork, but just in case the worst occurred and the quilt was gone forever, she'd ease her heartache by crafting a new one.

Energized by the idea of the new quilt, Sarah determined to go to the fabric store first thing in the morning, then straight to Pittsfield to see Andrew Blake.

CHAPTER SEVEN

G ood morning, Sarah. How nice to see you," Vanessa Sawyer said as Sarah entered the Wild Goose Chase. Vanessa sat on a stool behind the counter with a cup of tea and a romance novel.

"Hi Vanessa. Good book?"

Vanessa smiled, setting the novel face down to save her place. "The plot starts slow, but it's picking up pace. The story's set in the Caribbean. Just right for dreaming of sand and surf on a cold winter day."

"Oh I agree, there's nothing better on days like this than a nice cup of tea, a great book, and a roaring fire," Sarah said. "Unless, of course, it's a quilt hoop, instead of a book."

Vanessa laughed, a pleasant throaty sound. "Well, we may have lots of time for reading and quilting once that big storm gets here. I hear it's stalled over the Great Lakes, but gaining strength."

"I'm glad it's holding off, but my granddaughters won't be. They want snow for Christmas."

"Oh, so do my two, although the snow seems to lose its appeal to me after Christmas. 'Bout January, I start longing for the warm days of spring." Vanessa hopped down from her stool. Her copper-colored blouse enhanced the healthy glow of her dark skin and complemented her petite, trim form.

"Speaking of spring," Vanessa said. "I just got in the most beautiful pastel and floral fabrics. Want to take a look?"

"I'd love to, but I can't today. I've got a long list of specific fabrics I need from you, and then I'm heading over to Pittsfield," Sarah said, though she was thoroughly tempted. "I also wanted to return something of yours."

"Of mine?"

Sarah reached into her roomy quilted tote bag and pulled out the quilting book. "I found this at home. At first I thought it was mine, but I noticed your logo inside the front cover."

"Oh yes, that's a good book for beginners. I lent it to your boarder about a month ago."

"Belle?"

Vanessa nodded. "She'd come in one day to ask about fabric to decorate a ticket table and we started talking about quilts. She said something about researching the names of the quilt blocks that would be in the tour homes for some sort of game."

"She probably meant the treasure hunt."

"I showed her that book and she seemed excited about a couple of the patterns," Vanessa said. "She can keep the book longer if she needs it. The project is for charity, after all."

"Thanks. I'll tell her when I see her," Sarah said, praying that it'd be today. She slid the book back into the tote bag.

"Sure you don't want a cup of tea before you venture out in that nasty cold?"

"Maybe next time. I'm on a mission today." She reached into her purse and pulled out an enlarged copy of the family quilt she'd printed off the computer. "I want to re-create this quilt."

Vanessa eagerly studied the picture. "It's gorgeous. I love the starburst. I read somewhere that Lone Star or the Star of Bethlehem is one of the oldest patterns in America. I can see why it's such a favorite."

"Gerry's great-great grandmother, Rachel Hart, sewed this one in 1910. It was extra special because people didn't see this pattern much in the New England states back then. Rachel was a Southern belle from Georgia who married George Hart, a blue-blooded Yankee from Massachusetts. From what Gerry told me, she relocated to Maple Hill determined to civilize the brash Northerners with Southern manners."

"I tried that. It didn't work so well," Vanessa said with a roll of her eyes. She was from the South too. "Let's see. I know I have the fabric on hand to duplicate the colors. The patterns will be slightly different."

"That's okay. I know I can't re-create it exactly."

Vanessa rubbed her hands together. "Let's see what I have."

An hour later, Sarah left with bags full of fabrics and piled her purchases in the backseat. She climbed behind the steering wheel, filled with conflicting emotions. She was relieved to find it was Belle who'd left the quilting book in her attic, but also disappointed and anxious because this was more evidence that Belle was the prime suspect for stealing her Christmas quilt. The joy of starting a new quilt was quickly starting to fade in the face of the disappointment of Belle's potentially being a thief.

Sarah tried to shake off the bad feelings. No matter what happened with the quilt, she needed to focus on finding Belle. She was still worried about the girl. Sarah dug her cell phone out of her purse, and hit the speed dial button for Martha's phone. "I'm driving over to Pittsfield. Andrew Blake should be back at work this morning. I'm hoping Belle will be with him. If not, maybe he'll tell me more in person than over the phone. Up for a little road trip?"

"Thanks for coming along, Martha," Sarah said. After stopping off at the police station to fill out a missing person report, she and Martha had headed for Pittsfield.

"As if I'd let you go without me. We're in this together. I'm just hoping Belle is safe and sound. Maybe she's Belle Blake by now. Hmm, if I were Belle, I'd use Anabelle with that last name." Martha grinned.

"And even if she's not married, we know Andrew's been in touch with her over the last couple of weeks."

"Turn right in fifty feet," a mechanical female voice commanded.

Martha jumped in her seat. "I'm still not used to that thing just spouting off when it feels like it." She tapped Ernie's GPS on the dash, which she'd thought would be a good idea to bring. She peered at the little moving map. "Vine Street's coming up."

"Okay," Sarah said, obeying the more frequent urging of the GPS voice, and turned right as instructed. When they pulled up next to the Berkshire Heights Accounting Firm, they stared at the square glass and concrete architecture.

"Pretty modern building for Pittsfield," Martha observed as they hurried through the cold wind to the fifteen-foot tinted-glass doors. "Any services offered in there will be expensive. Andrew must do pretty well."

"Appearances can be deceiving, but judging from the marble floor, I think you may be right." Sarah's heel skidded as she stepped off the long gray carpet runner leading from the front doors to the elevators. She studied the building directory on the wall and located the accounting firm. It was the only listing on the third floor. They punched the button and the elevator door opened immediately.

Soft music serenaded them as they both repaired their wind-blown appearance in the elevator's conveniently mirror-lined walls. Sarah was wearing a soft pink turtleneck Gerry used to say complemented her rosy cheeks, a fitted navy jacket, and a calf-length skirt that covered tall black boots. Martha looked sharp in cocoa-colored slacks topped with an off-white Christmas sweater that was trimmed with gold.

The elevator flowed to a smooth stop and the door whooshed open directly in the reception area of the accounting firm. A young man in a pin-striped gray suit sat behind a desk with a headset wrapped around his head. He talked into the mic as his fingers flew over a keyboard. The name plate on his desk read Ted Yardley.

"Yes, Mrs. Tuttle, Mr. Henderson can see you this afternoon. Please bring your tax receipts with you, and he can advise you on any more investments you should make before the end of the year. Thank you, Mrs. Tuttle."

Ted's fingers stopped pounding the keys, and he acknowledged Martha's and Sarah's presence with a smile. "Some people are anxious to get a jump on the tax season."

"The new year will be here before we know it." Sarah smiled, although inside she grimaced at the thought of doing taxes. Maybe she should hire an accountant this year like Mrs. Tuttle had instead of struggling through the endless forms, trying to make sure she could justify all her quilting expenses. Gerry used to view tax preparation as a challenge. He loved to wrench every penny of their income back, but Sarah just wanted the whole thing over with so she could get back to quilting.

"Do you have an appointment?" he asked.

"No, I'm afraid not. I called yesterday asking to speak to Mr. Blake, but your answering service said he wouldn't be available until today."

Ted hit a button on the keyboard and studied the computer screen. "Mr. Blake is in, but I'm afraid he has a very busy schedule. Perhaps I can make you an appointment for later this week?"

"Oh dear, we live in Maple Hill and this is um ...," Sarah leaned across the desk and lowered her voice, "an urgent personal matter. If you could pass him a message that we're here, maybe he could squeeze us in. We promise we won't stay long."

The man frowned slightly. "Mr. Blake doesn't like to be disturbed when he's with a client. But I can let him know you're here when he's through, which," he glanced at the screen again, "should be in about ten minutes."

"Thank you so much," Sarah said, giving him another big smile.

He picked up a pen and message pad. "What's the message?"

"Please tell him we're friends of Anabelle Silver, and it's vital we speak to him today. I'm Sarah Hart and this is Martha Maplethorpe."

The man jotted down a note, and then gestured to some leather chairs lining the walls. "Please have a seat, and I'll let you know if Mr. Blake can see you."

Sarah and Martha stepped back toward the waiting area. While they talked, several more people stepped off the elevator. Ted allowed them quick passage to the inner sanctum through the door behind the reception desk.

Martha sighed, settling into a chair. "It'd be a shame if we drove forty minutes to be turned away."

"Even if we strike out here, I'd still like to try to find Belle's brother while we're here. I'm hoping Mr. Blake might have an idea where he lives or works," Sarah said.

"Mrs. Hart and Mrs. Maplethorpe, Mr. Blake will see you now." Ted took off his headset, and opened the door the previous privileged clients had entered. "Right this way."

He ushered them down a long hall of deep green carpet. Closed doors lined both sides. He stopped at the end of the hall and knocked on the door.

The door opened and a silver-haired woman exited, dressed in an elegant pink suit and pumps that made Sarah feel frumpy. Out of the corner or her eye, she noted Martha smoothing the wrinkles out of her sweater.

"Mrs. Steinbeck, I've called your driver," Ted offered the elderly woman his arm.

"Thank you, young man," she said. "Come along, Cookie." A Yorkshire terrier with a sparkling, gem-studded collar trotted at the end of an equally elaborate leash. The dog suddenly lunged forward. She ran to Martha, tail wagging, and planted her tiny feet on Martha's knees.

Martha scooped up the ball of fluff and patted the wiggling dog's ears. "What a beautiful dog you are." She laughed as Cookie tried to lick her face and handed her back to

Mrs. Steinbeck. "She's gorgeous. I had an aunt who raised Yorkies for a while. Wonderful dogs."

"Yes, yes she is, although she doesn't mind her manners all the time. Do you darling?" Mrs. Steinbeck cooed, holding the dog up so they were nose to nose.

Ted cleared his throat and Mrs. Steinbeck tucked the dog under her arm. "Yes, yes, I'm coming."

"Mrs. Hart?" a masculine voice asked.

Sarah turned. A tall man stood just inside the office. His thick, dark hair showed signs of receding at the temples, but his tanned face remained unlined and youthful. A double-breasted suit hung gracefully on his well-proportioned frame, which meant the cut was probably tailored.

He smiled and extended a hand in greeting. "I'm Andrew Blake." Sarah returned his firm handshake, noting that there was no wedding ring on his finger.

"It's a pleasure to meet you," he said. "Belle has said wonderful things about you and your home. She so enjoys living there."

"Thank you. That's good to hear." Sarah couldn't help smiling back.

He flashed his charming smile at Martha. "And then this must be Mrs. Maplethorpe." He shook her hand and gestured to two black leather chairs in front of a large mahogany desk. "Please have a seat and excuse the mess. Tax season is approaching and I'm trying to get organized."

He strode around the desk, which held a dozen stacks of neatly piled papers and an extra large computer monitor angled on one side. Centered on the wall behind the desk was a diploma from Harvard Law School. He settled in an elegant but functional high-backed desk chair. "Now what can I do for you ladies? Are you looking for an accountant? My appointment book is rather full for the next couple of months, but I would be willing to squeeze in any friends of Belle's."

"That's very kind of you, but," Sarah exchanged a glance with Martha, "actually we're here for an entirely different reason. This might sound a little strange, but we're trying to find Belle. We thought maybe she was with you."

He blinked his eyes several times. "Why me?"

"We know you sent her roses, Mr. Blake," Martha blurted out and sank back in her seat as his gaze shifted to her.

"Did Belle mention them to you?" he asked.

"We saw them at the Copy Shop where Belle works. Your card was on them," Sarah explained. "Someone suggested that she might have eloped."

"Really?" He seemed to ponder that for a bit, then said, "If she did elope, I'm afraid you have the wrong guy." He let out a dry laugh. "I sent the flowers in an apparently futile attempt to rebuild our relationship. Belle broke off our engagement quite some time ago."

"I'm sorry. I don't mean to upset you. We really have no idea if she eloped or not."

He gazed at the pen he rolled between his fingers. "Even if it's not true, I should've known better than to try to get involved with her again. She used me and then dumped me flat. Live and learn as they say. Problem is I still care." He looked up. "So, what's going on? Why would you think she eloped?"

"Belle seems to have…disappeared," Sarah chose her words carefully. "She left without informing me when she'd return. She isn't answering her phone. I try not to pry into my boarders' private lives, but the circumstances of her leaving are odd. I filled out a missing person report this morning."

"Do the police think something has happened to her?" His face seemed to pale.

"Actually, they're just beginning to investigate," Sarah said, omitting the part that they probably wouldn't continue beyond a few phone calls unless they found cause for concern.

"She's been gone for how long?" he asked.

"Three or four days, we think."

"Is that all?" His shoulders slid back against his chair. "She's probably on a little excursion. Belle never can relax like normal people. She likes to tromp through the woods or duck into caves to take photos."

"Normally I'd agree, but she cleaned everything out of her room, and yet left behind some personal items and her laptop. Do you have any idea where she could've gone?"

"That could be anywhere in the world. She loves to explore."

Sarah reached in her purse, searching for the photo she had printed that morning and held it up. "Is this her brother Ben?"

He glanced at the image of the sandy-haired young man in front of the mouth of a cave. "That's him."

"Do you know where this was taken?"

He studied the photo. Something flickered in his eyes, but he merely shrugged. "Could be any number of places. Probably in the Berkshires."

Sarah returned the photo to her purse. "I heard you enjoyed going caving with Belle."

"Let's just say out of Belle's numerous sports that was one I could tolerate." He glanced at his watch and rose. "I'm sorry ladies. I hate to cut our visit short, but I'm keeping a client waiting." He opened a desk drawer. "Let me give you my business card in case you have any more questions."

Sarah drew out her own business card and exchanged it with his as he walked them out the door. "Thank you for seeing us, Mr. Blake," Sarah said. "Would you happen to know where we can locate Ben?"

"You might try the Berkshire Museum of Art and see if he's still employed there. I know the curator, Mr. Warthorne, and gave him a nudge to give Ben a try. He hired Ben as a janitor a couple of months ago."

He escorted them halfway down the hall. "It was a pleasure meeting you both. Please keep me informed if you get new information on her whereabouts." He bid them good-bye and turned back toward his office as Sarah and Martha entered the waiting area, which was empty except for Ted. They thanked him for his assistance and headed for the elevator.

"If Mr. Blake had another client, then she or he is late," Martha said after the elevator doors closed.

"He probably just wanted to get rid of us. We go in there and announce that his ex-fiancée, whom he still cares for, may have eloped. Not exactly a topic a guy would warm to."

"He seemed like a nice man, and from the looks of his office, a successful one. Makes you wonder why Belle dumped him." Martha said.

"Who knows? He didn't seem all that worried about Belle's disappearance, but I did get the impression that when he looked at Ben's photo he recognized the location."

"Then why didn't he say so?"

"That's a good question."

The elevator slid to a stop, and Sarah and Martha made their way across the marble-floored lobby into the December weather.

The sun had broken through the cloud cover, but the wind still cut with a frosty edge. Sarah turned up the collar of her jacket and reached for her car keys. She unlocked the door and took one last look at the building they'd just exited.

"Martha, don't look now, but I think someone's watching us."

"What?" Martha looked over her shoulder anyway, and then waved at the small figure of Andrew Blake standing in the window of his office. He didn't return the wave, but stared down at them, a frown on his handsome face, before turning back into the depths of his office. A chill ran through Sarah that wasn't caused by the winter wind.

CHAPTER EIGHT

I haven't been to the museum since my kids were in high school," Martha said as she entered the revolving door.

When they'd emerged on the other side, Sarah replied, "Me either. I vaguely recall reading in the Sunday paper that their Christmas Tea fund-raiser raised thousands of dollars."

"Oh, a tea party. That sounds like fun. We should go sometime." Martha's voice echoed in the dome-ceilinged lobby.

"The tickets were a hundred apiece."

Martha coughed. "Pretty pricey for tea."

"I think they served a meal too," Sarah said as they approached a woman surrounded by a white counter.

The thirty-something employee, dressed in a navy blue uniform with a white collar, had the name Alice embroidered over her pocket. She smiled at them. "Welcome to the Berkshire Museum of Art. Will that be two tickets?"

"Thank you, but not at the moment," Sarah said, regret in her tone. "We're trying to locate one of the museum's employees, Ben Silver."

The smile weakened. "Ah yes, Ben. He usually works the night shift."

"Do you know how we can contact him?"

"You'll need to speak with our curator, Mr. Warthorne." Alice glanced at a clock on the wall. "But I'm afraid he's in a meeting right now. Perhaps you'd like to browse the exhibits while you wait. It should only be about ten minutes."

Sarah pulled out her wallet, intending to pay for tickets, but Alice waved her money away. "If you're here just to see Mr. Warthorne, the tickets aren't necessary." The phone on the counter behind her rang, and she turned to answer.

"Look over there," Sarah said to Martha, nodding toward a rack by the door holding brochures for local attractions. "Those leaflets look like the same ones in Belle's box."

"Maybe she picked them up here when she visited her brother," Martha said, selecting a map of the museum off the counter. "Oh look, there's a special Christmas exhibit in the west wing. 'Royal ornaments and treasures from the past,'" she read. "I bet this is where Belle got the idea for our treasure hunt. Let's pop in there and see what they have."

"That sounds like fun." Sarah waved at Alice and pointed to the west archway. She nodded.

As they entered the exhibit hall, Martha gasped. "What a gorgeous tree."

The Christmas tree, centered in the large domed room, towered at least twenty feet high. Colorful crystal ornaments sparkled in the branches. Martha wandered over to the information plaque.

"'The Royal Ornaments are on loan from Fredrik of Oldenburg, a distant cousin of Denmark royalty,'" Martha read, her eyes widening. "Wow. 'These ornaments contain real gold, silver, and precious stones.'" She whipped out her cell phone and snapped a couple of photos, leaning over the velvet boundary rope circling the tree.

"They're beautiful. And to think they were made just for Christmas. It'd be a shame to pack them away every year."

Martha lowered her phone. "But having them out only once a year makes Christmas extra special, just like when you display your Christmas quilt. You might get tired of it if it were out all the time."

"Good point," Sarah said, although she couldn't help thinking if she had the quilt out year round she would've noticed it missing sooner. Of course if Belle or someone else was determined to steal it, that would've made the quilt all the more accessible.

A whistle blew, and a miniature train engine and cars chugged down the track circling the tree. Martha hurried to get in front of it to snap another picture. "I bet Ernie would love an elaborate train set like this. It'd make a wonderful hobby."

"Yeah. He could tinker with trains as well as his cars," Sarah teased, knowing how Ernie loved to fix up automobiles for his grandchildren.

"He has time for both, believe me." Martha shot her a grin. "You know, one of the houses on the tour, the

Grenshaws, has a track around their tree too, only the train is bigger, more for a child. This miniature setup with the mountains and towns is a work of art." Martha followed the caboose as the train continued along the track around the tree. "Look at all the adorable miniature houses. There's a whole town back here."

Sarah's smile grew, loving how Christmas could bring out childlike wonder and anticipation even when one sported gray hair. She wandered over to the other exhibits lining the walls. They depicted various Christmas arts and crafts, some by local Berkshire artists and others by famous artists from other parts of the country. She spotted an original Norman Rockwell Christmas painting with a small plaque underneath mentioning it was on loan.

Martha had left the tree and was studying an antique music box painted with a Victorian house, horse-drawn sleigh, and sparkling snow-covered landscape. As Sarah walked up behind her, Martha said, "Listen to this." She pushed a button on the display case and the box chimed out the song "I'll Be Home for Christmas."

"That song always makes me teary." Martha blinked away barely formed tears. "It reminds me of when my brother was in the military, and oh, how we wanted him to come home for the holidays."

"And he did."

"Not the first year, but he managed to get leave for the second. My mother played that song over and over until he walked in the door. That was one of the best Christmases we ever had, and one of the last times we were all together as a family."

"What a wonderful memory." Sarah remembered what Jason had said about expecting Gerry to walk in the door and felt that familiar longing. The first Christmas without Gerry had been the hardest. Every little detail seemed to point to his absence.

Jason and Jenna had wanted her to visit for the holidays that year, but she wasn't up to leaving home yet. She hadn't anticipated how painful it would be to go pick out a tree, decorate, or attend the Christmas Eve service without Gerry by her side. Martha, bless her, had tried to make it easier for Sarah by popping in every day during the holidays and making her laugh.

Renewed gratitude filled her as she turned to speak to Martha, but her friend had moved on.

Sarah rounded the other side of the Christmas tree, and she noticed a guard in a navy uniform standing in the corner, stoically watching a woman push a mop around the floor.

Sarah nudged Martha. "Look, a janitor. She might know Ben."

"It's worth a shot," Martha said, leading the way over to the woman.

"Hi," Martha said with a friendly smile, but the petite, dark-skinned employee pushing her mop across the floor didn't answer.

Sarah moved closer and noticed tiny ear buds tucked above the janitor's earlobes, the cords discretely sliding under her collar. She tapped her on the shoulder and the janitor jumped, dropping the mop handle. A loud crack echoed through the room.

"Oh, I'm sorry." Sarah bent to retrieve the mop handle, aware the guard had taken a step closer to them. She smiled at the burly man; but his bushy eyebrows furrowed and he continued to glare down his long nose

"I didn't mean to scare you—" Sarah glanced at the name tag on the woman's pink uniform top, "—Kay."

Kay, who didn't look much older than a teenager, pulled the ear buds out. "It's okay. Hazard of listening to my iPod when working." She glanced over her shoulder at the guard. "Did you want something?"

"I'm Sarah Hart, and this is Martha Maplethorpe. We're friends of Ben Silver's sister. We heard that he works here."

"Yeah." Kay snapped her gum. "But he's usually on the night shift." Her gaze shifted to the guard again. "Look I can't stand here and chat. I'll get in trouble."

"Go ahead and keep working. We were just wondering if you knew how we can get in contact with him."

Her eyes narrowed as she plunked the mop into the large yellow bucket on wheels. "Why?"

"I'm concerned about his sister. We're hoping Ben might know where she is. Do you know what time he comes in?"

She hesitated, then leaned closer to Sarah and lowered her voice. "He may not be coming in anymore. I heard maybe he got fired."

"Really? Why?" Martha whispered.

"Who knows? I just heard the boss was angry." Kay lifted the mop head into the wringer and pulled the lever to squeeze out the dirty water. "Doesn't matter. We *all* may get canned soon anyway." Kay glanced up at the wall clock. "Listen, I gotta go. My break is coming up." She popped her ear buds back in and wheeled the bucket through a door into a small room where Sarah got a glimpse of a large sink and cleaning supplies. She wanted to follow, but the guard took a step in front of the door.

"Mrs. Hart?" Alice motioned to them from the archway, and Sarah and Martha joined her in the lobby.

Alice's fingers fluttered as she picked up a notebook and set it on the counter. "I'm afraid I have some bad news. Mr. Warthorne was suddenly called away, so he can't meet with you today. I'm sorry. I wouldn't have had you wait if I'd known."

"It's not your fault. Thank you for trying," Sarah said with a smile for the flustered woman. "Is there anyone else here we can ask about Ben?"

Alice shook his head. "I don't think anyone knew him that well. Charlie and Kay, our other custodial help, are never on the same shift with Ben. Joe Stout is the night guard. Mr. Warthorne can have Joe contact you if you think it's an emergency."

"That would be wonderful. Thank you." Sarah turned to go and then hesitated. "One of your employees said Ben may have been fired, and that they all may be out of work soon. Is that true?"

Alice rolled her eyes. "That was Kay, right? She's been saying that ever since it went public that a company is interested in buying the museum. Doesn't mean anyone is getting fired. Unless they're not doing their job, of course. As far as Ben is concerned, I couldn't tell you anything even if I knew. As far as I know he's been a good employee, but like I said, Mr. Warthorne is the only one who can share the appropriate personnel information."

Martha's elbow nudged Sarah. "How about we call Mr. Warthorne tomorrow, and if he does know where to locate Ben, we can always drive back if you think we need to."

Sarah smiled. She'd come back alone if she had to, but she was grateful for her friend's loyal companionship. "When would be the best time to call in the morning?" she asked Alice.

"After nine. He'll be finished with the security and staff meeting and still be in his office." She wrote a number down on a slip of paper and gave it to Sarah. "This is the direct line to this counter. I'll be here."

Sarah and Martha thanked her and headed out into the chilly sunshine.

"She seemed a little hesitant to say anything about Ben, which makes me think that he may have indeed been fired," Martha said as they climbed back in the car. "What are you smiling about?"

"Alice gave us the night guard's name. Joe Stout." Sarah retrieved her cell phone from her purse and called information. After she'd finished conversing with the automated service, she turned triumphantly to Martha. "Looks like we may not need to wait until tomorrow to continue our search for Belle's brother after all."

Martha swiveled in her seat as Sarah turned the car back toward Maple Hill.

"Aren't we going to find Joe Stout? We're going the wrong way."

"Information gave me an address in Maple Hill. Beecher Street, which isn't far from the high school. The phone number is a Maple Hill area code too." Sarah added.

"I thought the name sounded familiar, but then Stout is pretty common," Martha said, tugging at her seatbelt as she shifted back around in her seat. "Remember we had a Stanley Stout in our class in high school?"

"I imagine Stanley might be Joe's father."

"Could be. If Joe works nights, he's probably sleeping now."

Sarah nodded. "I thought I'd wait until later this afternoon and drop by the house."

"Less chance of him hanging up on you."

"Exactly," Sarah said, glancing in the rearview mirror. "See that beat-up, brown sedan two cars behind us? I think it's been following us since we left the museum."

Martha looked over her shoulder. "They must be heading to Maple Hill too."

"Maybe." Sarah said, but her unease grew as the miles flew by. The two cars between them eventually turned off, but the brown sedan hung back, making it impossible to see the features of the two shadowy outlines in the car. Martha fell silent and kept glancing in the side mirror.

Mountain Gap Road was just ahead. Sarah made a quick turn without putting on her blinker.

Martha grabbed the overhead handle. "Where are we going?"

"Mountain Gap doubles back as a loop to the highway. I want to see if that car follows." She remained cautious as the car sailed around the many curves, but tried to speed up a little on the straightaways.

When the highway came into view again, Sarah made another quick turn into a small gas station. She rolled past the gas pumps and parked on the far side of the building.

Martha unhooked her seatbelt and they both sprang out of the car. "Do you think they followed us?"

"I don't know. I'm starting to feel a little silly trying to evade a car I'm not even sure is following us." She paused at the corner of the building and poked her head around.

"There they are!" Martha exclaimed, peering over Sarah's shoulder. The brown sedan, a dented, old Buick, screeched to a stop at the intersection. Two men sat in the front. The driver had a pointy nose and wore a baseball cap. The passenger was shorter, and Sarah couldn't see his face. Judging from the quick jerks of their heads, she thought they were having quite a heated discussion.

Sarah's heart pounded. "The angle of the car is wrong. I can't see the license plate. Try to get the number when they turn."

The car idled for a few seconds and then took off, wheels squealing, toward Maple Hill.

"It was a Massachusetts license plate," Sarah said, "but I couldn't get the whole thing. I thought I saw J63."

"I thought it was TS3."

Someone cleared his throat behind them. Sarah and Martha started, bumping into each other.

A man in overalls, wiping a greasy blue rag on his greasy hands, walked slowly up to them. "Can I help you ladies?"

"Actually, we're fine." Sarah nudged Martha back toward the car. "But thank you." She hurried around the hood and slid into the driver's seat.

"We're going to follow them, aren't we?" Martha said, buckling herself in. She clapped her hands together. "I love it. The hunter becomes the hunted."

"Well, we're headed back to Maple Hill anyway. We might as well keep our eyes open for that car."

A loud rapping on the window caused Sarah to jump again. "Ma'am?" The man from the gas station pointed to her right back tire. "Did you know you have a flat?"

"Do you think someone tampered with your tire?" Chief Webber sat behind his cluttered desk, a thermos of soup and a half-eaten corned beef sandwich propped in front of him.

"Maybe," Sarah replied. She'd already given Chief Webber the description of the brown sedan and told him the circumstances. The man at the gas station had helped Sarah put on the spare, and then they'd retrieved Martha's car and dropped Sarah's off at Jack's Tires on Main.

"Jack said the puncture was caused by something narrow and sharp. Could've been a nail that later fell out, but he doesn't know. Don't you think it's coincidental that we'd get a flat tire and be followed after poking around, asking questions about Belle and Ben? My sense is that this is related to Belle's disappearance."

Chief Webber fiddled with an unopened mayonnaise packet that had been lying next to his sandwich. "I'm not ruling anything out yet, although it's not necessarily a crime to follow someone. Maybe the guys thought you two were cute." He winked at Martha.

Martha snorted. "Then they would've had to be desperate."

"Have you gotten any leads on where Belle might be?" Sarah asked, which was her main reason for stopping by the station.

"None yet. Without evidence of a crime, I can't put Belle into the National Missing Person computer bank yet. I did have someone check the accident reports and call the hospitals between here and Boston. There are no Anabelle

Silvers or any Jane Does matching her description. None in the morgue either."

Sarah blew out a breath of relief. The fear that Belle might be dead had been niggling at the back of her mind.

"I also ran a check on her brother. The address on his driver's license is still Boston, and apparently he's staying out of trouble in Pittsfield. There's nothing showing up on the computer. Not even a speeding ticket."

"Thank you for checking, Chief."

"If it's any consolation, I'm taking your concerns seriously. I'm just bound by standard procedures, and I've already stretched those. Until we have a strong reason to think Belle's in danger, I can't do much more. This is a free country, and if people choose to disappear, that's their right.

Sarah repressed a sigh. It wasn't Chief Webber's fault; he was doing everything he could.

"And ladies. Let us handle this. If anything new turns up, I'll let you know. And," he looked pointedly at them, "I suggest you don't travel out of town alone, especially at night. If that sedan attempts to follow you again, call us immediately."

"All right," Sarah said and Martha nodded her agreement. Sarah would certainly be careful, but she had no intention of stopping the search for Belle.

"Is there anything else?" Chief Webber asked, his hand reaching for his sandwich.

Sarah hesitated. Out of the corner of her eye, she saw Martha glance at her. It was on the tip of Sarah's tongue to mention the museum night guard who lived in Maple Hill. She stopped. If she told the chief, he might tell her not to talk to the guard.

"If we hear anything about Belle, we'll let you know." Sarah picked up her purse and stood.

Chief Webber opened his mouth as if to say something else, but then changed his mind. "Have a good afternoon."

Sarah followed Martha out of the office. She gave Chief Webber a little wave before shutting his door.

"When he looked down his nose at us, it felt like I was back in Principal Barnhart's office." Martha giggled as they walked through the station waiting area. "I wanted the chair to swallow me up."

"I wouldn't know," Sarah teased. "I never had to go to Principal Barnhart's office. I was a good girl."

"Baloney. You just never got caught."

As they passed through the station doors and down the outside steps, Sarah's purse vibrated, and she dug out her cell phone. Audrey's name popped up on the screen.

"Grandma?" she whispered.

"Hi, Sweetheart. Everything okay?"

"Yeah, but Mom just told us that the shop is going to be extra busy the rest of the week because tour buses are stopping in town. There'll be lots of people looking for antiques so...."

"You want me to pick you and Amy up today instead of Friday."

"Yes," Audrey replied, sounding relieved. "If you can."

"Hold on. I'll have to check. I don't have my car right now." She pressed the receiver against her chest and turned to Martha. "The girls want to clean house for the tour as a surprise for their parents."

Martha pulled out her keys. "I'll be happy to run you and the girls over to the house. I think it's great they're getting involved in the tour."

Sarah smiled her thanks and lifted the phone. "We'll be right over, Audrey." She climbed in Martha's minivan and they took off for the store, all the while watching for strange brown sedans.

CHAPTER NINE

arah rubbed some dust from her cheek as she took a moment to study Maggie and Jason's damaged wall. She had scrubbed the plaster, and the surface did appear cleaner; but it still needed to be covered. The Hart family quilt would've been perfect, but there was no sense dwelling on what might not be. Too bad she wouldn't be able to finish the new quilt in time for the tour. Hopefully by Christmas she'd have something to show Maggie, assuming they didn't recover the original Hart quilt.

She glanced at her watch. It was almost six. The afternoon had sped by. After Sarah and Martha picked up the twins from the store with the excuse they needed to Christmas shop, they'd dropped by a couple of stores to grab some gifts before heading back to the house so the twins could clean.

The girls wanted Sarah to take charge of the parlor. After a brisk decluttering of magazines and a thorough swipe of the duster, the furniture in the room gleamed. The

Christmas tree twinkled in the window with colorful packages underneath, and the embroidered stockings over the fireplace lent a homey holiday atmosphere. Scuff marks and scratches still covered the oak planked floor, but the large circular rug in the middle of the room concealed most of them. A quick mopping on Friday would finish the room off. Everything looked wonderful. Except for the wall behind the sofa.

"All done with the downstairs bathroom, Grandma," Audrey said, carrying a bottle of window cleaner and a roll of paper towels. "What should I do next?"

"Why don't you gather up all those paint cans and rollers in the hallway, and store them in the garage? Take the drop cloth too. Then we can dust mop the floor."

Audrey sighed and turned away. The twins' bouncy enthusiasm had faded about an hour into the cleaning process, but they still plodded along without much complaint. The vacuum cleaner hummed upstairs. Sarah wasn't sure how many of the four bedrooms Maggie wanted to display for the tour, so Sarah was having Amy do them all.

Sarah found a stool and stepped on it to dust the parlor's antique chandelier. Her gaze kept straying back to the wall. It seemed silly to get so worked up over what was essentially just a few hours out of the whole year, but she didn't want Maggie to feel any embarrassment over the unfinished wall or experience any more stress during a busy time.

She glanced outside at the sleigh positioned in the yard. Maggie or Jason had decorated the sleigh with garlands of holly, the bright red berries and tiny white lights looking warm and festive. A red sack with wrapped boxes peeked out the top of the seat. Her spirits lifted with the memory of Jason and Gerry working on the sleigh together.

"All done with the upstairs," Amy said, flopping onto the couch. "I cleaned our room, and even put Audrey's stuff away, and vacuumed *everywhere*."

Sarah smiled down from her perch. "I'm sure you did a terrific job! The house is going to look absolutely wonderful."

Amy smiled. "Now all we have to do is mop the floors on Friday. Mom said she was bringing some things home from the shop for more decorations too."

"Okay, all the paint cans and cloths are in the garage," Audrey said, trudging into the room and plopping down beside Amy. "I'm starving."

"I'm heating some stew your Mom had in the freezer. She called and said she'd be a little late, but we'll eat as soon as your dad gets here," Sarah said, waving the duster over the chandelier bulbs.

"He's here. I hear his car." Audrey bounced to her feet and raced to the kitchen.

The backdoor squeaked open. "Dad, you have to come see the house!" Audrey called.

Footsteps and exclamations of praise could be heard as Jason moved from room to room, and then finally up the stairs at Audrey's insistence. When they returned, he stepped into the parlor, his gaze landing on his other daughter.

Amy smiled contentedly at her father from her position on the sofa. "You like it, Dad?"

"Like it? I love what you did." Jason crossed the room to give her a hug and a kiss on the top of her head. He grabbed Audrey and pulled her in for a giant group hug. "Thank you so much. I'm so proud of my girls. The house looks great." He turned to Sarah. "Hi, Mom, I see you've been really busy."

"Oh this was the girls' idea. I didn't do much," Sarah said, stepping off the stool.

"We wanted to surprise you and Mom." Amy shifted over so Jason and Audrey could sit.

"You did. I thought we'd have to stay up most of Friday night cleaning. Now we just need to be careful not to wreck the place in the next couple days." Jason's gaze circled the room, and then back to Audrey. "Where's Mom?"

"She's working," Audrey said with a big sigh. "But Grandma said we could eat when you got here. I'm starving."

"Maggie will be here soon." Sarah gathered up the rags and cleaning supplies. "She had some last-minute customers, which actually worked out well since that gave Amy and Audrey extra time to finish the house. She said for us to go ahead and eat. I heated up some of her stew."

Jason smiled when he noticed the girls watching him. "Hot stew sounds great. It's freezing outside."

"I also found a cherry pie in the freezer to celebrate the girls' hard work," Sarah said.

"Oh yum, I'll go set the table." Audrey headed toward the kitchen. Amy slowly got to her feet and followed.

"They must've worked really hard," Jason said with warm fatherly pride in his voice. "I'll go get supper on the table. You just relax for a bit, Mom." He strode toward the kitchen. Sarah took one last survey of the parlor and followed.

Maggie arrived as they were finishing their stew, apologizing and explaining she had a customer who'd driven out from Pittsfield to pick up a dresser. She squealed with delight when she saw the newly clean house, and they all celebrated by eating cherry pie and vanilla ice cream.

Sarah settled on the couch in the parlor to watch *How the Grinch Stole Christmas* with the girls until Jason finished some chores and could drive her home.

During the commercial, Amy, who sat on the floor with her back against the couch, tilted her head to gaze at Sarah. "Thank you for helping, Grandma."

"You're welcome, Sweetie."

"Were you busy with Mrs. Maplethorpe today?"

"Some, but this was important too." Sarah just wished she'd been able to visit Joe Stout. She hadn't been able to pick up her car before the shop closed either, but she wouldn't trade the last few hours for anything.

"Is your quilt still lost?" Amy asked, ignoring Audrey's shushing as the movie came back on.

Sarah nodded. "For now."

"I thought it was really pretty when I saw it in the attic. It had gold pictures on it. Dad said each one had a story."

"He's right. It's a Hart tradition that each year someone embroiders on the quilt one symbol of something special that happened that year."

Amy sighed. "Wish I could see the quilt again."

"Me too. But you know what? I have a photo of the quilt in my purse."

"I'll get it." Amy scrambled to her feet, ran to the kitchen, and returned carrying the bag. She scooted close to Sarah and studied the enlarged image of the quilt.

"Your great-great-great-great Grandmother Rachel made the quilt. It's called Star of Bethlehem. They made the border wide so there's room to embroider on it." She pointed to the upper right corner of the quilt. "See the gold thimble with 1910 under it? That's the year the quilt was made."

"Wow, that's a hundred years ago."

Sarah nodded. "And over there, see this ship?"

Amy peered at the slightly blurry image. "Looks like a battleship."

"It is. The year was 1941 and your great-grandfather Jonathan Hart was stationed on a ship over in Pearl Harbor, Hawaii. On December seventh the Japanese attacked and blew up Grandpa Jonathan's ship."

"What happened to Grandpa?" Audrey asked, her blue eyes wide. Sarah had been speaking softly so as not to disturb Audrey's movie, but Audrey jumped up from the floor and sat on the other side of Sarah.

"Grandpa Jonathan was on shore leave that day. In fact he'd just written a letter to your great-grandmother and dropped it at the post office. The news didn't arrive until four days later that Jonathan was still alive, and then his letter came right before Christmas. Can you imagine how relieved and happy the family was?"

"Wow!" Amy said, her eyes shining. "I knew Grandpa William was in the war, but I didn't know Grandpa Jonathan was at Pearl Harbor."

Audrey picked up the photo print. "Cool story, Grandma! What does this rose inside a heart by 1937 mean?"

"That story isn't quite as exciting, but it's a nice one. You had a great-aunt Bethany who loved to garden, and she had a huge rose garden. In fact, you can still find descendants of the rose bushes she planted out on the old Hart farm. She entered the county fair every year and would get a ribbon. One year she grew a hybrid, which is making a new kind of rose. And guess what? She won first place at the county fair and then at the state fair. She got to name the rose too."

"What was it?" Audrey asked.

"'Harts Forever,' spelled like your last name."

Amy snorted. "Kind of mushy."

"I like it," Audrey said, tugging the photo her way.

"I didn't say I didn't." Amy grabbed the other end of the paper.

"Girls, before you tear it, do you see anything else you want me to tell you about?" They did and Sarah shared several more stories with the twins until Jason appeared. He smiled at the huddled group on the couch. "I'm glad to see the tradition of storytelling is continuing even without the quilt."

"Me too," Sarah said, giving the girls one-armed hugs.

"I hate to break up the party, but it's after nine. Time to get Grandma home."

"Aw, do you have to go?" Audrey asked, leaning on Sarah.

"I better, so your dad can get back to go to bed. Don't worry, the memories will still be there for next time."

Swaying bare tree branches cast shadows over the lamp-lit street as Jason turned the car down Main Street. He braked suddenly as a dog bounded across the street, and then proceeded forward at a cautious speed. "Any news on your boarder?"

"Not yet." She told him about visiting Andrew Blake and the museum. "I'm getting more worried. First Belle's gone, and then a janitor at the museum says Ben got fired. I wonder if he's in some kind of trouble and Belle is mixed up in it."

"What kind of trouble?"

"I don't know. What would a janitor working in a museum have to do to get fired?" But was he fired? After Sarah had talked to Alice, Kay hadn't seemed like the most reliable source.

"Lots of reasons. Being late for work all the time, talking back to his boss, not doing his work—hey, is that Pastor John?" Jason said, slowing the vehicle.

Sarah peered over the dash to see the pastor bent over one of four spotlights stationed around the nativity scene in front of the church. He tilted one spotlight to shine on the manger, then raced to another. As he adjusted the second one, the first light blinked out. He straightened, hands on hips, staring at something on the ground.

Jason pulled over to the curb. Sarah rolled down her window and called, "Pastor John, do you need some help?"

His face broadened into his usual welcoming smile as he hurried over to the car. "Well, hello. I didn't expect to see any of my parishioners out here this late."

Sarah spied his pajama bottoms crammed into his boots. She smiled. And was that his bathrobe peeking out from under his long coat?

"Having some trouble, Pastor?" Jason asked.

"Yes, unfortunately. Nothing serious, but Mrs. Bitty phoned me and said the lights had gone out on the nativity scene. The wind blew the star over and somehow discombobulated all the extension cords. Now I can't seem to get the spotlights to work properly." He surveyed the dark scene. "I suppose it can wait until morning, but with Christmas so close, I like to leave it on all night. That way people on the way to work in the morning can see it too."

"Would it help if you had someone hold one spotlight while you set up the rest?" Jason asked, opening his door.

"It might," Pastor John said.

Sarah stepped out of the car. "Three pairs of hands are better than two." The wind cut through her coat like her sharpest pair of quilting sheers. She shivered and grabbed hold of a spotlight by its two-foot pole and straightened it.

Jason grabbed another. "Hold on to it tight, Mom," he said, giving the extension cord a tug.

Sarah kept the pole firmly upright as the pastor ran to a third one. When they had all three lights upright, Sarah let go of hers.

"I'll try plugging the main cord in again," Pastor John called from behind the nativity scene.

The scene flooded with light. The Bethlehem star twinkled with tiny white lights from its perch above the roof of the three-sided backdrop. The hovering angel's crown and wise men's chests of gold, frankincense, and myrrh reflected the bright light. Baby Jesus, wrapped in swaddling clothes, lay in the manger, with Mary and Joseph by his side.

"Looks like everything's lit," Jason called.

Sarah stooped to pick up a handful of straw from the ground and tuck it back into the overstuffed manger. The church ladies must've added more straw since she sent it over. She hadn't filled it this full. They'd be lucky if the Baby Jesus doll didn't roll out.

Pastor John came around the corner. "Thank you so much for the help. I won't keep you any longer in the cold.

I'll see you on Sunday." He gave them a wave and turned, his bathrobe flapping like a flag behind him as he dashed toward his house at the edge of the property.

Sarah's numb fingers could barely feel the handle as she yanked the car door open and jumped back inside. Jason had left the heater on and the interior was toasty.

"This has got to be the coldest night we've had all December. I bet it's in the single digits." Jason's teeth chattered. He pulled off his wool gloves and held his hands in front of the heater vent. If I'd known it would be this cold, I'd have worn my heavier gloves."

"'Tis reason for the season."

"Huh?"

"Oh, sorry, I was reading the topic of this week's sermon," she said looking at the church sign. "But, yes, time to break out the heavier snow gear, especially if those storms hit us this week."

Jason released the parking break, and they resumed the journey back toward Sarah's house. "I'm thinking of buying another cord of firewood. Keeping the fireplaces going has kept our gas bill down. Do you need any more wood?"

"I think I have enough. I never used up last year's, so I have extra in case of an emergency."

Jason pulled into Sarah's driveway. "If you run out, just let me know. Why join a gym when I can get plenty of exercise splitting wood?" He paused. "Dad and I used to split wood for hours in the fall. In a weird way, I miss it."

Sarah pulled her keys out of her purse and protested as Jason got out of the car on his side. "You don't need to follow me to the door."

"Humor me. I want to make sure you get inside safely." Jason rounded the bumper of the car and opened her door.

"You sound like your father."

"I'll take that as a compliment."

"It is." Sarah sighed as she trudged up the steps. She'd heard Gerry in Jason's voice. "A gentleman always walks a girl to her front door and makes sure she gets in safely," Gerry used to tell Jason all through high school, and it looked like his instruction had stuck.

She turned her key in the deadbolt and pushed the front door open, stepping into the foyer.

"It's freezing in here," Jason said. "Look, I can see my breath. Is the furnace broken?"

Sarah paused, listening. "I don't know. I can hear it running." The thought of trying to get the furnace fixed gave her an instant headache. What if she couldn't get it done before the home tour?

"Let me take a look at it," Jason said, heading toward the kitchen. Sarah flipped on the hall light, and Jason stopped so short she bumped into him.

"What's the matter?" she asked.

"Mom, get your cell phone and call the police."

Sarah bustled about the kitchen, setting out coffee and cookies for the three police officers, despite Jason's pleas that she sit and take it easy. Staying productive was much preferable to dwelling on the horror that someone had broken into her home.

Although Jason had hustled her out the door and back to his car right after he'd told her to call the police, she'd caught a glimpse of the torn up living room. Not only was her furniture overturned and items scattered everywhere, her Christmas tree was gone.

They'd waited in the car until the police arrived on the scene and then entered the house when given the all clear. Sarah preferred to hover in the kitchen until the police finished their work in the rest of the house. The backdoor had been found wide open, which accounted for the frigid temperature in the house.

Chief Webber came through that door now, stomping his boots on the doormat. "We found your tree. Looks like they tried to haul it over the fence, judging from the mess on the ground."

"Who would try to steal a Christmas tree?" Sarah asked, flabbergasted. This whole situation was surreal.

"Your guess is as good as mine," Chief Webber said. "We don't see many deliberate acts of vandalism in Maple Hill. Do you know anyone who would want to cause you harm? Get back at you in some way?"

"Not that I know of," Sarah said, her mind sorting through possibilities and coming up blank, except . . . "I keep thinking about those men who followed Martha and me from Pittsfield. Do you think they could be connected to this?"

Chief Webber shrugged. "There have been incidents where people were followed home and robbed. But in this case, you lost them before you got here. When do you think those guys started tailing you?"

"What guys?" Jason asked, strolling into the room. He'd been checking on the progress in the living room.

"The last place we were at was the museum, but I didn't notice the sedan until we were on the outskirts of Pittsfield."

"Do you think you would recognize them if you came in and looked at mug shots?"

She shook her head. "I couldn't identify them. They went by us so fast, I couldn't even get the full license plate number."

"Mom!" Jason said, "Who are you talking about?"

Sarah placed her hand on Jason's arm and his muscles tightened as she told him about the brown sedan and two men.

"You said you had a flat tire. You never mentioned people trying to follow you. Why didn't you tell me?"

"I'm sorry," Sarah said, regretting she hadn't brought it up earlier. "I didn't want to worry you."

Chief Webber cleared his throat. "Sarah, do you remember if these guys had large or small builds?"

"They were sitting, so it'd be hard to tell for sure, but one guy was definitely taller than the other. The passenger's hat barely cleared the seat's headrest. The driver had big shoulders and a thick neck. I'd say he was overweight. Why?"

"Since whoever broke in came through the cellar window, they'd have to be quite thin," Chief Webber noted, referring to one of the two narrow cellar windows set about six inches above the ground. They'd been cut into the concrete to provide light in Gerry's workshop area. Sarah didn't think her hips would even get through them.

"We need to get bars installed on both of them," Jason said. I'll make a call in the morning." He headed toward the cellar. "I'm going to get some measurements."

"I suppose that would be best," Sarah said, knowing that action would make Jason feel better. Break-ins in Maple Hill were rare; and with having boarders, there always seemed to be someone in the house to help deter burglars.

"Mrs. Hart?" A freckled-faced police officer poked his head around the corner. "We need you to check if anything is missing from under the tree."

"Of course," Sarah said. She'd stayed away from the living room until the police crew finished their investigation, and steeled herself when she entered the room. Her once cozy living room was a disaster.

The Christmas tree had been ripped from its stand, and the stand lay tilted over. Water spread across the floor and seeped under the pile of gifts. Someone had torn the wrapping paper on most of the packages, revealing the contents. One of the lime green ski gloves she'd bought for Amy lay in the middle of the rug.

She stepped over pine needles and tinsel that created a path to the backdoor and counted the mangled packages, trying to remember how many had been there. She had a couple of gifts for Maggie and Jason, and four each for the twins. Plus she'd wrapped something for Martha. Thankfully she'd mailed off the presents for Jenna and her family and had already taken her father's presents to the nursing home.

"I don't think anything is missing," Sarah said with surprise.

"Let's do a walk-through of the rest of the house," the chief said and followed Sarah room to room. Her television hadn't been touched, nor had her computer. She looked in her jewelry box in the bedroom, and everything appeared exactly as she'd left it. They paused in Belle's empty room as Chief Webber circled the interior.

"Nothing seems disturbed here either from the last time I saw it, but then Belle had already packed up her belongings. She left a crate of books and other small items in the attic. And then of course the suitcase you saw in the basement."

Chief Webber turned to the door. "Let's have a look in the cellar again."

They were halfway down the cellar steps when Jason met them.

"Other than the broken window, everything looks the same as it was when I was here yesterday except—Mom, did you move Belle's laptop?"

"No. You told me not to in case it was broken," Sarah said reaching the bottom step. The light was on over the workbench, but the spot where she'd left Belle's computer was bare.

CHAPTER TEN

The roof groaned under the onslaught of the wind as Sarah set the teakettle back on her stove. Normally Sarah didn't even notice the old house talking to her, as Gerry used to say, but tonight every sound seemed accentuated, from the creaks in the floorboards to the refrigerator's hum to the click of the furnace.

A soft snore drifted in from the living room where Jason slept on the couch. Sarah smiled at the comforting sound of another human being. He'd insisted on staying over until the broken window in the cellar was fixed the next day, even refusing the upstairs bedroom so he could listen for intruders. Sarah had argued it wasn't necessary since she could lock the door at the top of the cellar stairs, but in truth she was glad he'd stayed.

Jason had helped her stack the torn Christmas packages on the dining room table and vacuumed up the glass and pine needles. In the morning they'd see if they could salvage her tree, which now leaned up against the house outside.

Sarah should've gone to bed hours before, but working on the new quilt was a comfort and helped organize her thoughts. She'd washed and ironed the fabrics and used her fabric pen to mark where to cut.

Sarah set out her cutting mat and rotary cutter, checked her notebook, and did some calculations. The finished diamonds would be two and three-quarter inches wide, so she needed to cut strips of fabric three and a quarter inches wide. She layered the red, green, and gold fabrics, lined them up along the measurement grid on the mat, and began cutting, the blade of the rotary cutter making swift, accurate slices.

As she worked, thoughts of Belle floated to the surface of her mind. For a while, she simply prayed for Belle's safety as she cut and stacked the strips. When she finished asking for blessings on Belle and her brother Ben, she said a word of thanks for the safety of her own family and whispered an amen.

She felt like she hadn't made much progress in finding Belle today, but at least she knew the girl hadn't eloped, at least not with Andrew Blake. He obviously wanted to rekindle a relationship with her, evidenced by the red roses and the assumption he'd been the one calling Belle at work. But it seemed odd that he didn't seem overly concerned about her disappearance.

And Sarah had no idea how he had gotten hooked up with Belle. It was possible something in their past could help her find a new lead to where Belle might be. Maybe she should find out more about this guy.

She made certain her rotary cutter's safety cover was on, and turned to her computer. She typed *Andrew Blake MBA CPA* into a search engine. All she found was the Web site for his current firm. There were other Andrew Blakes further down the list, but none of the sites seemed to connect with Belle's ex-fiancé.

Sarah tapped her fingers on the desk. She could ask Ted, the firm's office assistant, for more background information, but even if he would oblige, he might report her snooping back to Mr. Blake. If Andrew was involved somehow in Belle's disappearance, she didn't want to be too obvious. She needed to do more digging on her own first.

She sat up straight. What about the woman that'd been in Mr. Blake's office when they got there? What had Ted called her? Mrs. Steinbeck? It was a long shot, but maybe she'd be willing to answer some questions. She tried the online white pages and discovered telephone numbers in Pittsfield for Steinbeck. Tomorrow, she'd check them out.

She stood and resumed methodically cutting, strip after strip, and her pile of fabric grew. She hoped her pile of clues to Belle's whereabouts would grow as well.

"I hate to bring this up after your terrible ordeal last night, but I have a problem." Martha swirled the remainder of a peppermint mocha latte in her mug. "Have you seen the prizes for the treasure hunt anywhere?"

"You mean those gold frames?" Sarah smothered a huge yawn behind her hand. When Martha had dropped Sarah off last night at Maggie's, they'd agreed to meet at The Spotted Dog that morning to discuss the treasure hunt. She was still determined to help Martha out of the mess caused by Belle's disappearance even though her search for Belle seemed to be at a standstill.

"Yes. I'm afraid they're missing, unless you've seen the box at your house. Remember when Julia at the Copy Shop gave me the invoice? Yesterday afternoon I realized that I hadn't a clue about where they actually were. So I called the company, and they told me that Belle had signed for them last week. The delivery address was your home."

"I went through the entire house with the police last night and didn't see them, but I'll look again."

"I hate putting you to any more trouble. I can't believe someone would ransack your living room. If you need to pull out of the home tour, I'll understand," Martha said.

"I wouldn't dream of it." Sarah reached across the table and gave her friend's hand a squeeze. "When I woke up this morning, Jason had already set the tree back up. One side is a little squashed, but we turned it to the wall. I'll need to buy more ornaments, but I should be ready by Saturday evening."

"Only if you're sure."

"I am. I'm not going to let some troublemaker ruin Christmas," Sarah replied. "Now, let's see if we can figure out what Belle planned for the treasure hunt and what happened to those prizes. Maybe Belle already stashed them in their hiding place. Any idea where that'll be?"

Martha shook her head. "I was hoping you'd know. It's at your place somewhere."

"All right, let's take it from the top. Belle visited the tour homes to plan the treasure hunt, right?"

"Yes. I helped her set up appointments with each of the families. She was going to choose something in each house for the participants to count. What, I don't know."

"Well, I might have an idea." Sarah pulled her tote bag into her lap, and produced the quilting book and the ornaments she'd found in the attic. She set them on the table.

"These are what I found in the trunk. The book belongs to Vanessa Sawyer. She lent it to Belle." She opened the book and tapped the Wild Goose Chase stamp. "Vanessa said Belle wanted to learn the names of the quilts in the tour homes."

"Oh! Maybe she used the quilts as part of the game," Martha said, and then wrinkled her forehead. "But I don't remember which houses had quilts displayed."

"We can check that out. Also, these ornaments were stashed with the book, so I assume they might serve some purpose in the treasure hunt too."

Martha stroked the angel's gold-tipped wings. "It's pretty. Kind of reminds me of one of the royal ornaments we saw over in the museum."

"Only, of course, this is painted glass and not real gold."

"Too bad," Martha said with a sigh and grinned.

"Is that a guardian angel?" Liam asked as he cleared the table next to them.

"I think they belong to Belle," Sarah said. "And wherever she is, I hope her guardian angel is keeping her safe."

Liam paused, a water glass in his hand. "Still no word from her then?"

"No." Sarah sighed. "I filed a missing person report. Chief Webber's looking into it."

"He's a competent man. Good at his job. I'm sure they'll find her soon." He reached for their empty plates and his gaze zeroed in on the sheet by Martha's elbow. "Treasure map?" he asked. "You hunting for gold?"

Martha smiled. "This is for the Holiday Home Tour. It's Belle's project, but it looks like I'll have to finish it for her."

Liam continued to linger, so Martha filled him in on the details. "After participants finish counting the Christmas 'treasures' in each house they write the numbers down on this map. When they get to the last house, the numbers decipher the final clue—in this case a sentence—which leads them to a prize."

"Intriguing," Liam said. "So, the numbers they uncover correspond to these letters." He tapped a simple chart on the side. "And then they put the letters in those blanks."

"Twenty-one letters that make up seven words," Sarah said. "We might be able to figure out the clue by playing with the letters, but that still wouldn't tell us what they're supposed to be looking for in the homes." She looked at Martha. "Do the homeowners know what Belle was planning?"

"Nope. Last night I called the first three homes on the tour: the Sanders, Greens, and Grenshaws, and they all said that Belle hadn't told them. *But* she wanted to know if they changed any of their decorations. She was planning on returning this week to finalize the game. Since she had this treasure map ready to print, I'm assuming she already had everything all set up."

"Or she could've planned to add some items at the last minute," Sarah said, thinking about Belle's request to access the attic for the treasure hunt.

"Might I suggest that you consider walking through the treasure hunt yourselves?" Liam said. "You may get some of your questions answered that way."

"Good idea." Sarah smiled at Liam. The thought had crossed her mind too. "We can call it a trial run. They did say Belle would get back to them this week anyway."

"Yes, they did," Martha said with enthusiasm. "I'll give them a call, and see if I can set it up for today. Thanks for the suggestion, Liam."

"You're welcome. I hope you figure out what you need to know. It sounds fun." An eagerness in his tone caused Martha to look at him.

"Liam, would you be interested in helping out with the treasure hunt? With Belle's absence, I could use someone on the day of the tour to make sure it runs efficiently," Martha said, using the same sales pitch voice she'd used to convince Maggie to join the tour. "It's for a worthy cause. We're raising money for the Children's Home and—" Martha glanced at Sarah, who smiled.

Martha blushed. "There I go again, rattling away. If you're too busy, Liam—"

"No, no. I'm interested." He grinned. "I've been meaning to get more involved in community events, and a treasure hunt sounds more like play than work. Just let me know what you want me to do."

"Oh thank you," Martha gushed. "Sarah and I have our homes in the tour, and all of my committee members have jobs that'll keep them busy the whole evening. If you could take Belle's place, at least until she returns, it'll really help."

"Then consider me your treasure captain," Liam said with a mock salute.

"This is very generous of you, Liam," Sarah said. "Thank you."

His eyes twinkled at her. "You're welcome, but I think I'll be thanking you both in the end. Do you want me to visit the homes with you?"

"Yes, that would be perfect. We'll probably go this evening after everyone gets off work." She looked at Sarah for confirmation. "I'll call you."

"Aye, aye, maties. A treasure hunting we will go," Liam picked up the tray of dirty dishes and headed for the kitchen, humming a pirate tune.

Martha's step had an extra bounce as they walked up the sidewalk toward the Stouts' front porch. "With Liam taking over for Belle during the tour, I feel like a big burden has been lifted. Wasn't that sweet of him?"

Sarah grinned, glad to see her friend so happy. "Yes it is. He's a good friend."

"He might be more than just a friend with a little encouragement on your part," Martha said with a wink.

"Oh, Martha. He was intrigued by the treasure hunt," Sarah replied, but her stomach did a flip-flop. Liam had been a little extra-attentive lately. She wasn't sure what it meant, or how she felt about it.

Right now she needed to concentrate on finding Belle, which had brought them to the museum guard's home. She rang the bell, and a man answered the door.

"Joe Stout?"

"Yep, that's me." He yawned and scratched his stomach. Maybe it was his name that'd influenced Sarah's mental image, but she hadn't expected this extremely tall, skinny man to be the security guard they'd been looking for. Curly red hair puffed up on his head in a fuzzy halo, and freckles covered his youthful face and arms.

"My, you look just like Stanley Stout," Martha exclaimed, her hand pressed over her heart. "He led the basketball team to the championship our senior year. Was he your father?"

Joe blinked several times and focused his green eyes on Martha. "That's right. Have we met before?"

"Oh no, I haven't talked with your father since high school graduation," Martha said with a chuckle. "I'm Martha Maplethorpe, and this is my friend, Sarah Hart. Is your father still in town?"

"Nope. He and Mom split for Scottsdale, Arizona, about five years ago. I'm the only one living here now." He suddenly seemed to remember his manners, or maybe he noticed the cold wind kicking up leaves onto the porch, for he pushed the screen door open. "Would you like to come in? The place is a mess, though."

"Bachelor quarters don't scare me," Sarah said, stepping through the door. Scents of pizza, aftershave, and old socks floated in the air, familiar smells from Jason's law school days when he'd crammed his stuff into a two-bedroom apartment shared with four others. Sarah had been ecstatic when Maggie agreed to marry Jason, and the smells had gradually changed to grilled cheese and soup for his last semester.

The ladies maneuvered around a laundry basket with a gray-striped tabby cat asleep in the pile of clothes. The cat opened a yellow eye, scrutinized them for a moment, and then went back to snoozing. A scraggly Christmas tree stood in the corner, the few ornaments threatened to topple it any second. Sarah gave the young man credit for having some Christmas spirit.

"Um, do you want something to drink?" Joe shifted awkwardly in the doorway as Sarah and Martha pushed aside books and papers to sit on the threadbare couch.

"No, thank you. We just ate," Martha said and Sarah politely declined too.

"That's cool," Joe said, and dropped his lanky body into a beanbag chair.

"Are you in college?" Sarah asked, noting an accounting textbook on the couch.

"Pittsfield Community. I decided to go back to school and get a degree. I want to be a cop. Right now, I'm a security guard."

"That brings us to the reason for our visit," Martha said. "We were recently at the museum looking for Ben Silver."

The smile disappeared from his face. "What's the dude done now?"

"We're not sure, but one of the employees said he got fired," Sarah said.

"That's harsh. What'd he do?"

"We were hoping you'd know."

He shrugged. "Ben and I didn't really get along. He was always complaining about his life and looking for his big break. Like he doesn't have to work for it like the rest of us."

"When was the last time you saw him?"

He scratched his stomach again, appearing to be in deep thought. "Must've been after the Christmas Tea. We were both called in early."

"Did anything unusual happen?"

"Nope. I stood and did my thing. Ben helped take down decorations. Pretty boring."

"Who was there?" Sarah asked.

"The boss, Mr. Warthorne, and a bunch of ladies. Sam, the other security guard, stuck around for a while too."

"Is Sam the day guard? Heavyset, going bald? Frowns a lot?"

Joe nodded. "Ben clashed with him sometimes because Sam thinks he can order the cleaning people around." His eyes narrowed. "Why all the questions? Does this have to do with the sale of the museum? I already filled out the job survey and sent it back in. I don't want to get anyone in trouble."

"No, this is just a personal matter," Sarah said.

"A personal matter?"

"Actually, we're trying to find Ben's sister, Belle. She boards in my house. And we don't have an address for Ben. Would you know where he lives?"

"Sure. He let me stay over a couple times when they needed us to put in extra hours. I met Belle while I was there. Her fiancé helped Ben get his job at the museum."

"That would be Mr. Blake then," Martha said, glancing at Sarah.

"Has Ben been in trouble before?" Sarah asked.

"It seems like he's always on the edge of big trouble, but not lately. He told me some stories from Boston that'd make your hair curl like mine."

"These people in Boston, were they involved in ..." Sarah gave a little wave of her hand.

"Drugs? No way." Joe shook his head. "He's got a hot temper. He seems to stumble into things without meaning to, if you know what I mean."

"Naive?"

"Maybe. He always needs money too. In fact, he owes me a bunch, which I loaned him before I realized his promises aren't worth anything." He glanced at his watch and scrambled to his feet. "Almost forgot. I have a class in twenty minutes. I have to go."

Martha stood, startling the cat in the basket. "Thank you for answering all our questions. If you hear from Ben, can you let us know?"

Sarah fished out one of her business cards and gave it to Joe. "We really would like to talk to him. And if you could give us an address to Ben's home, we'd appreciate it."

"Don't know the address exactly, but I can give you directions." Joe ripped a sheet of paper out of his notebook. "I'll ask around tonight, and see if I can find out what happened. Not right him being fired. Something bad must've happened."

He hastily scratched out a map. Sarah looked over at Martha who gave her a nod. They both knew where they were heading this afternoon.

CHAPTER ELEVEN

T hat must be the place," Sarah said as they passed the shabby apartment complex for the second time. Many of the street names were missing on Joe's map to Ben's home, but he'd noted landmarks, mostly fast food places and gas stations, for the turns.

"I'll go around the block again." Martha flipped on her right-turn signal. Although Sarah's repaired tire seemed fine, they'd decided to take Martha's green minivan, just in case the brown sedan was still lurking.

Before they had left for Pittsfield, Sarah had dashed home for lunch. She'd found Jason's car and a white panel van advertising "Speedy Glass Repair" parked in front. Jason, clad in his usual suit and tie, stood by the side of the house talking to two men installing security windows for the cellar.

Jason also mentioned researching an alarm system for her. His interfering irritated her some, but Sarah didn't bother to argue. Last night's break-in had shaken Jason and taking action would calm his fears. She knew his heart was in the right place.

Martha finished circling the block and guided the car into a parking spot. The two-story square building resembled a motel more than an apartment complex. A row of doors, interspersed with wide windows, ran the length of the building on both levels. The stairs to the upper floor were outside, and all the apartments faced the parking lot.

A sign in a downstairs window identified the manager's residence. Martha set the parking brake, and they contemplated the building. "Well, at least the manager can see who's coming and going all the time."

Sarah smiled. Trust Martha to find something positive to say about the dismal housing. The manager's door stood only about fifteen feet away, but during the short walk, Sarah felt as though a hundred pairs of eyes were watching them. With all the windows facing the parking lot, it must be like living in a fishbowl every time you ventured outside.

Sarah rang the bell for Apartment 1A, and the beige curtains in the apartment next door parted and then swished together again. The fishbowl feeling grew.

Seconds ticked by before the door finally opened to reveal a short, greasy-haired man in a dingy white T-shirt and sweatpants. A cigarette with a long grey ash hung off his puffy lip.

"Yeah?"

"Are you the manager?" Sarah asked.

"Yeah, but I ain't got no vacancies. Come back next week after the rents are due, and I may have something for you," he drawled, the cigarette bobbing with every word.

"We're not here to rent. We're looking for one of your tenants. Ben Silver."

"You and everyone else. Who are you? His mother?"

Sarah shook her head. "Just a friend of his sister. It's important that we talk to him. Could you tell us which apartment is his?"

"I could, but it won't do you any good. That's what I told his brother yesterday."

"Brother?"

"Yeah, he seemed really annoyed when I told him I hadn't seen Ben around. He banged on his door until a neighbor yelled and threatened to call the police."

"I don't think Ben has a brother," Sarah said.

He shrugged. "Ain't my business anyway."

"Now, wait a minute," Martha said, her hands on her hips, using a tone she reserved for bossing children. "Are you sure he's not in there? Maybe he's hurt."

"No, lady, I ain't sure. It's none of—"

Her voice gentled. "Surely you can do something. Please. You're the landlord and you have some responsibility, if not to the people then to protect the building."

"I've got a passkey, and if there's trouble like fire, I can use it," he said.

"Could you check please?" Sarah asked. "I'm very concerned about him and his sister. No one can find them."

"His sister's missing too?"

"Yes. Do you know her?"

"I've seen her come to visit a few times. She's a real looker, but not very friendly, if you know what I mean." He stepped out of his doorway, and spat his cigarette onto the cracked sidewalk. "Tell you what, I'll open Ben's door, if you make it worth my while."

"You want money to open Ben's door?"

"Just compensation for my time. I'm real busy."

Sarah frowned. "How about we just call the police. I don't think they'll approve of your business practices."

"Go ahead. It'll be your word against mine. They'll take their sweet time getting out here, and even then, they probably wouldn't let you in." The man reached into his pocket and extracted another cigarette. He took his time lighting it with a grungy lighter. Sarah felt Martha shifting impatiently behind her as the acrid stench of tobacco surrounded them.

She opened her purse and extracted a ten and when the landlord didn't take it, she let out a huff and pulled out another. "That's all I'll give, Mr.—"

He took the bills in his yellowed fingers and slipped them into his sweatpants pocket. "Name's Tim. Follow me."

He shuffled along in slippers and led the way to the stairs. When they reached the top, he went into a coughing fit, and another cigarette hit the concrete walkway. "I really need to quit," he wheezed.

"Good idea. Those things will kill you," Martha said, keeping her distance behind him.

He squinted at Martha, then stopped in front of a door with peeling paint and the 4B plaque hanging by one nail. He knocked hard. "Ben! Are you in there?"

When there was no answer, he turned to the ladies and shrugged. He stuck the passkey into the lock, and with a click the door opened. The air inside smelled faintly stale.

The landlord flipped on the light. "Well, he's not getting his security deposit back, that's for sure." He stepped farther into the apartment that consisted of one main room with a kitchen in a tiny alcove at the far end. A shaded window over the sink let in enough light to reveal dirty dishes in the sink and a pizza box on the counter. The cupboards had been emptied. Cans and boxes of food lay on the floor.

Sarah ventured farther into the room. A sofa bed was shoved up against one wall, the bed out, mattress flung half on the carpet. A dresser with an ancient television propped on it claimed the other wall, along with a small table or desk.

"I'll check the bathroom," he said, weaving around piles of junk on the floor. Someone had yanked the dresser drawers open, and clothes spilled onto the floor.

"No dead bodies. Are you satisfied? He ain't here." The landlord ambled back into view.

Sarah gazed around at the destruction. It reminded her of her living room the night before. "I think you should call the police."

"For what? I've seen worse. You won't believe what tenants will do."

"I understand, but this room looks like it's been searched." Sarah inched farther in. The trash can had been emptied onto the floor near the door. Sarah toed the papers, moving them about. Most of them were candy or fast food wrappers.

He shrugged. "Or Ben's a slob."

"Most people leave the mattress on the bed," Martha pointed out.

He shrugged again. "As long as people pay their rent on time and don't burn the place down or put holes in the walls, it ain't my business."

Sarah stepped beside the door and ran her finger over the metal pad. "Looks like scratches to me, and the metal on the doorjamb is bent. Someone jimmied the door open."

"Listen lady, if you want me to call the cops, I will. Just don't expect them to do anything except waste my time."

"I think you should. There's a missing person report on Ben's sister Belle, so they may be coming by here anyway," Sarah said. "And who was this other brother you mentioned? Did he give his name? What did he look like?"

He shrugged. "Didn't ask his name and he didn't offer. He was taller than me. Short hair. Drove a black Toyota Camry. Looked new."

"What kind of clothes did he have on?"

"Lady, I don't pay attention to that kind of stuff. I suppose he had on jeans and a shirt. Wore a baseball cap. New York Yankees, I think."

Sarah stepped back out on the landing by Martha and glanced up and down the balcony walkway. "Did Ben have any friends in the building?"

Before he could shrug again and say it wasn't any of his business, Martha added, "Anyone he talked to at all? What about the people next door?"

"You can try. You can also ask the lady in 2A, Mrs. Corker. She's always home and pokes her nose into everyone's business." He backed out of the apartment and locked the door.

Sarah pulled a business card out of her pocket. "If Ben comes home or you hear anything, could you please give me a call?"

The landlord shoved the card in his front pocket and headed for the stairs. Cigarette smoke drifted up past the metal railing by the time he reached the ground.

Martha and Sarah split up and started knocking on doors on either side of Ben's apartment. Most people weren't home or didn't answer. The few who did said they didn't know Ben Silver.

They met downstairs by apartment 2A. Sarah could hear loud television sounds through the door. People talking interspersed with music.

Sarah knocked on the door. The television volume grew fainter, and the dingy beige curtain parted. Sarah caught a flash of eyeglasses before the curtain dropped back into place.

The door cracked opened, the safety chain in place. A little, wrinked lady with hair the color of mud peered out. "I'm not buying anything."

"Oh, we're not selling anything," Martha said.

Sarah gave the woman a friendly smile. "Mrs. Corker, we were just over there talking to the manager—"

"I saw you. What do you want?"

"We're looking for another tenant, Ben Silver."

"Well, I'm busy right now, but if you make it worth my while...."

Sarah exchanged an exasperated look with Martha, and reached into her purse. She held out a ten dollar bill. Mrs. Corker's thin fingers reached through the crack, and the bill disappeared before the door clicked shut.

Mrs. Corker took so long, Martha whispered, "Is she coming back?" Finally, the door chain rattled and the door opened.

"Come on in," Mrs. Corker said.

Sarah sidled past Mrs. Corker, Martha following. Mrs. Corker gestured to a couch slipcovered in a teal blue and sat in a recliner covered with the same fabric. Remote controls and magazines covered the side table by her chair.

The apartment layout was identical to Ben's, but of course cleaner, and Mrs. Corker owned a forty-inch plasma flat-screen television. The sound had been muted and the noon news was on.

"Mrs. Corker, your landlord suggested that you may have seen Ben Silver. He lives in 4B."

"Humph. Tim thinks I just sit here all day and spy on people."

"Well, he did mention that you're home most of the time, so he thought you might've seen something." Sarah glanced at the window. Through the crack in the two drapes she had a clear view of the parking lot.

"Like what?"

"At this point, anything might be useful." Sarah pulled the photo of Ben from her tote bag. "This is Ben."

"Oh yes. I've seen him and his girlfriend."

"Girlfriend?" Martha asked.

"Yeah, a blonde. Short hair. Carries a camera around her neck."

"That sounds more like his sister Belle." Sarah perked up. Finally someone who could tell her something about Belle.

She shrugged her thin shoulders. "Girlfriend. Sister. Makes no difference to me. Pulled up in a car and ran upstairs. I could've told her she'd missed him if she'd asked. She looked upset. I figured they must've broken up. Haven't seen her since."

Sarah leaned forward. "When was this?"

"I'm not sure. Oprah had George Clooney on as a guest. I remember because the girl honked the horn once right in the middle of the movie clip." She reached for a *TV Guide* on her side table.

"If it was George Clooney, then that would be Friday," Martha said. To Sarah, she added, "I had the TV on while I was cleaning."

"Yeah, that's right," Mrs. Corker said, adjusting her glasses and reading the print. "Friday."

"You said she'd missed Ben. When did he leave?" Sarah asked.

"Before Oprah came on. He showed up in that old wreck of his and went upstairs. Next thing I know, he dropped something on the stairs, and it made a terrible noise. Everything echoes around here. All that concrete. Anyway, it must've been the backpack he put in his car."

"Backpack as in a small daypack, or the kind you take on trips?" Sarah held out her hands showing the different sizes.

"Wilderness kind. It was big. I've seen him with it sometimes on the weekends."

"That's the last time you saw him?"

"Nah, he was there a little while longer. I fixed myself a snack, and when I came out of the kitchen, I saw him take off. He burned rubber and almost hit the telephone pole on the way out. His girlfriend, or I guess his sister, showed up not long after that." Mrs. Corker glanced at the television. "Anything else you want to know?"

"The manager said that Ben's brother visited him yesterday? Banged on Ben's door," Martha said. "Did you hear him?"

"Yeah, never got a good look at him." She gestured at the big screen. "Looks like we're in trouble."

The meteorologist stood in front of the US map, pointing to a huge swirling radar cloud of green and white. Martha groaned softly at the prediction for a record snowfall arriving on Saturday evening.

Just in time for the home tour.

"Chances are the weathermen are wrong again. They've been predicting that storm to build and move east for four days and so far, nothing," Sarah said as they settled back in Martha's car after bidding good-bye to Mrs. Corker. "You watch, tomorrow they'll say something different."

Martha fired up the engine and smiled. "You're right. I'll just keep praying the storm will hold off."

"I will too. We don't want a blizzard after everyone worked so hard," Sarah said, gazing through the windshield at the cloud cover. "And I'm worried about the storm hitting when Ben and Belle might be out in the wilderness somewhere."

"You think they'd stay out in this cold?"

"I don't know, but I heard Belle once say she's gone winter camping up on Mount Washington."

"Incredible. And here I get annoyed when the car won't heat up fast enough." Martha flipped the heater lever over to high.

"Mrs. Corker said Ben had taken his backpack. When we searched the house, I didn't see Belle's backpack, tent, or sleeping bag," Sarah said, her fingers tapping the armrest. Belle might be able to camp in the snow but a blizzard could be deadly.

"At least now we know they must've left last Friday. And they weren't together, at least not initially. Sounds to me like someone is after Ben or Belle or both."

"I think so too." Sarah nodded, her stomach twisting. Things were not looking good.

"Now where to? The museum?" Martha asked.

"Yes, I was supposed to call the curator this morning, but it might be more productive meeting him in person."

As Martha's minivan rolled down the highway toward Pittsfield, Sarah tried one of the numbers she had for Mrs. Steinbeck. She answered after the fourth ring.

"Mrs. Steinbeck, you may not remember me," Sarah said, "but we met at Andrew Blake's office. My friend Martha was with me and your cute little dog ran up to her."

"Oh yes." Her voice warmed. "Your friend mentioned an aunt who raised Yorkies."

"This may seem a bit nosey but I wanted to ask some questions about Andrew—"

"You must want a reference," Mrs. Steinbeck said. "I've given them out for Andrew before."

"Well, actually—"

"I don't mind at all. I know Andrew's grandparents. Good people. Of course I wouldn't be using him unless my lawyer was absolutely sure. You can rest assured that any rumors you may have heard about Mr. Blake's situation are false. He was completely cleared of embezzlement. It was his partner all along."

Embezzlement?

Sarah was speechless as Mrs. Steinbeck continued. "Poor Andrew, he's been trying to rebuild his life. I'm just glad he came back to where people care about him."

"That's good," Sarah agreed. "Where was he working before this?"

"Manhattan."

Sarah mouthed the word to Martha and she shot Sarah a look that indicated they were thinking the same thing.

Yankees ball cap.

CHAPTER TWELVE

Martha turned the minivan down Main Street into the historic downtown of Pittsfield. Tiny white twinkle lights decorated the stores. Giant glittery snowflakes adorned the street lamps, and red ribbon wound down from the top to the base of each one, making them look like candy canes.

Sarah stared out the window contemplating who Tim might have seen and mistaken for Ben's brother. Mr. Blake could probably fit Tim's vague description, but so could thousands of other men. And anyone could own a Yankees baseball cap.

They turned on Museum Drive and wound up the hill to the stately building. The parking lot contained only three cars and a delivery truck. Business was probably down due to the Christmas season, Sarah mused, as they entered through the revolving door. Alice White stood behind the reception desk.

"Well, hello," she said with a smile. "I thought you were going to call this morning."

Sarah returned the smile. "Since we were in Pittsfield today, we thought we'd check again to see if Mr. Warthorne was available."

A commotion sounded behind them as three men in beige coveralls came through one of the side doors, pushing four-foot cubes on rollers. When they got closer, Sarah realized the cubes were lockable storage containers. The man in the lead addressed Alice. "Excuse me, ma'am. Where do you want these?"

"I don't want them anywhere in here right now," Alice said, hands on her hips. "We don't need them until the day after Christmas."

The one who appeared to be the boss talked around his gum, "Sorry, but our orders say today."

Alice lifted the counter partition and walked through. "There has to be a mistake."

The man picked a clipboard off the top of one of the containers and scrutinized it. "Nope, it says December twentieth."

"You'll have to take them away and come back December twenty-sixth," Alice insisted.

"We're booked up until after New Year's. We can take them back to the warehouse, but then we can't deliver them again until January second."

"I'll have to get Mr. Warthorne," Alice said, picking up the phone and hitting a button. She turned her back to them and murmured into the receiver.

A minute later, footsteps sounded in the hall beyond the reception counter and a distinguished-looking man appeared. He wore a navy suit and a white shirt, and had a red handkerchief in his breast pocket. A light frosting of silver streaked his dark hair. His grey eyes scrutinized the packing men.

"Gentlemen, I'm Mr. Warthorne. What seems to be the problem here?"

"We brought the travel chests you reserved. We're ready to assist with packing," the man with the gum said.

"No, no, this won't do." Mr. Warthorne furrowed his forehead, his eyebrows forming a V above his long, chiseled nose. "The ornaments are for our *Christmas* display. That's why I arranged for them to be picked up on December twenty-sixth."

The man lifted his clipboard. "Well, as I was telling the lady here, we pack now or we pack after the New Year."

"Fine. We'll wait until then."

"Um, Mr. Warthorne?" Alice said, holding up a black notebook. "We can't wait until the second. The exhibit is due back in Denmark by the thirtieth, or the museum pays a significant fine."

"Are you sure?" Mr. Warthorne asked.

"Yes, sir. It was specified in the contract. That's the date you gave me."

Mr. Warthorne sighed. "My mistake. We'll have to do something else. Any suggestions, gentlemen?"

The boss glanced at the other two men who were standing off to the side, looking bored. "Well, I suppose we can leave the cases here. We won't have anyone available to pack until after the first, but you can do it yourselves and we'll send someone to pick them up. But I'll have to have you sign a waiver releasing us from liability in case anything breaks."

Mr. Warthorne continued to frown. "I'll expect a discount, then."

The man shrugged his beefy shoulders. "Talk to the office."

"Put the shipping units in the back storage room. I suppose we can work around them for a couple of days. Alice will show you the way."

Alice skirted around the counter, and gestured for them to follow her down the hall. The men trailed her like train cars.

Sarah cleared her throat. "Mr. Warthorne, can we speak with you for a few minutes? I'm Mrs. Hart, and this is Mrs. Maplethorpe."

He turned around, some of the annoyance etched on his face fading. "Ah yes, Alice mentioned you were here yesterday. Please come on back to my office." He led them down the hall and ushered them into a narrow room with tall French doors and windows overlooking a stately Greek garden.

"Can I get you some coffee or maybe tea? Water?" he asked.

"Nothing for me, thank you," Sarah said, gazing around the tastefully decorated office.

"I'd like some tea, please," Martha said, unbuttoning her coat before settling into one of the winged burgundy leather chairs set in front of an antique desk.

"Lemon and cream?" Mr. Warthorne asked, backing to the door.

"Lemon, please."

"I'll be just a minute. Alice usually gets the refreshments, but she's probably still detained." He stepped into the hall, giving Sarah more time to explore the room.

The surface of his marble-topped desk was fastidious, all the papers at right angles. An antique divan upholstered in a paisley gold pattern rested next to the wall flanked by a cabinet on one side and an end table on the other. The side table held several art magazines and a brochure from the Metropolitan Museum of Art.

Sarah wandered over to study a stormy seascape that hung above the divan, and her shoe crunched on something hard. She lifted her foot and picked up a diamond-shaped piece of glass. The edges had crumbled, leaving a powder on the floor. She placed it on the table and bent over to pick up the rest of the fragments.

"Is something wrong?" Mr. Warthorne asked from the doorway. He held a silver tray with a petite silver teapot and cups.

Sarah straightened. "I'm so sorry. I stepped on something and broke it. Looks like glass."

"Oh, don't bother cleaning it up. It's nothing. Probably a piece of Christmas decoration that didn't get vacuumed up. The decorating committee used the office to store some things from our last fund-raiser."

He crossed the room and set the tray on a small round table by Martha's chair. "Here is your tea, Mrs. Maplethorpe. The lemon is in the covered bowl."

Sarah sat in the chair next to Martha as she squeezed a lemon wedge into her tea. A clean, refreshing scent filled the air.

After Mr. Warthorne settled behind his desk, Sarah spoke, "Mr. Warthorne, we came to ask about one of your employees."

He nodded. "Ben Silver. Yes, Alice told me. I'm afraid personal information about our employees is confidential."

"We understand," Sarah said with a smile. "We're not trying to pry into anything confidential, but merely hoping for some information that might help us locate his sister, Anabelle Silver. We think, maybe, they're together. Anything you can share with us about Ben may be useful."

Mr. Warthorne's lips turned down in a frown. "Is his sister in trouble of some kind?"

"We're not sure, which is why we need to find her. She's a boarder in my home and has been missing for several days," Sarah said. "We heard you fired Ben from his job here."

"Really?" Mr. Warthorne asked in a flat tone, moving one neat stack of papers to another. "Where did you hear that?"

Sarah glanced at Martha. She didn't want to get the janitor in trouble. "I'd rather not say. Could you at least tell us if he's still employed here?"

"He is not. But I didn't fire Ben Silver. He quit."

"Quit?" Martha set her teacup down so quickly, drops of her tea spilled on her lap.

Mr. Warthorne opened a drawer, pulled out a box of tissues, and gave it to Martha.

"Thank you," she murmured, dabbing at the dark stain on her slacks.

"Why did Ben quit?" Sarah asked.

He leaned back in his chair. "Ben hasn't been in since last weekend. He didn't call in sick or ask for time off. So in my mind, he quit. If he does show up to work without an excellent explanation for his absence, then he's fired anyway."

"Has he done this before? Not shown up?" Sarah asked.

"Ben's employment information is confidential, but I can tell you that this isn't unexpected."

"Then why did you hire him?" Martha asked.

He sighed. "As a favor to a business associate. One of the community goals of our museum has been to hire the less fortunate for hourly positions. Besides, Ben's family has a connection with museums. I don't know if you know it, but Ben's father is a world-renowned archeologist."

"So you thought maybe his dad might contribute somehow to the museum," Martha blurted out, and then covered her mouth with her fingers. "I'm so sorry. I didn't mean to make you sound like an opportunist."

Sarah bit back a laugh.

"I'd be lying if I said the thought didn't cross my mind," Mr. Warthorne said with a nod. "Donations are the lifeblood of museums. As the curator, my job is to seek out funding opportunities whenever possible."

"I saw the museum had a recent fund-raiser. The Christmas Tea. That night was the last shift Ben worked. Correct?"

"How do you—" His eyes narrowed, but then he shrugged as if he found it easier to just answer, "That's correct."

"Did anything happen that night? Something that would warrant Ben suddenly leaving his job?"

"I saw nothing out of the ordinary. Ben and some of our other staff came in early to clean up after the fund-raiser. That was the last time I saw him." He glanced down as a light lit up on his phone. "I'm afraid I have a phone call coming in. If you'll excuse me."

"Thank you, Mr. Warthorne, for your time." Sarah stood.

"I apologize for not being more of a help to you." Mr. Warthone picked up the receiver.

"That's okay. I haven't had much luck so far in locating them. I hope the police will have more."

"The police are involved?" Mr. Warthorne nearly dropped the phone. He asked whoever was on the other end of the line to hold and came around the side of the desk. "I didn't realize this was so serious. Of course. If I learn of anything, I'll let you know."

"I would really appreciate it," Sarah said and paused on her way to the door. "One last thing. Is it true the museum is being bought out by a private company?"

"Yes, it was announced several weeks ago, although the transaction hasn't actually taken place yet."

"One of your employees said they were all afraid of losing their jobs." Martha said. "Is that a possibility?"

"Not that I'm aware of. Nothing has been decided yet, but there's no need for worry," Mr. Warthorne said emphatically. He ushered them into the hallway.

Sarah turned and before he could close the door, asked, "Are you a Yankees fan?"

Mr. Warthorne made a small exasperated sound. "I don't have time for baseball. Please excuse me." He shut his door with a firm click.

"Baseball?" Martha asked and then her mouth dropped open. "Oh! Do you think he was the man who went to Ben's apartment?"

Sarah shrugged. "I don't know. I was just fishing."

Alice leaned against the reception counter. Her hair had pulled loose of its bun, and brunette wisps formed a halo around her head. She gave Sarah and Martha a weary smile. "I'm sorry about earlier. I had no idea the packers would be here today. I hope Mr. Warthorne was able to help you."

"He confirmed some things for us." Sarah said, and then got a closer look at Alice's red-rimmed eyes. "Is everything okay, dear?"

She glanced around them at the empty hall, her eyes brightening with tears. "Sorry. I was informed because of the clerical mistake on the dates for the exhibit, I have to come in on my vacation to pack up the Christmas display. Mr. Warthorne doesn't want anyone else touching the ornaments and he'll be on vacation out of the country. He'd already postponed his trip from last week and says he won't again. The ornaments have to be shipped back to Denmark next week." She sniffed. "My boyfriend is going to be upset with me. We were planning a trip too. It wasn't my fault. I'm sure I gave the packers the right date. Someone else goofed."

Martha pulled out a tissue from her purse and handed it to Alice.

"Some of those ornaments are worth thousands of dollars apiece, which is why we use the bonded packers and special foam-lined cases. It'll take me hours because each one has to be checked for damage and signed off on. I don't want the responsibility. What if I dropped one? Each one is probably worth a month of my salary."

"The ornaments are insured, right?" Sarah asked.

She nodded.

"Surely Mr. Warthorne considered that, no matter who packs them."

She sniffed. "I suppose you're right." The sound of footsteps and chatter came from the exhibit hall. She quickly wiped her eyes and smoothed her hair. "Thank you for listening," she whispered as a family wandered into the lobby.

"You're welcome. And we appreciate all your help," Sarah said. Martha gave Alice a wave as they headed out the door.

They paused on the steps, the cold air nipping at their cheeks. "So now what?" Martha asked.

"I'm not sure. We'll just have to keep digging." Sarah sighed. All the clues they'd been collecting were tiny fragmented pieces of information like the glass she'd picked up off the office floor. None of them seemed to fit together.

Yet.

Twilight had settled over Maple Hill by the time Sarah and Martha reached the Sanders' residence. Sarah's gaze swept over the Colonial Revival House. Light from the multipaned windows glowed warmly in the gloom of the dreary night. Smoke drifted from a chimney that rose out of the gabled roof.

Martha had contacted the owners of the first three houses on the tour, and they had agreed to let them do a run-through of the treasure hunt. Tomorrow they would tackle the last three homes—Martha's, Maggie's, and Sarah's. Sarah glanced down the street at the houses as, one by one, residents turned on their Christmas lights.

Sarah couldn't seem to shake the uneasy feeling that had plagued her since they'd left the New England Museum of Art. They'd kept an eye out for any brown sedans, but no one had followed them home from Pittsfield this time.

A black pickup truck turned the corner, its headlights washing over them. Liam hopped out of the cab and waved. "Sorry I'm late."

"We just got here." Martha smiled. She'd called him when Sarah and she had arrived back in Maple Hill.

Liam strode up to them, his boots crunching on the dry leaves the wind tossed onto the sidewalk. He carried a clipboard. A pencil was stuck over his ear. "How are you both doing this chilly evening? Any progress on finding Belle?"

"Nothing significant," Sarah said as they walked up the brick sidewalk to the porch. "But I'm still waiting for a call back from her father. Maybe he'll know something."

"I hope so too. I'd be frantic if my daughter were missing," Liam said as Martha pushed the doorbell. Chimes sounded behind the stately door.

Liam cleared his throat. "Before we go in, do we have any idea what we're looking for?"

"Not really. We're just hoping we'll know it when we see it." Martha said with a laugh.

The door opened and a slim, middle-aged woman said, "Come on in. Sorry it took me so long to answer. I was in the back getting supper ready." The smell of pot roast wafted on the air, causing Sarah's stomach to growl.

"Smells delicious," Martha said. She introduced Liam and Sarah to Joyce Sanders and explained Liam's new role in the treasure hunt.

"Nice to meet you both," Joyce said as a buzzer rang in the distance. "Oh dear, that's my timer. If you'll excuse me for a minute, I need to check the roast. Go on into the parlor, make yourselves at home, and do what you need to do. I'll be back soon." She hurried down the long hall.

Martha led them into a large room on the left side of the entryway. A fire crackled in the fireplace, heating the room to a comfortable level. Sarah unbuttoned her coat as they all gathered to scrutinize the elegant furnishings.

Sarah turned slowly, her gaze scanning the details. Her eyes were drawn to a lovely log cabin quilt above the mantle. Green fabric strips had been cleverly sewn in sequence around two or four sides of each square, then the squares had been joined to construct a Christmas tree with brightly colored ornaments in the centers of the squares. The border was a red holiday pattern with tiny stars. The challenging part must have been getting the ornaments to line up correctly in the pattern. Of course, the pattern wasn't as unique as her Star of Bethlehem quilt, but it was beautiful all the same.

Liam roamed the room, tapping his clipboard with his pencil. "I've been thinking about this all day," he said. "I assume Belle was planning to provide the participants with a clue before they began. Perhaps someone at the booth where people make their donation and pick up the treasure hunt form would give them a verbal or written clue to get them started."

"That's very possible," Martha said, thinking for a moment. "The map I gave you both is only a draft. Miss March said there's a colored border that'll be around the outside edge on the final copies."

"Maybe that's the clue we're missing," Sarah suggested.

"Doesn't hurt to ask. The Copy Shop's still open." Martha pulled out her cell phone. "Be right back." She wandered toward the entryway, chatting on her phone, and then returned, a smile on her face.

"Guess what? Belle designed a swirling musical score as a border on the top and bottom of the map with little carolers in the corners. Both scores are the beginning verses to Christmas carols. At the bottom of the map is a verse to 'Angels We Have Heard on High.'"

"Angels!" Sarah said. Sarah circled the tree, her eye gazing at the wide array of ornaments, and bumped into Liam. "Oh, sorry."

"Quite all right." Liam took a step back, looking at the top of the tree. "Isn't that an angel like the one you had at the café, Sarah?"

Her gaze narrowed on the glass angel with gold-tipped wings, "Yes, it is! What's the other carol?"

"Above the first house listed, which is the Sanders' of course, is the first verse to 'Ding Dong Merrily on High,'" Martha said.

"*Ding dong merrily on high. Christmas bells are ringing*," Liam sang in his deep voice. Martha and Sarah looked at each other and smiled. The poor man couldn't carry a tune, yet something about his deep voice tugged at Sarah's heart.

"There's a bell on the tree right next to the angel," Sarah said.

"Excellent. I think we've got the beginning to the treasure hunt. Belle must've meant the songs to be the first clues." Liam scribbled on his clipboard. "We can think of a clever way to point this out to the participants as they start the tour."

Sarah crossed to the tree. "There are bells all over the tree and another silver one on the side table."

"Bells?" Joyce asked, standing in the doorway. "Is that what people are supposed to hunt for in the treasure hunt?"

"Yes, but you mustn't tell unless someone really needs help," Martha said in a loud conspiring whisper.

"Oh I won't. How fun!" Joyce clapped her hands together.

"We need to get a total of how many bells are here to see if it corresponds with this chart and the last clue," Liam said. "Let's all count individually, and see if we come up with the same number."

They each started counting as Joyce approached the tree. "You know what? I don't remember this many bells being on the tree."

"Belle probably added some," Sarah said, again remembering Belle's request to look around in the attic for extra decorations.

"That could be. She did ask if she could tweak a few things," Joyce said. "I expected her to drop by this week. I saw her at the gas station at Tillman's Corner and waved, but she didn't see me."

Sarah stopped counting and shifted her attention to Joyce. "When was this?"

"Couple days ago. Probably Monday. She was pulling out as I was turning in and didn't see me. At least, I'm pretty sure it was her."

"Was it a red car?"

Joyce nodded. "A compact."

"Was there anyone else with her?"

"I think there was someone else in the car. Why are you asking?"

"I haven't seen her since last week, and I've been wondering where she's off to."

"She was headed east out of town, so no telling. Could be heading for Boston."

"I get nine ornaments and the one on the table makes ten," Martha called from across the room.

"I got ten too," Liam said.

"Actually, there are eleven if you count the bell on the quilt." Sarah pointed to the log cabin quilt over the mantel.

"How clever," Joyce said with a smile as Liam noted it on his clipboard. "I bought that quilt while I was in Washington, DC, when Harry attended a sales conference. I'm so looking forward to the tour. I can't do the treasure hunt since I'll be hosting here, but I do want to hear all about it when it's over."

"I'll make sure you do," Martha said. "We'd better run on to the next house. We so appreciate your participating, Joyce."

"My pleasure," Joyce said, opening the door for them.

After Joyce closed the door, Sarah's phone vibrated in her purse. She took it out, noting she had a voice message.

"Excuse me a moment," she said pausing on the sidewalk. The phone connected with her message service.

"Mrs. Hart. This is Dr. Silver." Static roared in her ear and then his voice returned, "Trouble reaching you. Reception terrible. Will try your home phone again at six PM your time."

"Oh dear." Sarah said and hurried to the street.

"What's wrong?" Martha asked.

"That was Belle's father. He must've called when we were in the dead spot on the highway. I don't know why it didn't come through until now. But he's going to call my house again at six," she glanced at her watch, "which is in ten minutes."

"Here, take my car and go home." Martha tossed Sarah her keys. "Liam and I can handle the treasure hunt from here. It's more important you work on trying to find Belle."

"Good luck," Liam called as Sarah jumped in Martha's minivan and raced toward home.

Sarah charged into the house a minute before six. She was shaking off her coat when the phone rang.

"Mrs. Hart?"

"Hello, Dr. Silver," Sarah said, sinking onto a kitchen chair. "Thank you so much for calling me back. The reception is better."

"For the moment." His words were clipped. "You were calling about my daughter?"

"Yes, I am. Belle is my boarder, and I was wondering if she's been in touch with you lately."

"Not for a couple of weeks. We usually e-mail back and forth."

"Do you know if she was planning a trip?" Sarah stalled, trying to figure out a gentle way to say his daughter had disappeared.

"Mrs. Hart, what exactly are you trying to tell me?"

Sarah took a deep breath. "Your daughter left here almost a week ago, and I'm worried." She filled him in on all the details she'd collected, including Joyce's possible sighting of Belle on Monday.

"So Ben's gone too?"

"As far as I can tell. He hasn't been at work since last week. Do you have any idea where they could've gone?"

"Not really, but being the holidays, I'm sure they're together. I'm afraid I haven't been around much the last few years and Belle took a parental role with Ben. They were always very close. Ben's misguided at times, but overall he's a good kid."

"Belle's been a delight to live with. I haven't met Ben yet. I did visit with Belle's ex-fiancé. Do you know Andrew Blake?"

"Only from a distance. I haven't been in the States for over two years. I've talked to Andrew on the phone." His voice rose. "Why? Does he have something to do with this?"

"I'm not sure." Sarah wished she had better answers for the man.

She told him what little she knew; and when she finished, he said, "I appreciate your checking into this. I'll do some investigating from here. Make some phone calls, and if I locate them, I'll let you know," he said, his voice tight with tension, the earlier impatience gone.

"I'll do the same," Sarah said. "Before you go, Belle's former Pittsfield roommate mentioned Belle had an aunt, but she didn't know her last name."

"Ah yes, that would be Lisa, my wife's sister. I doubt very much they'd go there. But if you want to contact her, her last name is Stuart. Lives in Stoneham, outside of Boston. Her phone number should be listed."

"I'll try it. Thank you for calling back."

"No, thank you for your concern."

Sarah thought about Martha and Liam as she hung up the phone and wondered how they were doing. It'd probably take them at least an hour before they arrived at her house.

She turned on her computer. The online white pages were proving to be very useful in this case. Only one L. Stuart popped onto the screen for Stoneham. A woman answered on the first ring.

"Lisa Stuart? I'm Belle Silver's landlady. Her father gave me your name as someone to call about Belle and Ben."

"*Who* is this?" a shrill voice asked.

Sarah patiently explained again, and asked her when she'd seen or heard from her niece and nephew.

"I haven't talked to Benjamin since he called here a couple months back asking for money. Can you believe that? After all I did for him."

"Why did he need money?"

"Gambling, most likely. Always wanted to get rich quick. He always got into trouble, even in school, although Belle helped him there. He was out of control. I finally had to kick him out and he moved over to where his sister is. I tried to warn Belle about him, but she wouldn't listen."

Sarah rubbed her forehead with her fingers. "Do you know of any friends of Ben's or Belle's I could call?"

"No, sorry."

"If you hear from them or think of anywhere they might be, please give me a call." Sarah rattled off her home and cell numbers before saying good-bye. She highly doubted the woman would ever call back.

For supper, Sarah sliced cantaloupe and topped it with cottage cheese and then spent some time rewrapping the packages that the vandals had ripped. She heard Martha's voice before the doorbell rang.

"We did it!" Martha said with a laugh as she and Liam entered the living room.

"All the objects are accounted for except for here. It was fairly easy. All we had to do was look for an angel at each house, and the object that we were supposed to count was right next to it. Belle was clever not to use an angel ornament each time. At the Grenshaws', she used a little angel statue, and the Greens had an angel quilt. At my house it was an angel nutcracker."

Sarah smiled and gestured for them to sit on the couch. "Sounds like fun!"

"I think everyone will like it," Liam agreed with a warm smile in return. "As you know, at the Sanders' the Christmas objects to count were bells. At the Greens' they were Christmas trees, and at the Grenshaws', toy trains."

"Nutcrackers at my house," Martha said. "We figure we'll use hourglasses at Maggie's, since she only needs one or two objects. Now we just have to figure out what Belle had planned for here."

"I think I know," Sarah said. "The ornaments I found were an angel and a star. My quilt, which she knew was going to be displayed, is the Star of Bethlehem pattern. I'm guessing stars were supposed to be counted here."

"That would work great," Liam said, consulting his clipboard. "You only need three items—to make your house the number three in the puzzle—for the correct answer."

"So what was the last clue at the bottom of the map?" Sarah asked.

"Oh!" Martha clapped her hands together. "We figured it out after only a few letters. It's a Bible verse. 'For unto us a child is born.' Do you know what she was referring to?"

A smile tickled Sarah's lips. "The prizes are in the manger. The one that Gerry carved."

Martha's eyes rounded. "But I didn't see your nativity scene out front."

"That's because I lent the manger to the pastor last Sunday. Your treasure is in front of the church, buried in the straw."

CHAPTER THIRTEEN

Sarah stared at the computer screen and yawned. She wanted to check a few things online before she headed to bed, but her eyelids were drooping.

After Liam, Martha, and she had retrieved the little photo frames from the manger, she called Jason. He'd promised to fix the church's manger, so Sarah could use Gerry's for the home tour. Martha was ecstatic to be able to cross the treasure hunt preparation off her list, and Sarah and Liam had been happy to help.

Sarah spent the rest of the evening cutting the last of the diamonds to form one point of the star for her quilt. The next step was to lay out the diamonds in the star point shape, and then move the different fabrics around until she'd decided on the most pleasing pattern of colors. She could then use a shortcut to construct all eight star points. She would sew together strips of fabric in the order she'd decided on, then cut those bands of fabric into presewn strips of diamonds.

She glanced at the framed photo of Gerry she kept on her desk. Gerry hadn't had much use for shortcuts. When he worked with wood, he took his time, perfecting each step, which is why his furniture lasted. Like the manger she'd lent to the church.

He'd taken his time courting her, too, which was why she had been shocked when he'd proposed. She smiled as the memory filled her thoughts.

It was spring break in her senior year of college and they'd decided to go for a drive in his convertible. He'd put the top down, and warm sun and crisp air felt great after the long winter. She had wanted to invite Martha and Ernie along too, but Gerry insisted they go alone. Later, she understood why.

They'd driven to Shadow Lake, high in the Berkshires and secluded, a favorite spot of theirs. Gerry had been quiet for most of the trip. But after their picnic lunch, he started talking about the future as he often did. He discussed his goals in life and plans to open his own accounting practice after he passed his CPA. Sarah lounged next to him on a boulder, contentedly listening, watching the sunlight play across the crystal clear lake water. Suddenly she realized he wasn't beside her any longer, but kneeling at her feet.

He took her hands in his and asked softly, "Sarah, darling, nothing in the future matters unless you are with me. Will you marry me?"

She nearly fell off the rock, and the next thing she knew she was in his arms, saying yes.

Sarah blinked. A tear, a happy one, rolled down Sarah's cheek and dropped onto the back of her hand resting on the keyboard. Gerry might not be with her now, but he'd always be in her heart and memories.

She wiped away the tear and focused on her computer search. She typed *Berkshire Museum of Art* in the online search bar. It still bothered her that she'd gotten two different versions of Ben's departure from the museum. Granted, Kay, the museum janitor, may have jumped to paranoid conclusions, but Sarah didn't completely trust Mr. Warthorne's version of the story either.

She couldn't believe that Belle would support Ben's suddenly going off without even asking for the time off. Both Kelsey and Dr. Silver had mentioned how protective Belle was of her younger brother. If Belle had gone off with Ben, maybe she was protecting Ben from something. Or someone.

Joyce had seen Belle at Tillman's Corner, which could mean they were headed for Boston, although taking the interstate would've been faster. But Tillman's Corner wasn't far from the entrance to a popular drive into the Berkshire wilderness, the same route Gerry and she had taken to Shadow Lake. Sarah certainly hoped they weren't backpacking, especially with the huge storm that was predicted for this weekend.

The museum home page finally finished loading, and Sarah scrolled through the options. Her cursor landed on the *recent news* link. There was a brief press release reporting that an official offer had been made to buy the museum. She clicked on the link to the company's Web site and scrolled through some of their other projects. They owned several museums throughout the country, and there were articles about their renovations and improvements. She studied a photo of the CEO. The man looked to be in his early thirties, as did the rest of his staff.

She went back to the museum site and clicked on the *Christmas Tea* link. Several pictures showed groups of people gathered in front of the spectacular Christmas tree. One caption mentioned the mayor of Pittsfield, so Sarah assumed some of the others were important town officials also. Judging from some of the sparkling dresses and jewelry these were wealthy patrons of the museum.

Tables with white tablecloths had been set around the room, each adorned with poinsettias and gold candles. One photo captured the buffet table, piled with traditional holiday fare of turkey, ruby bowls of cranberry sauce, snowy mounds of potatoes, sweet potatoes, and green vegetables.

She flipped to the next section on the history of the special exhibit. The close-up shots of the bejeweled gold, silver, and crystal ornaments reminded her she needed to pick up some more for her tree. Not all of hers had been broken. Jason had retrieved several that had been scattered across the grass in the backyard. The whole thing still seemed surreal. Why on earth would anyone want to destroy her Christmas tree? She turned her attention back to the screen as a tiny flicker of suspicion lit in the back of her brain.

She was so deep in thought, she only dimly heard the phone ring. She glanced at the time on the computer. Her heart thumped. Who would be calling after eleven at night? She ran to the kitchen and snatched up the phone.

"Hello?" she said, her voice louder than she intended.

A long pause ensued, and then a distant female voice said, "Mrs. Hart?"

"Yes, I'm Sarah Hart."

"Oh good. I couldn't find your number, and I had to call information. I wasn't even sure if I dialed right. I'm a little shook up."

"I'm sorry. Who is this?"

"Oh! I'm sorry. This is Kelsey Manning, Belle's old roommate."

"Oh Kelsey, hi. Are you all right?"

"I-I think so. I'm sorry to call you so late, but you said to call if I learned anything about Belle."

"Did you hear from her?" Sarah asked, gripping the phone hard.

"Not exactly."

Sarah sank down on a chair, her knees rubbery. "Belle's not...?"

"Oh no, no, no. She's fine as far as I know. Sorry. I'm so scattered. I can't seem to think," Kelsey said. "My apartment was broken into, and I surprised them when I came home."

Sarah sucked in a deep breath. "Well no wonder you're upset. Are you okay?"

"Yes, luckily my neighbor heard me scream, and she hollered out her door that she'd called the police."

"Thank the Lord for that."

"I didn't know what to do. I opened the door and they were standing by my tree, ripping open the gifts. I screamed, and one of them grabbed me before I could run out the door. He kept asking me, 'Where are they?' The jerk left bruises on my arms."

"You poor girl. Do you think he was referring to Belle? Her brother is missing too."

"I guess. If Ben's gone...that makes even more sense. I said I didn't know, but I don't think they believed me. That's when my neighbor hollered. They shoved me and ran out. I fell and cut my hands because there were broken ornaments all over the place."

"I'm so sorry. Do you need to go see a doctor?"

"I don't think so. I'm okay." Kelsey said. Her voice had gradually lowered to a more normal pitch.

Sarah leaned back in her chair, relieved the girl seemed relatively unhurt. "Do you have any idea who those men could be?"

"No, but...okay, this is weird. Remember when you asked about Belle's ex-fiancé Andrew? He came by here yesterday, wanting to know where Belle was, and if she'd left anything of hers here. He was pushy and seemed angry. Or maybe just upset. I don't know."

"I told him Belle was missing, but I never expected him to bother you," Sarah said. How strange.

"Well here's another weird thing. He said she'd called him."

Sarah's pulse raced. "When?"

"I'm not sure, but he implied it was recently."

Sarah's heart thudded. "Is there anything I can do for you Kelsey? I'll come over if you don't want to be alone."

"No, I'm fine now. Thanks. The super's going to install a stronger lock. I just wanted to tell you. I think Belle is in trouble."

A tremble shook Sarah. "So do I, dear. So do I."

"People are going to think we don't cook at home anymore," Martha said, sliding into a chair at a table for four at The Spotted Dog. The red of her sweater cast an even rosier glow on her cheeks than they usually had, and her hazel eyes sparkled.

"We're only doing our civic duty by supporting the small businesses of our town." Sarah draped her coat on the back of the chair before sitting. The coatrack by the door was full, and they wouldn't have gotten a table if Liam hadn't put a reserved sign on the one he ushered them to.

Behind Martha, Karen set down plates in front of a young couple. She gave Sarah a quick smile and lifted a finger, indicating she'd be with them in a minute.

"I made breakfast for Ernie, but one of those huge, yummy cinnamon rolls is calling my name," Martha said, her attention fixed on a plate of the delectable pastries on the table next to them.

"Mine too," Sarah said, almost drooling. "I shouldn't though." She patted her waist.

"Hey, it's almost Christmas, and after all the work we've done we deserve a treat."

Sarah smiled. "I've always loved your logic."

"I'm a practical woman." Martha grinned, unfolding her polka-dot napkin and dropping it in her lap. "Only one day left before the home tour, and Ernie finally got a fire lit under him. He chucked the giant tangled ball of house lights and set off in search of some new ones. Since he likes to bargain shop, I figure that'll keep him busy most of the morning."

"I need to pick up some ornaments. I'm going to see what Maggie has left at her store because I don't really want to go shopping. Only four days until Christmas and the stores will be packed, especially if everyone's trying to beat the snow."

Martha glanced around the café and bookstore. "I hope the threat of that storm doesn't scare off all the tourists before tomorrow," she said, picking up the menu. "Of course I don't want people to get caught in bad weather, but you know what I mean."

"I do. After everyone's hard work, you want the tour to be a success. What did the latest weather report say?" Sarah had meant to check online last night, but Kelsey's phone call had distracted her.

"It's still stalled east of the Great Lakes. Those poor people are getting dumped on. Something to do with a low pressure system, or maybe it was a high pressure wave." She flicked her fingers in a shooing gesture. "I don't care as long as it stays away for one more day."

Liam arrived with three steaming mugs. He smiled and handed them each a sheet of paper before taking a seat at the table. "I created an answer key for the treasure hunt. The participants will count bells at the Sanders', Christmas trees at the Greens', trains at the Grenshaws', and nutcrackers at the Maplethorpes'. I called Maggie this morning, and we agreed to use hourglasses in her home. Sarah, I assume you're still okay with stars."

Sarah nodded. "I have three, and I'll make sure they are placed before tomorrow. Jason's going to repair the church's manger, and I'm going to put the nativity scene on the porch, so we don't have to change anything. We can return the prizes to the manger. However, Belle was going to take photos of the participants for souvenirs."

"I think I can find someone to cover that," Liam said. "I have a camera, but we'll need a computer and printer on site."

"You can use mine," Sarah offered.

"We're all set then," Martha said. "I'll drop by the Copy Shop and pick up the treasure hunt maps. I had Julia print them on card stock, so they'll be easier for everyone to write on."

"I bought some golf pencils they can use too."

Martha shot him a big smile. "Bless you, Liam, you have been such a huge help."

"Yes, this is wonderful of you," Sarah said. "I'm sure Belle will be grateful you carried on for her."

"I keep hoping she'll just waltz in that door any minute," Liam said, pushing back his chair as some customers made their way to the cash register. Murphy sat by the counter chewing on a rubber bone, and one of the ladies bent to coo over what a pretty dog he was.

"Excuse me," Liam said. "As much as I'd love to stay here with you lovely ladies, I have to get back to work." He headed into the bookstore.

"Good morning, Mrs. Hart and Mrs. Maplethorpe. What can I get you?" Karen asked, looking fresh in blue jeans and a hunter green blouse. She'd tucked a red flowery comb in her hair. Tiny bells dangled by ribbons from the comb and jingled softly when she turned her head.

"I'll have one of those delicious cinnamon rolls," Martha said.

"Make that two," Sarah added.

Karen hurried off and returned with water glasses and the pastries. Sarah breathed in the fresh baked scent, rich with cinnamon. Years ago, she used to make homemade rolls for Gerry and the kids every Christmas morning.

"You look all dreamy-eyed. What are you thinking about?" Martha asked, picking a pecan off the top of her roll and popping it into her mouth.

"Baking. I'm thinking of making cinnamon rolls for the twins for Christmas morning. Maybe cranberry-orange bread too."

"They'll probably love both."

"I just need to check with Maggie and make sure I don't accidently tread on any of their Christmas traditions."

"My mother always made rice pudding for Christmas. It would simmer for hours and smelled so good. But hey, if Maggie doesn't want those cinnamon rolls, I'll take 'em."

Sarah laughed. "I'll make you some too."

They polished off the rest of their rolls and finished their cappuccinos while chatting about more of their favorite Christmas traditions.

Finally Martha leaned back and studied Sarah with a practiced eye. "Okay, you've been trying to be extra cheerful this morning, but I can tell something is bothering you."

Sarah blew out a sigh. "I didn't want to spoil anything with bad news, especially with the home tour tomorrow."

Martha leaned forward. "Hey, that's what best friends are for. You can spoil my mood anytime." She grinned. "So what happened?"

"Kelsey, Belle's old roommate, called last night." She filled Martha in on the conversation.

"That's awful. And you think Mr. Blake might be involved?"

"Maybe. And the feeling I have to find Belle keeps growing." Sarah reached for her purse under the table.

Martha let out a troubled sigh. "So, what are your plans for today?"

Sarah looked up from digging for coins in her purse to leave for the tip. "I'm thinking of going spelunking."

"How do we know where to look?" Martha asked, staring at the map Sarah spread out on her kitchen table. "There must be dozens of caves and campgrounds in the area." After they'd left the café, Martha had insisted on going with Sarah to search for Belle.

"Well, I have a hunch on how to narrow down the selection." She'd brought out the maps and brochures of the Berkshire's natural attractions from Belle's box. "Remember we saw these same brochures in the museum while we were waiting to see Mr. Warthorne? There were three rows with four brochures in each, which would make a dozen. I count only nine here."

"I see. So you think Belle might've taken them with her?"

"Maybe. Or maybe they were places she went frequently and she didn't need the map."

"How do we know which ones are missing?"

"We don't, but someone else may be able to tell us." Sarah reached for her phone and the piece of paper Alice had given her at the museum with the direct phone number.

"Berkshire Museum of Art. How may I help you?" a female voice asked.

"Alice?"

"Yes, this is Alice White."

"This is Sarah Hart and—"

"Hi, Mrs. Hart," Alice said. "I'm afraid Mr. Warthorne is not available—oh wait, I just saw his car pull up outside. If you wait a moment, I'll get him."

"That's okay. I wanted to speak to *you*. I was wondering if you could do me a small favor. In the foyer there's a rack of brochures of the Berkshire's natural attractions."

"Yes, I keep the display stocked. Do you wish me to mail you some?"

"Actually, I already have most of them. I was hoping you could read off the ones you have on the rack."

"Well...sure, give me a moment." She put Sarah on hold, and Christmas music floated across the airwaves.

Martha was busy studying the photos Sarah had left on the table. Sarah pointed to the one with Ben standing at the mouth of a cave. "That particular cave came up in several photos."

"You think Belle and Ben might be hiding there?"

"There's a chance. If you were running from something or someone, wouldn't you go someplace you know well to give you an advantage? Belle spent most of her free time exploring areas like this," Sarah said. "It can't hurt to look. If they've left the area, then it's out of our hands. But at least we can say we tried."

"Mrs. Hart?" Alice's voice came back on the receiver. "Sorry to keep you waiting. I grabbed a copy of each brochure. You want me to read the names to you?"

"Please," Sarah said, and as Alice named the different attractions, Sarah set the matching brochures aside and made note of the missing ones. "Thank you, this helps a lot."

Alice gave a small laugh. "Wish all the requests that came through here were as simple."

Sarah said good-bye and turned to Martha, who read off the three names. "Goose Meadow, Tumbling Rock, and Mother's Den. Goose Meadow is a campground, and the other two are caves. Mother's Den sounds rather cozy," Martha added, "but I don't like the sound of Tumbling Rock."

"Me either, but I wasn't planning on going in the cave, maybe just drive around and see if there are any signs of Belle or her car in the area."

"Okay, I'm feeling better about this adventure." Martha rifled through one of the brochures. "Caves are dark and damp, and I really, really don't want to encounter a bat." She plunked the pamphlet down on the table, and the page opened to a photo of two tiny bats hanging from a rock ceiling.

Sarah laughed. "I think bats are cute in their own way. The small ones anyway."

"They look like flying mice to me." Martha shivered and stood. "If we're going to do this, I need to change clothes and find my hiking boots."

"You don't have to go if you don't want to. I know you must be busy."

"Who says I don't want to? Besides, someone has to protect you from the bats," Martha said with a wink, as she went out the kitchen door.

CHAPTER FOURTEEN

I think this is the place," Martha said, holding up the caving photo of Ben and peering through the windshield. "The rock face on the mountain looks the same."

"I hope so." Sarah parked between two pine trees. She'd done a quick search on the computer for Goose Meadow, Tumbling Rock, and Mother's Den and printed out directions.

Goose Meadow had been easy to locate and actually contained a few adventurous or perhaps foolish campers huddled up close to fire pits. None of the people they'd questioned recognized the photos of Belle or Ben.

The entrance to Tumbling Rock cave was barricaded with a locked grate. A posted Park Service sign stated that due to the danger of shifting rocks during temperature changes, the cave was closed until summer.

The directions to Mother's Den were rather obscure, citing forks in the road and a giant oak as turning points.

They'd been driving down the dirt road for over an hour, backtracking until they found the two tire tracks that constituted the "road" to Mother's Den.

No other vehicle occupied the small clearing, but with the dense forest and large boulders strewn about, it'd be easy to hide a car.

"I can see why this was a great hiding place during the Revolutionary War," Martha said, referring to the information they'd found online. "If someone wanted to disappear, this would be the place."

They zipped their jackets. "Got your flashlight?" Sarah asked.

Martha patted her right pocket. "Yep." She tucked her cell phone in the other. "I still have no service. We're pretty isolated."

"The mountain must be blocking the signal." Sarah opened her mud-splattered door and breathed in the pine-scented air. When she let it out, a cloud of her warm breath wafted upward. The temperature had certainly dropped since their last stop.

She slid on her gloves and struggled into the small backpack she had borrowed from Amy. The pack barely fit around her down coat, and the sleeves puffed out on either side of the padded straps. She turned to see Martha grinning at her. "I wouldn't laugh if I were you."

"Oh, I already know I look like the Pillsbury Dough Boy. These down coats look ridiculous, but it's sure nice not to have to wear so many layers. I hope we don't have to stay out long."

"Me too." Sarah gazed at the rugged mountainside. "Supposedly, there are several small caves in the area. Let's hope we can find Mother's Den first."

"Hey, we're mothers. You'd think the cave would be calling to us, welcoming us home."

Sarah snorted and took the lead through the woods. "There seems to be a path here."

"Good, paths lead somewhere."

After about a half mile, the trail disappeared into a rock bed. "Now where?" Sarah asked, peering up at the craggy cliff. Huge boulders had tumbled down into a giant pile which they couldn't see over.

"Look, a soda can," Martha said, pointing at a shiny green object wedged in some rocks. "I think we need to go that way."

Sarah turned where Martha pointed, making a mental note to pick up the can on the way out. They climbed over the rocks and rounded the corner.

"That's it!" Martha said. "See those two rocks that look like steeples? That's where Ben Silver was standing for that photo."

"Good eye," Sarah said with happy relief. A dark hole yawned near the base of one of the rocks. Footprints marred the path leading into the cave. They scrambled down the incline, boots slipping on the gravel until they hit dirt.

They stopped at the mouth opening. A dank, earthy smell rose from the interior.

Martha wrinkled her nose. "People like to camp in there?"

"So they say," Sarah said with a shrug. "Hello? Anyone in there?" Her voice echoed as the sound bounced into the depths. She called a couple more times and then dug a flashlight from her pack.

Martha's eyes widened. "You're not going in, are you?"

"Just in the entrance." She ducked and took a few steps in, the walls closing around her. "Belle?" Her flashlight beam swept the interior. A narrow tunnel shot off into the depths of the mountain.

"Sarah?" Martha said anxiously.

Sarah sighed and turned, bumping her head on an outcropping. "Ouch!"

"Are you okay?"

"Yes. Just hit my hard head. I'm coming out." She searched the ground for her flashlight. Spying it, lying beside some rocks, she snatched it up. Something pink glinted between two rocks. A cell phone that looked very familiar. Her heart sank to her stomach as she examined it. She recognized the flowery case cover.

"Sarah, do I have to come in there?" Martha asked. Her shoulders relaxed when Sarah came into view. "Are you sure you're all right?"

"I'm fine, but..." Sarah popped out of the hole and held up the phone. "This looks like Belle's."

"Are you sure?"

Sarah turned the phone over to reveal a cracked screen, but the phone still powered on when she held down a button. The wallpaper shot was a photo of Ben, Belle, and an older man she assumed was their father.

"We should call Chief Webber," Martha said. "When we can get a signal, that is."

"I agree." Sarah hesitated. "Do you think I should at least take a quick look inside first? I don't have to go far. What if she's trapped in there or something? I'll be right back." She started into the cave.

"Wait, I'll go with you. I'd never forgive myself if you got lost in there," Martha said, taking off her pack and opening the cover. She pulled a blue ball out of her pack. "We can use this to lead us back out if we lose our way."

"You brought yarn?"

Martha smiled. "Of course. You never know when an opportunity to crochet might come up. Isn't it pretty? The color is Blue Lagoon. I'm going to make an afghan with this color for Lexi for her birthday," she said. "Tie it to something, and we'll use it to find our way back out."

"You are quite the woman, Martha Maplethorpe." Sarah said with a chuckle as Martha wound the yarn around a large rock, knotting it. She tucked the yarn back in her backpack pocket and zipped it, leaving space for the yarn to come out. She walked to the cave entrance and the yarn unraveled, leaving a blue trail behind her.

Sarah flipped on the flashlight. "Here goes." She ducked into the cave entrance. Her flashlight beam pointed the way down the long, narrow passage. The low ceiling caused both women to hunch over. By the time they reached the end of the passage, Sarah's back ached from bending over and trying to walk without knocking her head. The ceiling lifted, and Sarah straightened her back. Relief turned to dismay when she found herself facing a wall.

"Dead end?" Martha asked from behind her.

"Maybe." Sarah shone her light around and spied a hole off to her right. "I think we have to go up."

"Up?" Martha paused. "How far?"

"Not far. See the hole there?" Sarah tilted her head back and as she shone the light upward, the beam swept a brown object on the wall.

"A bat!" Martha screeched.

"Shh. Bats hibernate. If we're quiet, we should manage to get around it without waking it."

"Sorry little bat," Martha whispered and started softly humming the lullaby song.

"Will you cut it out?" Sarah asked, suppressing a laugh. "You've been in a giddy mood all day."

"Just trying to get some of the pretour jitters out."

"Not that I don't love seeing you more relaxed, but we have a problem here. How are we going to get up to that hole?" Her fingertips touched the edge, which was forehead level.

"I could boost you," Martha suggested.

"And chance throwing your back out? No way."

Martha put her hands on her hips. "Well, what do you suggest then? I don't suppose there's a rope in your backpack."

"I didn't bring a rope because I didn't plan on going anywhere we'd need one. We're not exactly professional spelunkers."

Martha grinned. "I'm satisfied with not ever turning professional. I explored a cave and saw a bat. I can check those items off my life list. Oh yuck, and now I have cave water dripping on my face."

"Okay, we can go back, but I really want to see what's in there first. If I just had another six inches, I could pull myself up." Sarah looked back down the passage. "See that rock? If we drag it over here, I can stand on it."

They crept back down the passageway, and huffed and puffed until they managed to push the rock against the wall. Sarah stepped on top. The rock gave her another eight inches, and she slid her elbows over the edge. She jumped and Martha gave her feet a hefty shove, just enough so she could scoot the rest of her torso onto the ledge. She wondered if this was the way the experienced cavers got up here.

She crawled forward on her elbows until most of her body was in the tunnel. Breathing hard, she rested her face on the backs of her hands.

"Well?" Martha called.

Sarah lifted her head. Were her eyes playing tricks on her? She blinked several times. "I think I see light ahead. And I hear running water." She crawled forward, unable to even get up on her knees. Her pack scraped the tunnel ceiling and stuck. She pressed forward but the shoulder straps dug in, halting her. She wiggled her arm, but she was wedged in and couldn't slip her arms out.

Oh Lord, please don't let me become a permanent fixture in here.

Trying not to panic, she scooted backward until she felt the ledge with her toes. Taking deep breaths, she managed to shake her backpack free from her arms, leaving it balanced near the place where she had jumped up.

On the second try, Sarah managed to get through the low-ceilinged tunnel and dropped somewhat gracefully over another ledge onto the floor of a large room. She brushed her damp jacket off and sat back on her heels. Light shone through some deep cracks in the ceiling of the basketball-court-size cavern.

"Sarah? Are you okay? What do you see?" Martha called, her head bobbing up and down at the other end of the tunnel.

Sarah turned back to gaze around her. "You're not going to believe this!"

"Okay, I've changed my mind. I'd go spelunking again if other caves are as pretty as this," Martha said, slowly turning. With Sarah pulling on Martha's arms, she'd managed to climb up the wall and get down the passage into the large cavern. Her coat and jeans, like Sarah's, were covered with mud.

The walls sparkled with mineral deposits that glinted in the daylight pouring through cracks in the ceiling. Through a natural archway, a trickling waterfall cascaded into a small pool before flowing into the depths of the earth.

A fire pit had been dug in the middle of the floor, the rocks blackened from years of smoke. Boulders lay around the room like discarded furniture. Sarah marveled that Mother's Den had hid members of the militia army. Tingles ran up her arms. She could be sitting on the very same rock a Revolutionary soldier had sat on as he cooked his supper over the fire.

"You can tell campers have been here," Martha said picking up a soda can top. "But no way to tell if one of them was Belle."

Sarah stood up and put her hand near the black wood in the fire pit. "The ashes are cold, but it smells like a fire burned here recently." She turned her attention to the three passageways that branched off the room. "You know? This place is well hidden, but with only one way in and out, would soldiers stay in here knowing it could be a trap?"

"You're thinking there might be an easier way to get out?" Martha asked. She obviously didn't relish the idea of crawling back through the tunnel.

"Maybe. But I think we've had enough adventure for today. Let's get back in cell phone range and call Chief Webber. The police would be much better equipped to check out the other passages."

"You're right," Martha said. "Let's head back—uh-oh!"

"What?" Sarah asked, turning to Martha.

"You don't want to know." Martha had taken off her pack. "The yarn unraveled all the way, and I didn't notice." She swung her flashlight beam behind them. "I don't see it any-where! What are we going to do?"

"First thing is not to panic," Sarah tried to say calmly, but her voice squeaked. It had been a really dumb idea to come in here unprepared. It could be hours before anyone missed them, and no one would even know where to search unless their car was found. A cave would be the last place they'd think of.

Jason would never let her forget this. She took several deep breaths, trying to calm her racing pulse.

Martha moved closer to her. "You're right. All we have to do is try to retrace our steps. The yarn is prob-ably not far back there. We haven't been in here that long."

"Right." Sarah agreed as they both gazed at the maze be-hind them. They turned their flashlights to the path behind them and moved cautiously forward. Sandy sediment cov-ered the ground and the path grew narrow. Sarah's toe con-nected with something solid. "Ouch!"

Sarah shone her light on the ground to see what she had stubbed her toe on and found instead the blue thread. "I found it," she called.

"Thank goodness. Now let's get out of here. My knees are sore, and my back is going to be stiff tomorrow as it is. Of course, soreness would've been well worth it if we'd found Belle."

"We found her cell phone, so we know she was here. That's progress. Now we need to call in reinforcements."

The narrow tunnel seemed longer on the way back, but at least Sarah could see the dim shadowy outline of the drop to the main part of the cave. She managed to dangle her legs over the edge and fall gently onto the boulder they had placed below. Martha quickly followed.

By the time they emerged from the cave, winding the blue yarn as they went, both Sarah and Martha were a little winded.

Martha tilted her head back and gazed up at the mountain peaks, taking a deep breath. "The fresh air feels so good. I didn't realize how musty the cave smelled until we got back out."

Sarah agreed. They started to trudge back down to the car, but as soon as it came into sight, they noticed a black car pulled up next to it. "There's a black car down there. Belle's car was red, wasn't it?" Martha asked. Before Sarah could answer, Martha continued. "And what's that beeping sound?"

"It's coming from my backpack." She pulled it off and unzipped the pocket. "Belle's phone. It must have an alarm on it." She held it up to see if she could figure out how to turn it off, when a hiker came up over the rise and headed straight for them. Dressed in jeans, tan jacket, and baseball cap, the hiker was hard to identify as male or female. As the person drew closer, the head lifted revealing his face.

Sarah gasped. "Mr. Blake? What are you doing here?"

"I was going to ask you the same thing." Andrew's gaze zeroed in on the cell phone she clutched. "Is that Belle's phone?"

"Um…maybe." Her gaze narrowed on his Yankees cap. Her heart rate accelerated and she felt light-headed.

He held out his hand. "Let me see it."

Sarah took a step back, holding the phone against her thigh. "The screen's cracked, and it's probably best not to handle it anymore. We just called the police to let them know we were bringing it in." Sarah slipped the fib in, hoping for some insurance just in case Mr. Blake was the one Belle was hiding from.

Martha inched closer to Sarah. "You never said why you're here, Mr. Blake."

"Same reason as you." His handsome face appeared more lined than when they'd seen him the other day. He glanced around them as if checking to see if they were alone. "Belle called me."

That confirmed what Kelsey had told her, but she still didn't know if she could trust Mr. Blake. "When? Is she okay?"

"Last night, not that it's any of your business. She left a message but it was garbled like she was losing the signal. But I got the gist of it. She was in trouble. I tried to call her back, but she never answered. I figured she might come out here. It's a favorite spot of ours."

"Why didn't you call the police?" Martha asked.

"If she wanted the police involved, she would've called them herself."

Sarah felt Martha nudge her gently with her elbow, but she wasn't ready to let Mr. Blake go without asking a few more questions. "Did you try looking in Mother's Den?"

"Yes, I went there first and then checked out some of the smaller caves in the area. The mountainside is riddled with them. You can spend forever exploring."

And disappear forever.

"Now, give me the phone, or I'll be forced to take it," he said again, tension strung high in his voice.

Sarah wasn't about to give him the phone. It could be evidence. Or at least it might give a clue to where Belle had gone. She backed up a little until her hand brushed an outcropping of rock, riddled with stone fragments. Her hand grasped one loosely.

Her hand with the cell phone slid slowly behind her as Mr. Blake stepped forward. "Why did you go to Kelsey's? What were you looking for?" Sarah asked. "Did you send those men over to ransack her place?"

He froze. "What are you talking about? I went to Kelsey's looking for Belle. I thought maybe she'd been in touch with her. That's all! You know what? I've had enough of this. I need to find her. Give me the cell phone or—"

"Then catch!" Sarah whipped a rock the size of the cell phone toward him. Andrew threw up his hands to catch it, tripped, and stumbled backward over the embankment.

Martha and Sarah tore down the trail. Sarah thought her lungs would burst by the time they reached the safety of the car. She jumped inside, ready to hit the automatic locks as soon as Martha shut the door. Sarah looked up the trail. Andrew was nowhere to be seen.

Martha panted. "He's not coming. Do you think he's all right?"

"There wasn't that far to fall." Sarah leaned forward, trying to catch her breath. Her heart pounded in her ears, but gradually her pulse slowed.

A hawk cried overhead, swooping along in the wind. Dusk darkened the eastern sky. It'd be night soon. They needed to get out of there. But where was Andrew?

She glanced down the empty trail. Maybe she'd hurt him after all. "I'm going to go look. Wait here and be ready to lock that door."

Martha nodded, looking too worn out to argue. Sarah crept back up the trail and peered over the edge of the embankment.

At the bottom of the shallow ravine, Andrew knelt over some blue and green cloth. Sarah gasped.

He looked up at her. "It's Belle's backpack and there's blood. Go call the police."

Sarah backed away, her heart in her throat, and motioned to Martha to come. Was Andrew trying to trick them? Or was Belle down there somewhere badly hurt? She couldn't take the chance. She had to go for help. Martha joined her and they hurried back to the car together. They had barely shut their doors when Sarah pulled out and raced out of the clearing.

"Do you think he's just lying to buy time to get away?" Martha asked.

"We'll find out soon enough," Sarah said as they cleared the mountain valley and sped toward town. "There should be a cell signal now." She pulled over to the side of the road and called the police station. They put her through to Chief Webber. She quickly informed him about the cell phone, Andrew, and Belle's backpack.

"He's sending a squad car right away," Sarah said to Martha. "Now, let's see if Andrew is telling the truth." She picked up Belle's phone. The bars indicated it was receiving a signal, and she studied it, trying to find the call record.

"Here, let me. I used to have a phone like this." Martha clicked several buttons and then scrolled through a line of numbers. "It's hard to read with the crack in the screen but he's on here. She kept his name in the saved numbers section. If her phone was out of range, then it may not have picked up his call, but..." She pushed the number one. "Voice mail would've caught it if he left a message. Here, listen."

Sarah leaned her head close to Martha's, the phone between them. There were several messages including a couple from Sarah and Kelsey. The last message was from Andrew sounding frantic.

Belle, are you okay? What's going on? I could barely hear the message. I'm heading out now. Call me.

"He was telling the truth," Sarah said. "And to think I threw a rock at him."

"Well, he didn't have to act so scary even if he was frantic with worry." Martha said with a huff. "He could've said please."

Sarah sighed. "After all that, there isn't anything else on here to help us find her."

In the distance, headlights approached. Two squad cars. One pulled alongside Sarah's car. Chief Webber sprang out of the passenger side and strode toward her.

Sarah quickly recapped the afternoon, ignoring Chief Webber's question about what they thought they were doing going into the cave alone. She handed over the cell phone, hoping he wouldn't bring up that they had tampered with what was now evidence.

"Go home," Chief Webber said. "I've already notified the forest service and they'll organize a search if we determine she may still be out there."

"What about Mr. Blake?" Sarah asked. She was starting to feel more and more guilty that she'd thought he would hurt Belle. The look on his face as he knelt over Belle's pack was pure anguish.

"We'll take care of him, don't worry. We shouldn't need to keep him too long. Drive safely."

"Thanks, Chief," Sarah said, rolling up her window. She turned on her signal, although there wasn't another car on the road, and headed toward Maple Hill.

Martha leaned her head back. "He didn't sound very happy with us, not that I blame him. But at least maybe we're a step closer to finding her, right?"

"Right," Sarah echoed, although a heavy feeling of despair settled over her. It seemed even more certain now that Belle could be hurt. Or worse.

CHAPTER FIFTEEN

ervous energy propelled Sarah out of bed at six
AM. She did some stretches to relieve her sore, stiff
muscles, and read her devotion for the day while
she drank strong coffee. She tried to focus on prayer, but she
couldn't help watching the clock. Chief Webber had told her
he'd call if they found Belle. She prayed that no news was
good news.

Last night she'd started to sew together the diamond
strips that would form the star points for her Christmas
quilt. Needing a larger area for the next step—laying out the
starburst pattern—she'd taken the fabric to the dining room
table.

Perfectly matched seams are the sign of a good Star of
Bethlehem, and some of the diamonds were giving her problems. Just like the mystery surrounding Belle, something
didn't fit. With Belle, the key piece that joined all the other
pieces together was missing.

As she pinned the diamond strips together to create the first star point, she went through what she and Martha had learned.

Andrew had been the most obvious suspect in Belle's disappearance. He had the most obvious motive: a scorned fiancé wanting to get back at his ex-girlfriend. But now it appeared he'd only been trying to help find her.

So that brought her back to Ben. Conflicting information swirled around him. Dr. Silver had said that Ben was a good boy, just misguided at times. Kelsey talked about how Belle had helped Ben get through school. His aunt had painted a picture of a boy out of control, a budding criminal. But he had a good job at the museum and a place to live. Now apparently something had happened to make him disappear along with his sister.

Sarah started work on the second star point, carefully lining up and pinning the fabric strips to match the pattern of the first.

Her mind kept returning to the museum. Something wasn't adding up. Alice had said Ben was a good employee, but Mr. Warthorne hinted he was not surprised by Ben's absence. It seemed he knew something he wasn't telling.

By the time she'd gotten half the fourth star point pinned, she couldn't think anymore and had headed to bed.

Now she needed to move the star pattern off the dining room table so she could get that room ready for the home tour. The easiest thing to do would be to slide everything onto a large sheet of cardboard and move it somewhere out of sight. Her leg muscles protested the short climb to the attic, where she'd stored several flattened boxes.

As she passed the quilt trunk, she noticed the drops of dark stain on the floor she'd forgotten to clean up. Good thing it was winter or the sticky spots might attract ants or other bugs.

Sarah hauled a large flattened box downstairs, slid her starburst onto it, and set it in her sewing room. She'd move the quilt pieces back to the dining room after the tour.

She tackled the living room next. She switched on the radio to a station with Christmas music as she gave the furniture a final flick of the duster. At the top of the hour, the weatherman reported a twenty percent possibility of snow showers by evening. Martha would be relieved that the major front wouldn't reach them until Sunday or Monday night.

She did a quick cleanup in the kitchen, and then returned upstairs to make her bed and put that room in order. She opened the vacant bedroom that was awaiting a new boarder. Sarah smoothed the quilt, and removed dust from the antique furniture.

She crossed the hall to Belle's room, did another quick inspection, and swiped the room with the duster and dust mop. Since Belle had cleared the room of personal belongings, she decided to leave the door open. The white walls, peacock quilt on the twin bed, and mulberry curtains gave the room a welcoming, comfortable feeling. She hoped the room would be welcoming Belle back soon.

By noon, the house looked presentable and ready for the tour. She added garlands to the staircase railing and the fireplace mantel, but she still needed to pick up the wreath she'd ordered for the front door. Maggie was closing the store at two this afternoon, and had said she'd bring home the ornaments she had left over to replace Sarah's broken ones.

Sarah glanced through the window at her outdoor decorations. So far the wind hadn't knocked down any of her lights on the bushes in the yard. Jason had brought Gerry's manger home and re-created Sarah's nativity scene on the porch. Sarah tossed her coat on and darted out into the cold with the bag of gold photo frames, placing it in the manger at the feet of Baby Jesus.

As she unbundled from her coat, she noticed Liam's black scarf still hung on the coat rack. Granted, he'd told her to keep it as long as she liked, but she'd intended to give it back to him right away. She ran her hand over the soft wool. She decided to ignore the warming feeling that crept up her spine when she thought about a possible relationship with him. He was her friend and she didn't want to ruin that. Liam might stop by tonight while running the treasure hunt, so she could return the scarf to him then with an apology for keeping it so long.

As Sarah started toward the kitchen for a quick lunch, the phone rang. She picked up the receiver, and Chief Webber's deep voice said, "Sarah? I have good news."

"It's the perfect size," Maggie exclaimed as she and Sarah admired a four-foot wreath on the wall behind the couch.

Sarah smiled. "When I went to pick up my door wreath, I saw this one behind the counter. The supplier had sent an extra one by mistake for one of the churches in town. The clerk gave it to me at a bargain."

"Well, I'm thrilled. It covers the marks on the wall and looks great opposite the Christmas tree."

Audrey shuffled into the room, picked up her pack of drawing pencils, and paused. "Pretty, but I think it needs more sparkle," she said and continued on her way out of the room.

Maggie tilted her head. "I like the simplicity of just the red bows, but maybe it does need a little more pizzazz. Something gold or silver. Just a little sparkle since the tree has a lot of glittery stuff on it."

Sarah studied the circle of pine for a moment and then glanced in the box of antique ornaments from Magpie's. "What about these?" Sarah held up a tiny silver ball, the size of her thumb. "There are gold and red ones here too. We can hook them on tightly rather than letting them hang."

"I like that idea." Maggie dug into the box and pulled out about a dozen miniature ornaments. She tried a silver one on the wreath and stepped back. "What do you think?"

"I think Audrey was right. A little more sparkle is just what it needed," Sarah said. When she'd arrived, the twins had been assigned to go through the house and pick up any of their belongings that'd been left out. Jason had run to the grocery store to pick up fresh lemons to garnish the punch they were serving to the guests.

Maggie twisted a red ball onto the wreath. "I've been meaning to ask if there's been any news about your boarder."

"Chief Webber called me this morning. They haven't found her, but at least we know she's not in the ravine near Mother's Den."

Maggie almost dropped an ornament. "What?"

"Oh yes. A lot happened yesterday." She updated Maggie on her and Martha's cave adventure. After a gasp when Sarah mentioned crawling through the tunnel, Maggie shook her head.

"I can't believe you two went into a cave. What were you thinking?" she asked, trying to contain a smile.

"Well, I was so worried about Belle," Sarah explained. "One thing led to another." She told Maggie about Andrew Blake and finding Belle's backpack.

Maggie sighed. "So, you don't think Mr. Blake was involved in her disappearance?"

"Doesn't appear so. Chief Webber interrogated him. Mr. Blake claims he'd heard from Belle, thought she was headed for Mother's Den, a favorite spot of hers, and went to meet her. Other than the two backpacks and the cell phone, they didn't find any other traces of Belle or Ben. The Forestry Service helped scour the area and they sent out search dogs, but they didn't find anything." The chief had called this good news—relative to what they could've found, at least.

Maggie wrapped her arms around Sarah. "I'm so sorry. I wonder where they could be."

"I wish I knew."

"I'll keep praying for them."

"Thanks, Maggie." Sarah turned her attention back to the wreath and helped Maggie finish decorating. With the whole family chipping in to clean and Maggie's tasteful holiday touches, the rambling old Victorian house looked homey and full of Christmas cheer.

Maggie gazed around, a smile on her lips. "You know, I was a little stressed about doing the home tour during the store's busiest time, but it all worked out wonderfully. We've been missing some of our California holiday traditions, and of course family and friends, but this has been fun. I wouldn't have put this much time and effort into getting ready for Christmas if it weren't for the tour, and now the place really feels like home. Different from what we're used to, but sometimes change is good."

"You've done a marvelous job, Maggie." Sarah smiled.

"Thank you. I appreciate all your help." Maggie looked at her watch. "Oh dear, we have only a couple hours left, and I've been monopolizing your time. Do you think the rest of these ornaments will work on your tree?" she asked, gesturing to the decorations remaining in the box.

"They'll do perfectly. I better run. I need to get cookies out of the freezer to thaw." Sarah called a good-bye to the twins and hurried home.

Once home, she dashed to the freezer and reached for the containers of the cookies she and the twins had baked. Right before the guests arrived, she'd pop a dozen of the cherry chocolate chip cookies in the oven to warm and make the kitchen smell wonderful.

Since Karen would be using the dining room to take photos of those completing the treasure hunt, Sarah had decided to set up her snacks on the kitchen table. She topped the surface with a green, lacy tablecloth and set out her silver trays. A Crock-Pot would keep her apple cider warm and she'd also put out a pitcher of ice water.

She placed the assorted antique ornaments on the tree. One particular ornament caught her attention. The beautiful hand-blown blue glass encircled with bands of gold paint reminded her of the ornaments she'd seen in the museum.

That Belle had used ornaments as part of the clues for the treasure hunt didn't surprise Sarah. Belle could've gotten the idea when she'd visited Ben at the museum. Sarah thought about her own destroyed tree and then remembered that Belle's old roommate Kelsey had said her ornaments had been smashed too.

She grabbed her cordless phone and hurried into the office to turn on her computer. She called Martha. "I'm sorry to bother you right now with the tour about to start, but I need a quick favor."

"Of course," Martha said rather breathlessly. "Do you need something for the tour?"

"Actually I think I'm ready. This has to do with our trip to the museum. Can you send me the photos you took on your cell phone of the Christmas tree?"

"Sure thing. I'll do it right now. If I weren't so busy with last-minute preparations, I'd ask why," Martha said. "Promise to tell me later?"

"Of course."

Sarah's cell phone beeped a few minutes later, and Sarah looked at the tiny images. Martha had snapped two photos of the Christmas tree and the royal ornaments.

Sarah brought up the museum's Web site and zeroed in on the photos of the fund-raiser and the one close-up of the tree. Anticipation and excitement mixed in her chest. Of course this could mean nothing. Or everything. But she needed some assistance from an expert on antiques, and she didn't want to interrupt Maggie right before the tour started.

She called the *Country Cottage Magazine* office on the chance Chester Winslow was working late. Relief flooded through her when Chester's voice came on the line.

"Sarah, I was delighted to see your name pop up on my caller ID. It's been too long since we've talked. I was just thinking about you this morning. How are you?" His deep, friendly voice sounded so familiar.

"Things could be better in some respects," Sarah said, "but I'm fine. Thanks. And you?"

"I've been traveling too much this month and looking forward to taking some time off for Christmas after I get my last column done. Which reminds me, have you decided on the topic of your next one? Your last article was superb."

Sarah's cheeks warmed. It'd been Chester's influence that'd given her the courage to write a quilting article for *Country Cottage*. "Actually I was calling for some information," Sarah said, hedging. With Belle and her quilt missing, she still hadn't found the inspiration for her next column.

"Well, fire away. Glad to help if I can."

Sarah took a deep breath. "Chester, what do you know about antique ornaments?"

"Sarah, the home tour has been so much fun. I'm sad I've made it to the end already," Vanessa Sawyer said, popping the last bite of a cookie into her mouth. "Yum, what is this cookie called? Is it my imagination, or does it taste like licorice?"

"Pfeffernuesse. My great-grandmother's recipe. I make them every year and think of her," Sarah said with a smile. "The licorice flavor is anise."

"They're wonderful, but I've already eaten way too many." She wiped the powdered sugar from her lips with a napkin, and took a sip of mulled cider. She waved at someone in the hallway. "I better go. I think my friend is ready to leave."

"I'll be over to see those spring fabrics pretty soon," Sarah said as she checked the refreshments on the kitchen table. The cider steamed in a Crock-Pot surrounded by platters of cookies. Periodically throughout the evening, she'd replenished the drink from the large stockpot on the stove and retrieved cookies from the freezer. Now that the tour was winding down, she figured she didn't need to add any more.

Outside the snow had started to fall, reflecting green, blue, and red in the glow of the Christmas lights. One of the lanterns Sarah had lent Martha flickered at the end of the walk next to a sign that proclaimed Sarah's house as Old Town Holiday Home Tour #6.

She turned from the window and strode into the living room. The room glowed with firelight and lights from the tree. She touched Gerry's old stocking lovingly. He might not be with her, but so many reminders of his presence remained.

The deep, rich red of the poinsettias and the holly berries in the garlands seemed to glow against the dark green foliage. She'd lit candles on the mantel. The only thing missing from the scene was the Hart family quilt.

Despite the bittersweet feeling that dogged her steps, Sarah kept smiling and making small talk with the guests. Those participating in the treasure hunt were working out the last part of the puzzle. Sarah loved to see their faces light up as they filled out the verse on the bottom and realized that the clue led to the manger on the porch.

She waved to Karen Bancroft stationed in the dining room, on hand to steer people in the right direction if need be. Karen had kept busy, checking treasure hunt sheets, and handing out additional prizes of candy to children. A friend of hers took snapshots of tour participants with a digital camera and printed out the results using equipment they'd moved from Sarah's office.

Sarah noted that several young men who'd come through the tour tended to linger around the dining room, hoping to be noticed by the girls rather than explore the rest of the house, which was fine with her. Every time a stranger paused too long by the tree, Sarah's stomach knotted, and she thought of Belle. She was sure the break-ins at her home and Kelsey's were related to the disappearance of Belle and Ben. And she had a hunch about why. She just needed proof.

She hadn't heard from Chief Webber the rest of the day, not that she'd really expected to. She'd picked up the phone a couple of times to call him, but then put it back down. The chief was an excellent policeman and now fully on the case. He certainly didn't need her checking up on him.

Sarah said good-bye to some of the tour guests, and stepped back to let more in. Being the last house on the tour meant she'd be the last to close down. She started to shut the door when she saw another man coming up the walk. Liam.

He lifted a hand in greeting and bounded up the steps. "I've been following the last group, so you're almost done. I'm going to help Karen pack up. How are things here?"

She stepped back to let him in and shut the door. "Went better than I expected."

Liam took off his navy jacket and looked particularly handsome in a royal blue cable-knit sweater and black jeans.

He brushed snowflakes off his red hair. The warm tingle crept up Sarah's spine again.

"How's it going elsewhere?" she asked.

"From what I can tell, the tour's a huge success. Martha's as happy as can be. She's making the rounds, seeing if anyone needs assistance with cleanup. She was at Maggie and Jason's when I left."

The doorbell rang, although Sarah had placed a sign on the door to come right in.

"Oops. I guess I'm not the last one after all," Liam said as Sarah turned to the door. "I'll go help Karen." He headed to the dining room.

Chief Webber stood on the threshold. "Sarah, sorry to bother you now. I know you're busy."

"Actually, this is the last group. Come on in. There's cider and cookies in the kitchen."

"Thanks." He pulled off his gloves and unzipped his black jacket as he followed her.

She waited until an elderly couple helped themselves to cookies on the way out before asking, "Did you find Belle?"

"No, but we're checking out leads." He cleared his throat. "I need Belle's suitcase and whatever else she left."

"Of course, but can I ask why?"

He hesitated. "I have a contact in Boston in the precinct where Ben used to live. Although Ben was never convicted of a crime, he had some friends who have been charged with gambling, petty theft, and stealing cars. From what I understand, Ben owes people—bad people—money."

"So he ran, and Belle is either trying to protect him or cover their tracks."

"Those are plausible conclusions."

"But why would she call Mr. Blake?"

He shrugged. "Needed money. Maybe a place to stay. Who knows?" The chief's attention shifted to the cookie tray. He selected a peppermint pinwheel and took a big bite.

"Now what? Do you think those men caught up with them?"

"Something happened up there at Mother's Den." Chief Webber took another bite of cookie and must've noticed Sarah's alarm because he swallowed quickly. "But there's no evidence that they were harmed or ... worse."

"What about the blood?"

"The lab confirmed it wasn't human. Possibly two animals fighting over the food supplies in the pack."

Sarah let out a deep breath of relief.

"We had the tracking dogs cover the area pretty thoroughly, and it appears they returned to the parking lot and left in a vehicle. Chances are they headed out of the area and aren't planning to return. The Boston police have already been notified."

Sarah fiddled with the cookie tray, her mind working over the puzzle pieces that simply didn't fit. She wasn't ready to share her hunch yet. Not until Chester called. "I still can't see Belle involved in something like this. She had plans for her life. She was saving to buy a house and get more into her photography."

"Family loyalty is a powerful motivator."

"Can I ask who shared this tip?"

"I'd rather not say. He isn't the most reliable source, but we may need him later." He selected another sweet. "Great cookies. I haven't eaten anything since this morning."

"You poor man. Can I fix you a sandwich?" Sarah asked. "I have some turkey slices in the refrigerator."

"Thank you, but I need to get going. I'll pick up something later. I have paperwork at the station to fill out before heading home."

"I'll get the suitcase. The box of Belle's things from the attic is in the sewing room, if you want to get it." She pointed to the door across the kitchen and went down the stairs to the basement. The suitcase was still by the workbench. She hauled it upstairs to where Chief Webber waited with the box under one arm. He took the suitcase from her, and she walked him to the door.

"I appreciate your stopping by personally and informing me about the police's progress."

He shrugged. "No problem. Merry Christmas." He gave her a smile and strode down the walkway.

Sarah ducked into her office, shut the door, and hoped no one would notice the hostess was missing. She couldn't shake the question of who was after Ben. Tim, the apartment manager, would know where Belle lived if Ben had used her for a reference. He could've sent people in this direction, if the price was right. Tim had also seemed pretty keen on convincing her and Martha that nothing was wrong. She could imagine him selling out Ben to the highest bidder, or any bidder at all.

She quickly looked up Mrs. Corker's number. She let the phone ring and when no one answered, she called again.

"Hello!" Mrs. Corker's annoyed tone rose above the television blaring in the background. "I don't care who you are. I'm not buying anything."

"Mrs. Corker, this is Sarah Hart."

"Who?" she yelled into the phone. "Wait just a minute." The volume of the background noise decreased. "This better be good."

Sarah took a deep, calming breath. "Mrs. Corker, this is Sarah Hart. Martha Maplethorpe and I talked to you about Ben Silver's disappearance?"

"Oh, yes, I remember. What about it?"

"I need to ask you a favor."

"Well, I don't know—"

"Mrs. Corker, please realize this is for a good cause. We still haven't found Ben or his sister. I have a question to ask about your landlord Tim."

"Well, in that case, I'll tell you whatever you want to know. I never liked him. Called me a spy again while he's the one who's always meddling in everyone else's business."

"Do you know where he was yesterday?"

"Sure, he was here. Making fussing noises about the carpet cleaners who came to clean 5B."

"Did he ever leave?"

"His car's parked next to mine, and from what I can tell, it hasn't been moved in over a week. I saw a police cruiser come around, but that's not unusual around here. Why? Is Tim in trouble?" Mrs. Corker asked. She sounded pleased.

"Not that I know of." At least not where it concerned Belle. "Thank you, Mrs. Corker. If you happen to see Belle or Ben Silver, please give me a call." Sarah hung up. The idea that Tim might be personally involved in Belle's disappearance from Mother's Den was still a possibility, and she needed to follow up.

She opened the door a crack and peeked out. Everything appeared to be running smoothly. She looked up the number for Ben's apartment complex and dialed the manager. Tim answered on the third ring.

"Tim, this is Mrs. Hart. I was wondering if you've seen Ben Silver since I talked to you."

"Mrs. Hart, I already told you everything I know. Police too."

"Please don't hang up. Perhaps the police would like to know how you sold Ben out. I think he and his sister have been kidnapped, which makes you an accessory to a crime. I think my next call should be to the Pittsfield police station."

There was a loud sigh and a muttered curse, but she gave him credit that he hadn't slammed down the phone yet.

"Who were the men you gave Belle's address to?" She pressed.

"What men?" When she didn't reply, he sighed. "I didn't ask. It's none of my business. Ben owed me money, and I'll probably never see a red cent of it or the interest I charge. Figured they were looking for him for the same reason. They offered cash, and I took it."

"What did they look like?"

"Regular guys. Nothing special. One wore a baseball cap."

"What kind of car did they drive?"

"Tan Buick, I think, or maybe it was a GMC. I didn't really care." Especially if all Tim saw was green.

"Whatever they paid you isn't worth the trouble you'll be in if Belle and Ben are harmed. If you can help the police in any way, I suggest you do that now."

She hung up, even more convinced her hunch was right about the museum. Chester still hadn't called her back, and she needed his help before she proceeded.

Sarah headed back to the living room and stood by the tree. A hollow feeling rose in her chest. Without the suitcase and the box, all traces of Belle were effectively gone from her house.

She turned and met Liam's gaze. He said something to Karen and came across the room. "You look upset. I assume they haven't found Belle yet?"

"No, and she and Ben may be in deep trouble." She updated Liam, leaving out the specifics Chief Webber might not want shared.

"Poor girl. I do hope she isn't fighting a lost cause with that brother of hers."

"So do I, Liam."

He gave her a pat on the arm. "I'll say an extra prayer for them tonight."

"You're a good friend. Thank you."

He held her gaze for a long moment, and she drew comfort from the kindness reflected in his eyes. She looked away, suddenly feeling shy. "We appreciate all you did for the home tour."

"It was my pleasure." Liam smiled. "Martha said we raised over five thousand dollars to donate to the Children's Fund. There were lots who donated money who didn't bother playing the game."

"That's wonderful!"

"It was fun. I think Belle will be pleased when she hears how her hard work paid off."

"I think we're finished," Karen said, coming over with a box in her hands.

"Everyone's gone?" Sarah asked, suddenly realizing how quiet the house sounded. She could even hear the words of the Christmas music playing softly on the stereo.

"Looks like it," Karen said. "Although I thought I heard someone upstairs while I was getting my coat."

Liam frowned. "I'll go check to see if there are any stragglers." He headed for the stairs.

"I had fun. I'd love to do this again next year," Karen said. A muffled shout sounded overhead and footsteps pounded down the stairs. The front door opened and slammed shut.

Sarah and Karen froze for a moment, and then rushed to the foyer as Liam arrived at the bottom of the stairs, breathing hard. He wrenched the door open and peered out into the falling snow.

"What happened?" Sarah asked, her heart thumping.

"A man was up there, loitering. I simply asked if I could assist him with anything. He shoved past me and knocked me clean over. Took off like a shot. Looks like the hooligan's long gone now."

"Are you okay?" Karen asked.

Liam shut the door. "Yes, just my pride was hurt."

"I wonder if he was trying to steal something." Karen's blue eyes flashed.

Sarah looked up the stairs. "What room was he in, Liam?"

"The bedroom with the white walls."

"That's Belle's room." She climbed the stairs with the others following her.

"At least there isn't anything left in here worth stealing," Sarah said, glancing around the bedroom. "But the closet door was closed before the tour, and it looks like someone rumpled the covers on the bed."

"The top drawer isn't shut all the way in the dresser," Karen noted. "If I were a thief, that's where I'd look. I hear people sometimes hide money in their underwear and sock drawers, which is pretty dumb, since everyone knows about doing that if they watch TV or movies. I hide money in my Bible sometimes. I figure if they're desperate enough to steal my Bible or look through it for cash, then they need money—and the Bible—more than I do."

"Never thought about it that way before," Liam said with a smile as he turned to peer through the crack in the curtains to the street below.

Sarah checked the bathroom. The cabinet under the sink wasn't shut all the way either, but time and moisture had slightly warped the old wood, making it difficult to tell if someone had opened it or if it had just come unstuck by itself.

"I don't suppose we need to call the police," she said returning to the bedroom, although she intended to inform Chief Webber. "There isn't much they can do at this point anyway. Besides, other than shoving Liam, we can't prove a crime was committed."

"And that was my own fault for not getting out of the way. I suppose I could've just startled him and he panicked."

"I still think he was up to no good. Why would he hang around upstairs when everyone else was gone?" Karen asked. "If you do find something missing, can the police dust for fingerprints?"

Sarah nodded. "They could, but there've been a couple hundred people through here today."

"Well I hope he gets caught whoever he is." She yawned. "I guess I better get going. I'm on the early shift tomorrow, and I'm getting sleepy. I have to drive in the snow too."

"Luckily it isn't sticking much yet. I heard the storm front stalled again." Liam dropped the curtain back into place.

"I'm pretty sure that fellow is gone, but just to be on the safe side, you wait until I can walk you out."

"Yes, boss." Karen grinned and whispered loudly to Sarah. "He's overprotective at the café, too, when it gets dark."

"Lucky you," Sarah whispered back.

Liam let out an exaggerated sigh. "Old habits die hard. I still remind my daughter to be careful when I talk to her."

They all shuffled out of the room. Sarah turned the light off and closed the door before following them down the stairs.

Liam turned to Sarah in the foyer. "You're going to mention this to the chief, right?"

Sarah nodded. "He may want to get a description from you."

"I didn't get a good look. Tall and skinny. Looked like a kid, but he could've been in his twenties."

"Oh I think I saw him when he came in. He was wearing a green wool hat," Karen said. "I remember because it was the wrong kind of green for his complexion. Made his freckles look all blotchy.

Liam opened the door. Karen said good-bye, bounded down the steps, and dashed to her car across the street.

"Such energy." Liam grinned. "Is there anything else I can do for you, Sarah, before I leave?"

"You've already done enough. I'll be fine. I'm going to call Chief Webber before I turn in."

"Good. Have the chief call me, or I'll drop by the station tomorrow if something needs to be filled out. Now, make sure you lock up good and tight. Good night." He strode down the steps to the sidewalk.

"I will. Thanks again for filling in for Belle."

"My pleasure," he called back over his shoulder. "That's what friends are for." He hurried through the snow to his truck and gave her a final wave.

His black pickup had rolled down Hillside Avenue and turned the corner before Sarah realized she still had his scarf.

CHAPTER SIXTEEN

I can't believe the snow melted." Audrey moaned as she stared out the bay window at her house. "It didn't even last through church. I wanted to build a snowman this afternoon."

"The snow was a little too wet to hold together anyway," Sarah said from her position on the sofa. The main storm had stalled again over New Hampshire, and last night had been only a small taste of what was to come. "Don't worry, lots more is on the way tonight or tomorrow."

"I hope so. I want to go sledding on *Christmas*."

"How about you, Amy? Do you want snow for Christmas?" Sarah asked, attempting to draw the girl into conversation. She hadn't said much on the way home from church and was unusually quiet through dinner.

Amy shrugged as she flipped the channel on the television past several holiday movies, finally settling on a rerun of a Disney sitcom. "Yeah, I guess."

"What are you drawing?" Sarah asked Audrey.

Audrey glanced at the sketchbook and pack of colored pencils lying in front of her on the carpet and shook her head. "Nothing right now. I can't think of anything I want to draw."

"Why don't you sketch the Christmas tree?"

"Okay." She picked out brown and green pencils to sketch with.

Amy flopped on the rug not far from Audrey, studying the presents under the tree. The fire crackled and bathed the room with toasty heat. Potpourri in a crystal bowl on the mantel scented the air with apples and cinnamon.

Sarah sighed with contentment. If a stranger looked in the window at the Christmas decorations and the family, he might think the scene was straight out of a Norman Rockwell painting. But Sarah couldn't shake her melancholy over Belle's disappearance. The girls were uncharacteristically subdued. And something was going on between Jason and Maggie. They hadn't smiled much through dinner, although they kept the conversation flowing pleasantly.

One topic had been the success of yesterday's treasure hunt. All had enjoyed the home tour, and they'd met many new friends and potential clients. The stack of Jason's business cards on the small table in the foyer had decreased by half.

Amy yawned and her eyelids began to droop. Sarah yawned in response. Maybe everyone was just overtired. She could relate. After calling Chief Webber about the stranger in Belle's bedroom, she'd crawled exhausted into bed. For the first time since Belle went missing she'd fallen into a deep, dreamless sleep.

She just wished she felt more refreshed. The massive energy expenditure of the last week must've finally caught up with her, or maybe it was just the letdown from not solving the mystery surrounding Belle's and Ben's disappearance. And she still missed the Hart family Christmas quilt. Losing the quilt was like losing an old friend.

Sarah glanced at her watch. She'd planned to visit her father at the nursing home this afternoon, especially after neglecting to get over there this week.

Footsteps sounded in the foyer. Jason entered the room. "I'm heading into town for a while."

Sarah looked up in surprise. "Now?"

"Yeah, it shouldn't take too long."

Audrey dragged herself to her feet. "Are you going out to buy us more presents?"

"Don't you think you have enough under the tree already? In fact, I think there are too many," Jason said sternly, but a smile lingered in his eyes. "Maybe we should send some back."

"Dad!" Audrey protested, slapping him lightly on the arm. "You're kidding, right?"

Jason grinned, gave Audrey a hug, and then turned to her sister who was still sprawled in front of the TV. "What's wrong, Amy?"

"Nothing," she answered without looking at him.

Maggie came down the stairs and exchanged a look with Jason. "Hey, Amy, why don't you and Audrey go finish wrapping the presents you made for great-grandpa. We can take them over to the nursing home to put under their tree this afternoon." She looked at Sarah. "If that's okay with you. We're still planning on going on Christmas, but I thought it'd be nice to get out this afternoon."

"I think it's a wonderful idea," Sarah said. "Dad will be thrilled to have you and the girls visit. I hear they're having cake and tea at three o'clock."

"Cake?" Amy perked up.

Audrey stepped back from her father. "Okay," she said grudgingly. "Come on, Amy, let's go get our presents." They climbed the stairs.

"Good luck, Jason," Maggie said quietly.

He kissed her on the cheek. "Everything's going to be fine. Bye, mom."

After he left, Maggie's shoulders drooped, and she starting tidying up the already neat parlor. After restacking the magazines for the third time, she sat on the couch with a big sigh. "You're probably wondering what's going on. You know the two girls who were in the store and left with Martha's grandkids?"

"Amy's friends."

"Yes. Brita and Pam. Brita's mother was looking for something in her daughter's closet this morning and found some items that didn't belong. Apparently they took some things from a couple of stores."

"Shoplifting." Sarah's stomach dropped. "The girls know?"

Maggie nodded. "That's why Amy's so upset."

"Poor kid," Sarah said and then sucked in a sharp breath. "What about Lexie, Pru, and Trina?"

"They were shopping with them, but claim they didn't know anything about the stealing. Their parents were called and nothing was found in their possession, so they're in the clear."

"That's a relief," Sarah said. Martha would've been so upset if her granddaughters were involved.

"But that's why Jason went into the office. Brita's mom had picked up Jason's business card last night. The parents want to approach the stores and see if they can work out consequences for the girls without legal action. The fact that Jason is a lawyer may also help the girls realize how serious this is."

"I hope so," Sarah said, feeling sympathy for the girls' parents.

Maggie ran a hand through her auburn hair. "I keep thinking that if I'd let the girls go with them, Amy could've been involved in this by association. They're getting to the age where peer pressure can be even harder to handle. I don't think my girls would ever steal, but I'm sure neither did those girls' moms." She heaved a deep sigh and glanced toward the stairs. "I can't believe they'll be teenagers soon. Did you worry about being able to parent teens?"

"Oh yes. I don't think you can be a parent without a huge dose of worry." Sarah smiled. "Maggie, you're a great mom. All kids make mistakes. The fact that Amy's upset by this is a good sign—she realizes how wrong it was. But if you ever do want to worry out loud, I'm here."

A small smile lifted Maggie's lips. "Have I told you lately how much I appreciate you, Sarah?"

"You don't have to. That's what family's for," Sarah said, recalling how Liam had said the same about friends last night. "But I like hearing it sometimes. I appreciate you too, Maggie. I'm so glad Jason brought you into this family."

"Mom, where's the ribbon?" Audrey hollered from upstairs.

Maggie went to the bottom of the staircase. "Look in the hall closet. I think there are a couple of rolls on the shelf."

"I found some," Amy called.

Maggie glanced at Sarah's hunter green pantsuit, and looked down at her white blouse and jeans. "Maybe I should change."

"Only if you want too. You look lovely as always, Maggie. If it would make you feel better, we can stop by my house and I'll change to jeans too," Sarah said and then added, "Actually *I'll* feel better if I change. The temperature will be dipping back into the thirties by this evening."

"Great. Let me check on the girls' progress and fix my hair. Then we can go." She hurried up the stairs.

Sarah wandered back into the parlor. She picked up the fire poker and pushed the dying embers and glowing log fragments to the back of the fireplace. Pulling the draw chains, she carefully closed the mesh screen so no sparks could escape.

The elegantly carved wooden hourglass on the bookshelf caught her attention. She turned it over, watching the snowy white sand shift and flow to the bottom.

A psalm from the memory text in a devotion she'd read a couple weeks ago floated through her mind. *How precious to me are your thoughts concerning me God!...Were I to count them, they would outnumber the grains of sand—when I awake, I am still with you.*

The words soothed her troubled soul. God knew where Belle was, and Sarah just had to trust he'd put his protective hand over her.

"Lord, if I can help Belle in any way, please show me how," she whispered.

She sat on the couch, her mind drifting over the previous evening. She'd mentioned to Chief Webber how Liam and Karen had described the man who had searched Belle's room. Tall, freckled, and skinny, which was a good description of Joe Stout, the museum guard. Was he involved in this mess? He had mentioned that Ben owed him money.

Whoever had broken into the house through the cellar window had to have been skinny too. Joe was thin enough. But he'd seemed so nice when Martha and she had visited him. But then, how could you really know a person after spending only twenty minutes with him?

She drummed her fingers on the armrest as another thought occurred to her. If one assumed that the man from last night was the same person who'd broken into her house earlier, then her hunch might be correct. If only Chester Winslow would call. As an antique expert he had access to information she didn't.

"Grandma, we're ready," Audrey called.

"So am I, honey," Sarah said.

"Look at the angels!" Audrey exclaimed, leaning over the back of the front seat of Sarah's car. She pointed to the majestic flying angels attached to each of the four white columns bracketing the front entrance to the Bradford Manor Nursing Home.

"How'd they get that star up there so high?" Amy asked.

Sarah gazed at the giant Star of David centered below the peak of the brick colonial-style building. They must've put the decorations up since last Sunday.

"There may be an attic vent there," Maggie said, buttoning up her black coat. "Or they lowered the star from the roof. Big, isn't it?"

"I bet it looks so cool at night. We have to come see it," Audrey said, grabbing one of the bags holding presents.

"We could do that," Sarah said. "I'm thinking we might be able to see the star from town too. We'll have to check it out." She stepped out of the car, her boots crunching on the gravel that covered the private drive. Behind the building, the mountains rose majestically, reminding her of Mother's Den and Belle again. She said a quick prayer for Belle and strided to the front door with Audrey.

Amy hung behind, her breath rapidly puffing out steam.

"Amy, what on earth are you doing?" Maggie asked, humor and exasperation in her voice.

"Trying to fill up with fresh air," she said and glanced around them, her expression covert. "It smells like medicine and old people in there."

"Amy, you shouldn't say—" Maggie started to admonish, but she caught Sarah's amused look and coughed to cover a laugh.

Sarah smiled. She loved the open honesty twelve-year-olds possessed. "That's because they are old. Just be polite, okay?"

"Breathe out of your mouth," Audrey whispered loudly. "Try not to use your nose. That's what I do."

Sarah dug in her purse and produced two strong cinnamon candies. "Try this."

Each girl popped one in her mouth, and Amy's eyes lit up. "All I smell is cinnamon now."

"That's the idea. Do you want a candy, Maggie?"

She shook her head, smiling. "I'll try Audrey's suggestion of breathing through my mouth if need be."

In truth, the personnel at the Bradford Manor Nursing Home kept the facility very clean, or Sarah wouldn't have even considered letting her father live there. She'd really wanted him to move in with her after her mother passed away eight years ago, but her fiercely independent, considerate father, warrior of World War II, hadn't wanted to be a burden.

They entered the large sitting room where several residents and visitors lounged on the sofas and overstuffed chairs on both sides of the door. A large Christmas tree dominated the far wall, dwarfing the console piano.

"Can I put Grandpa William's gifts under there with the others?" Audrey asked as Amy beelined over to a cage filled with small, colorful birds.

"Go ahead, honey. I made sure they were labeled correctly," Maggie answered, and then paused to speak to a petite woman wearing a bright purple sweat suit who was exclaiming over how pretty the twins were.

Sarah motioned to Maggie she was heading back to her father. They'd already planned that Sarah would take her father to the sitting area rather than all four of them trying to cram into his small room.

Maggie nodded. Audrey was still searching for the perfect spot for their gifts under the tree while chatting with a man hunched over a cane who offered advice. Amy had shyly sidled close to her mother when another resident attempted to speak to her and smiled politely.

Sarah hurried down the hall and paused by the nursing station in the center of the building where one of the nurses, Grace, was standing filling out some paperwork. "Hello, Grace. I just wanted to let you know I'm taking William Drayton to the visiting area."

Grace smiled. "That'll be fine. At four, a children's group is coming in to sing Christmas carols with the residents."

"Thanks. Dad will like that," Sarah said and strolled down the hall to William's room. Her father sat in his wheelchair in front of the small desk in the corner.

"Hi, Dad." She bent and kissed him on the cheek.

"Sarah, sweetheart, I'm glad to see you. Is it cold outside?"

Sarah unbuttoned her coat and draped it at the foot of William's bed. "Not as cold as it will be when the next storm gets here. Sounds like we're going to get buried tomorrow." Sarah squeezed his sweater-clad arm and looked over his shoulder. "What are you doing?"

"Signing some Christmas cards for the nurses."

"How thoughtful," Sarah replied, thankful her father was lucid today. At ninety-six, William's memory often slipped.

"It isn't much, but they do a lot for us that they don't have to." He slowly signed his name.

"Like decorating your plant?" Sarah said with a laugh at the tiny ornaments made out of jelly beans hanging from the leafy house plant on the windowsill.

She reached into the paper gift bag she'd brought and pulled out a tin decorated with a snowman. "The girls and I baked some Christmas cookies."

"Thank you. I love your cookies." He set down his pen and took the tin. "Would you mind if I shared these with the nurses?"

Sarah smiled. "Not at all. In fact, I'll bring more over on Christmas. We baked huge batches for the home tour and Maggie's store. I still have some in my freezer." She took hold of the wheelchair handles. "Maggie and the twins are in the front room. Ready to go see them?"

"Wonderful. Let me wash the ink off my fingers first," William said. Sarah pushed him to the small sink. His large capable hands seemed shrunken, and his fingers trembled slightly as he reached for the soap. A couple of white drops fell down the front of his navy sweater. Sarah grabbed a hand towel and swiped them up.

"You look very handsome in that Christmas sweater, Dad. Turns your eyes a deep blue. All the ladies out there are going to want to sit by you."

"There you go teasing your old father again."

"I mean it." Sarah hugged his shoulders and then pushed the wheelchair into the hallway. As they passed the nursing station, Sarah smiled at Grace.

They made their way slowly to the front of the manor. When they reached the visiting area, the twins were playing dominos at a table with the bearded man with the cane, while Maggie watched from a distance.

Audrey glanced up from her game and saw him from across the room. She shoved the chair back, bumping the game table. Dominos flew in all directions.

"Be careful," Amy exclaimed, trying to grab the flying rectangles before they hit the floor.

"Sorry," Audrey said and raced across the room to give William a hug. "Grandpa William, Merry almost-Christmas."

He held her out at arm's length. "Now which one are you? Audrey or Amy?"

She giggled. "I'm Audrey."

Amy came up behind her, and William pretended to rub his eyes. "Landsakes, it's like seeing double."

Amy smiled. "Hi, Grandpa William."

"Do you two ever switch places and fool people? Now if I had a twin, I'd—"

"Grandpa, don't give them any more ideas," Maggie interrupted him.

William chuckled. The front door opened and a group of Girl Scouts entered. Audrey recognized one of them and headed over to chat. Amy settled on the floor in front of their grandfather's feet as the Girl Scouts gathered around the tree. One of the adults accompanying them sat at the piano and struck a chord. The group started singing "Jingle Bells." William joined in with his deep baritone. Eventually the singing wound down, and a kitchen attendant wheeled a cart in with a big snowman-shaped cake. They doled out pieces of cake and apple juice to the residents and guests.

Sarah finished her cake and took her plate to a trash can. Audrey and Amy chatted with a couple of Girl Scouts. A customer of Maggie's had cornered her, literally, discussing antique armoires, and several female residents had positioned themselves by William. He said something and they laughed. It was good to see her family engaging with others and enjoying themselves. She just wished Jason could be here. She hoped everything was getting straightened out between Amy's friends and the stores they'd stolen from.

The room had gradually gone from pleasantly warm to hot and stuffy, and Sarah needed some fresh air. She stepped outside, welcoming the cold air that bathed her cheeks.

Dusk had fallen, and someone had switched on the white lights on the angels and the star. A few snowflakes twirled down from the sky, teasing her with what was to come. She gazed down at the town. Street lamps defined the crisscrossing streets and house windows glowed.

The door opened and Amy stepped out. "Grandma, are you okay?"

"I'm fine, sweetie. Just needed some fresh air."

"Me too." She wrinkled her nose. "But it didn't smell too bad in there today. Do you think it's hard growing old?"

"Oh, I suppose it can be if you're not in good health, but every stage of life can be enjoyed. Right now, I'm enjoying having you and Audrey and your parents close by," Sarah said, and then turned to Amy with a teasing smile. "Why? Do you think I'm starting to smell old too?"

Amy hugged her, burying her nose in Sarah's sweater. "No, you smell good. Like cookies, cinnamon, and my grandma. I love you."

"I love you too, sweetheart," Sarah said, hugging Amy back.

"Grandma, you're vibrating." Amy giggled and pulled away. Sarah grinned, pulling the phone out of her blazer pocket. She glanced at the screen, and her heart skipped a beat. Chester Winslow.

CHAPTER SEVENTEEN

The parking lot held only two other cars when Sarah pulled up to the Berkshire Museum of Art. Dark clouds rolled past, casting a shadow over the building. Sarah suppressed a shiver. The second wave of the snowstorms was due that evening, and she hoped she'd be back in Maple Hill by then.

She glanced at her watch. The museum would be closing in a half hour for Christmas Eve. Last night on the phone, Chester said he'd found something interesting in his research about the royal ornaments. Rather than divulge the information over the phone, he'd insisted on meeting Sarah at the museum.

She rubbed the corners of her tired eyes. She'd spent another late night working on the quilt, double-pinning each seam, sewing the diamond strips together to form the star points, and then joining the eight star points first into four pairs, then into the two halves of the starburst. Now she had to sew the two halves together, first pinning all the seams

263

carefully, with special attention to the center seam. She'd been tempted to rush the process of sewing the starburst together, but if she missed lining the points up exactly, the whole quilt could be thrown off. If she wanted this quilt to honor the Hart family quilt, she needed to be meticulous and put as much care into it as the Hart women had put into the heirloom quilt. Now wasn't the time to rush.

She remembered the first baby quilt she'd made for Jason. She'd started cutting the fabric two weeks before his due date. Gerry had cautioned her about taking on a new project, especially the complicated pattern she'd chosen when she was already dealing with so many changes. But she was determined to finish that quilt before the baby arrived.

The result had been many tears as she ripped out seam after seam of mistakes. Gerry had been a rock during the surges of hormonal emotion, and his mother had patiently offered some tips but wisely refrained from offering to finish the quilt for her. Sarah realized later the quilt, for her, had been part of the nesting phase most women experience during pregnancy.

She'd nearly driven herself and Gerry nuts, but she did finish the quilt the day before Jason came kicking and screaming into the world.

A silver BMW coupe rolled into the parking lot and parked next to her. Chester Winslow emerged. His cheerful, confident smile lifted her spirits despite the growing gloom.

"Sarah Hart, always a pleasure to see you," Chester said, one hand on his slightly battered, bowler-style hat to keep it from flying away in the gusty wind. He looked distinguished as always in his tweed jacket and dark khakis.

"Likewise, Chester. I so appreciate your coming."

"Glad to. I find this mystery of yours intriguing." He placed his hand on the small of her back as they ascended the stairs. "Careful, it's icy in places."

"I just hope this isn't a wild goose chase," she said.

"Even if it is, I'm glad for the excuse to see you again," he said and Sarah smiled. He let her pass through the revolving door first.

Alice stood behind the counter. "Mrs. Hart, you're back."

"I see you're known here." Chester smiled down at Sarah and she felt a little flutter in her chest.

"Hi Alice. Yes, I'm back. I brought a friend," Sarah said, stepping up to the counter. "This is Chester Winslow, he's an antique expert from *Country Cottage Magazine*."

"Oh yes, I've seen that magazine at the store, but I've never read it," Alice said.

Chester turned his charming smile to Alice. "If you'll remind me later, I'll be happy to get you a copy of the current issue from my car."

Alice smiled back. "I'd like that. I'm trying to convince my fiancé that we should decorate with antiques, but he's more into big, comfortable, ugly stuff. Are you here to write a story about the museum?"

"I might, if I find something interesting." He pulled out his black leather wallet. "How much for tickets?"

Alice glanced at the wall clock. "You do know we're closing in twenty minutes?" Alice asked.

Sarah nodded. "We're here to see just the royal ornaments. This may be our last chance."

"In that case, just go on back," Alice said with a dismissive wave of her hand. "I know Mr. Warthorne's always glad when someone from the media visits."

"I appreciate the generosity, but I prefer to pay. That way if I do include a mention of the museum in my column, no one can accuse me of being biased," Chester said. "Besides, I think it's important to support the arts."

Alice's cheeks pinked. "Oh yes, I see your point. In that case it will be twenty-two dollars." She took the bills and gave them tickets. "Have fun."

"I should buy the tickets since I'm the one who needs your help," Sarah said as they stepped away from the counter.

"Not a problem. It's a business expense. I've always meant to check the museum out anyway," Chester said as Sarah led the way into the exhibit hall.

Joe Stout stood in the corner, but otherwise the room was empty of visitors. Sarah waved at Joe who looked startled to see her. He gave her a little wave back as Chester and she rounded the tree to where Martha had snapped the photos.

Sarah felt like her heart had slid to her throat. "I know I may be totally wrong about this, but see the turquoise blue ornament up there? Next to the red one? Now look at this photo from the Web page." She handed him the sheet she'd printed off. "See it's slightly off to the left now. Same with the silver one, it's down a branch."

"You're right. But someone may have cleaned and moved them."

"I thought about that too, but Mr. Warthorne is adamant only certain people touch the ornaments because of the liability. They even have special packers who transport them. Mr. Warthorne seemed very upset the day they came too early. Granted, he could've just wanted the exhibit to stay up until after Christmas, but what if he didn't want anyone getting close to them?" She quickly summed up her theory of what had happened.

"I see." Chester stroked his chin. "So you think these may be forgeries, and your boarder's brother stole them?"

"Not exactly. I don't think Ben is capable of doing such a thing by himself. At least not the forgeries. They have a guard on duty twenty-four hours a day, and they watch the janitorial staff." She nodded toward the corner where, as if to prove her point, Joe shifted his position so he could observe them.

"So it would have to be someone who wouldn't arouse suspicion and who can access this room when other employees can't. Someone the guards might not watch too closely."

Sarah nodded, pleased that Chester was following her line of reasoning and seemed to trust her intuition. "Mr. Warthorne was planning a trip out of the country last week, but suddenly postponed it about the time Belle and Ben disappeared. I also discovered the museum is being sold. Mr. Warthorne's job may be on shaky ground."

"So you think he decided to retire in style."

"Yes, only something went wrong. I think he may have used Ben in some way to steal the originals, only Ben took off with them." She gazed at the sparkling ornaments on the tree. "Do you think you can tell if they are forgeries?"

"Possibly. In my research I found out that most of these ornaments are signed with a tiny, almost imperceptible signature. If you didn't know what you were looking for, you'd miss it altogether. I need to examine one up close."

"But how?" Sarah said, surveying the scene. The tree was barricaded by a velvet rope and the elaborate miniature village and train track. "Do you want me to distract the guard? I know him."

Chester glanced over at Joe. "Would he shoot me?"

Sarah laughed. "I don't think he has a gun. Just that big billy club."

"Well then . . . there's a quick way to do this." He ducked under the rope, stepped over the train track, and snagged a turquoise ornament off the tree.

Sarah gasped, and Joe ran toward them. "Sir. Put that back. Now!" He gazed wild-eyed at Sarah as if he didn't know what to do.

"It's okay, Joe," Sarah said. "We're stopping a crime."

His Adam's apple bobbed. "Doesn't look that way to me."

Chester stood straight, dignified. "My good man, I'm Chester Winslow, an antique expert for *Country Cottage Magazine*. I have good reason to believe these ornaments may be forgeries."

Joe's mouth dropped open. "Forgeries?"

Chester nodded. "I want you to take me to the curator immediately."

"He's right," Sarah said, her heart thumping. "We need to see Mr. Warthorne. If these ornaments are fake, I wouldn't want to be the one who stood in the way of letting him know immediately."

Joe still hesitated, his gaze shifting from Chester to Sarah.

"If we're correct in our assumption, you'll want to make sure you've done everything you can to aid in the investigation of this crime," Chester added.

"Besides, do you think we'd try to steal the ornaments with you standing right there?" Sarah pointed out.

"I guess not," Joe said, his body relaxing some as he took a deep breath. "All right. We'll go to the curator's office. But I still have to report this to the police. I tripped the silent alarm."

"That's perfectly fine," Chester said passing the ornament to Joe, who cupped it delicately with both hands. They marched down the hall to the lobby.

"How could you tell it was a fake so quickly?" Sarah whispered to Chester.

"I don't actually know for sure yet. I didn't have a chance to examine it," he whispered back and Sarah's pulse did a tap dance. "But we'll know in a few minutes," he said, answering her unspoken question.

"What's going on?" Alice said, flying out from behind her counter, her hands fluttering. "Joe?"

"We need to see Mr. Warthorne," he said, his face as red as his hair. "Now."

"Okay, okay...."

Mr. Warthorne was at his desk when they entered. He looked up, surprised. "Yes? What is it, Joe?"

"Sir, this gentleman took one of the royal ornaments off the tree. He claims it's a fake." Joe gently set the blue ornament on the desk and stepped back. He swiped at his glistening forehead.

Mr. Warthorne stood and gaped at Chester. "What? Who are you?"

Sarah stepped around Chester. "Mr. Warthorne, you remember me, don't you?"

"How could I forget?" He replied. "Did you ever find Benjamin?"

"No, but I think you already know that."

Mr. Warthorne sat back in his chair. "Joe, go back to your post. I'll handle this ridiculous situation."

Joe hesitated. "Yes, sir, but—"

"Now!" Mr. Warthorne waited for the door to shut and then glared at Sarah and Chester. "All right, what is going on here?"

"Exactly what it sounds like," Chester said with a small smile. "You have forgeries on your tree out there."

"And you are?"

"Chester Winslow from *Country Cottage Magazine*." He stuck out his hand, which Mr. Warthorne ignored.

"He's an antique expert," Sarah added.

"I see," Mr. Warthorne said. "And for some reason you thought to come here and accuse this museum of what?"

Sarah took a deep breath. "I believe you switched ornaments on the tree with forgeries and were going to take the real ones out of the country."

"This is absurd. Why in the world do you think I would steal from my own exhibit?" Mr. Warthorne asked.

"Maybe you needed the money. I looked up the company that's buying the museum and they're pretty progressive and innovative. Young. No one on their company page looked over thirty-five. You were probably afraid you were going to be replaced."

"Or you could just be greedy," Chester said with a shrug.

A flush stained Mr. Warthorne's neck. "This is all absurd speculation. You have no proof."

Sarah flicked a glance at the small side table by the divan, wondering if the piece of glass was still there. "I think I do. Remember when my friend Martha and I were in here? I stepped on some glass, which I believe now was a fake jewel. Similar to the fake jewels on that ornament on your desk. I suspect if the police were to search, they'd find other similar material around here."

A commotion sounded in the hall, distracting Chester. Mr. Warthorne jumped up and ran for the door leading to the garden. Chester charged after him and was shoved backward over a chair, knocking Sarah onto the floor next to the divan.

Sarah struggled to her feet. Chester tackled Mr. Warthorne and they rolled and struggled on the floor. The door burst open.

"Mr. Warthorne?" Alice cried out, running into the room with Joe.

Two police officers shoved past her. "Everyone, freeze!"

Chester held up his hands as the police hauled him to his feet.

Mr. Warthorne got to his hands and knees, sputtering. "Officer, this man attacked me. I want him arrested."

"If you let him go, he won't be here tomorrow." Chester said, straightening his jacket. "He'll leave the country. I'm sure you'll find a plane ticket in his name, the thief. He stole from the museum."

"They have no evidence, officers," Mr. Warthorne said, standing, shaking Joe's hand off his upper arm.

Chester looked over at Sarah who was frozen where she stood. "Sarah! Are you all right?"

"More than all right." She smiled. "And yes, we have evidence. She reached far under the divan and pulled out a silver ornament. "I believe you'll find the fake version of this on the tree."

"We're lucky the blue ornament was a forgery after all." Chester said as they stood on the front steps of the museum. "I don't think we could've convinced the police so quickly if we'd grabbed one of the real ones."

Sarah nodded. "Mr. Warthorne was smart enough not to try to take them all."

"Just enough to live in a Central American country for the next twenty years or so," he said with a wry smile. "Don't worry. Finding the real ornament under the divan will cement the case for them. I suspect his fingerprints are all over it."

"I just wish he'd tell us where Ben and Belle are. I think he knows."

"He may. That might be a bargaining chip he can use if he wants to take a plea."

Sarah looked up at the cloud-covered sky while big puffy snowflakes cooled her face. The storm had finally arrived during the last hour and a half they'd spent in the museum with the police.

The museum door opened behind them, and an officer led Mr. Warthorne down the steps to a squad car. Chester and she would've had to go with them to the station if Chief Webber hadn't vouched for their integrity over the phone. For now they were allowed to go home and return after Christmas to sign their statements at the police station.

A screech of brakes, and the sound of a car hitting metal reverberated across the parking lot. A brown sedan had slid into a lamp pole. The back door opened and a person fell out, then a second body rolled to the ground. The car sped off.

Sarah recognized the curly blonde hair and pixie face. She ran down the steps, Chester on her heels. "Belle!"

The man beside Belle scrambled to his feet and appeared ready to flee. Belle grabbed his shirt. "No, Ben. No more running. We're going to face this."

"Belle, are you all right?" Sarah said as she reached the girl.

Belle stared at her with a dazed expression. Her sweatshirt was streaked with mud and her jeans were torn at the knees.

"Mrs. Hart? What are you doing here?"

"Me?" Sarah laughed shakily. "I've been looking for you for a week. Are you hurt?"

"I don't think so. Not really."

"Who threw you out of the car?" Chester asked, gazing down the hill at the fading tail lights.

"One of them works here as a guard, and the other I don't know. When they saw Mr. Warthorne in handcuffs, they shoved us out of the car." Belle looked past them at the police officers.

"This is your brother?" Sarah asked, gesturing to the guy Belle still had a death grip on.

"Yes, this is Ben."

"I didn't steal the ornaments," Ben said, his gaze on the police. "I didn't even know they were real."

"We know, Ben," Sarah said gently, "but you may have to prove you weren't helping Mr. Warthorne."

"If you didn't steal the ornaments, then how did you get them?" Chester asked.

"I was helping to clean up after the—" He tensed and gripped Belle's arm.

Sarah looked over her shoulder. Mr. Warthorne was gesticulating wildly in Ben's direction while speaking to the police officers.

"Go on, Ben, tell her," Belle urged. "Now."

"I was cleaning up after the fund-raiser and packing the ornaments they used for the little trees on the tables and around the punch bowl. I never touched the exhibit. We weren't allowed. Joe was there. He can tell you."

"We talked to Joe," Sarah said. "He said he saw you helping clean up."

"I didn't steal anything!" Ben insisted again. "I was filling a box with the ornaments they used on the table trees when one of the ladies who donated the decorations asked me if I wanted them. I said yes. I thought Belle would like them. So the next day, I took them to her. I thought she might like to use them in her treasure hunt."

Belle nodded. "That's what he said when he came to the house, but I could tell they weren't cheap ornaments after all that research I'd done for the home tour. They seemed heavier, and the jewels looked real. I thought it was a mistake. We were going to take them back. I–I–" She swallowed hard. "I couldn't go right then, so I was going to meet Ben at his apartment so we could go talk to his boss together."

Ben nodded. "Belle convinced me to go, but I didn't think anyone would believe me. Nobody ever does. But when I got back to my place one of the guys who kidnapped us was waiting. He shoved me around and kept asking where the ornaments were." Ben's fists balled and his face grew red. "My landlord suggested I might have left them with my sister. Told them he could provide them with Belle's address for a little compensation. I got away and called Belle."

"Why didn't you go to the police?" Sarah asked as two officers started toward them. Chester intercepted them, talking quietly.

Ben noticed and shivered. "They wouldn't believe me. I overheard one of the guys talking to someone on the phone, and they mentioned Mr. Warthorne. It was my word against his. And who would believe me?"

"He ran, and I panicked," Belle said. "I had to figure out a way we could prove he didn't take the ornaments on purpose. So I hid them and went after him. I never thought we'd be gone so long, or that they'd catch up with us at Mother's Den."

Sarah sighed. She had a hunch Mr. Warthorne had overheard Alice's phone conversation with her when they discussed the natural attraction brochures and had put it together just as she had.

"Where did you hide the ornaments?"

"Under your tree in one of the boxes."

"Someone broke in last week and tore the packages up."

Belle's face scrunched like she was trying hard not to cry. "Must've been those guys."

"But wait," Sarah said. "If they'd found the ornaments, then why did they still go after you?"

"They must not have found them. They kept threatening us to tell them where they were, or they'd hurt us. The ornaments have to still be somewhere in the house," Belle said as the police left Chester's side and strode toward Ben.

"Benjamin Silver?" One of the officers said. "You're under arrest." The other motioned for Sarah to back away.

"Mrs. Hart, I have to go with Ben. You need to find the ornaments," Belle said. "*Please.*"

"There's nothing we can do right now." Chester slid his hand under Sarah's arm and gently guided her toward their cars. "You're half frozen. Let's get you somewhere warm."

Sarah looked up at his snow-covered hat and coat. She gave him a trembling smile. "You look like Frosty the snowman."

He grinned. "And you look like Mrs. Frosty." He pulled out his key fob and beeped open the door of his BMW.

The sound of "Silent Night" floated through the air.

"Wait. Do you hear that music?" she asked.

"Sounds like carolers down the hill."

Sarah stopped short. "I think I know where the ornaments are."

"Ma'am, visiting hours are over," the security guard said, his body blocking the entrance to Bradford Manor Nursing Home.

"But it's Christmas Eve," Sarah said. "Surely you can make an exception."

"Only if it's an emergency," he said. "Otherwise, doors will open at six tomorrow morning."

If the ornaments really were under the tree, then someone might very well open the package before she got there the next morning.

"John, it's okay. I know her." Grace, wearing her pale blue scrubs, came up behind the guard. "Why don't you go check the back doors. Someone said they'd had trouble locking the one in the north hall."

Grace stepped back and gestured for them to come inside. "Come in out of the cold."

"Thank you," Sarah said, stomping her boots on the mat. An inch of snow already covered the ground, and it was still coming down heavily.

"You're William Drayton's daughter, Sarah, right?" she asked. "I think your father's asleep, but if it's important I can go check."

"Actually we need to look at the gifts under the Christmas tree in the front room." Sarah introduced Chester and gave Grace a summary of Belle and the stolen ornaments.

"Oh my goodness. Sounds like a mystery movie," Grace said with a little shake of the head. "So, the ornaments may be in a package you brought for your father?"

"I know it seems a little crazy, but yes."

"Well, go ahead. I don't see any harm in your looking." She led the way into the front room. "No one's in here at the moment. Most of our residents retire early."

They crossed the room to the colorfully lit tree. Grace hovered behind them. "Anything in particular to look for?"

"Any packages addressed to my father. I don't know which one she stuck them in. I used several different kinds of paper," Sarah said, gently pulling out packages.

"Here's one with gold paper," Chester said, from behind the tree. "But I don't think it's what you're looking for. It's too small. Wait, here's another."

The gift wrapped in blue was from her. New pajamas. Sarah squeezed gently. The package felt squishy. No ornaments in there.

Chester handed her a red box next. Sarah recognized it as the one she'd packed with a bottle of aftershave, comb, shaving cream, and other small necessities. She didn't remember it being this heavy. Her heart gave an extra thump.

She carefully unwrapped the paper and lifted the lid. There, nestled in a pile of new socks, were about a dozen royal ornaments.

CHAPTER EIGHTEEN

arah pulled the tray of cinnamon buns out of
Maggie's oven. The hot, sweet smell mingled with
aromatic coffee perking. She grabbed a pastry brush
out of the drawer and painted frosting over the pastries.
Sounds above indicated the girls were up. She glanced at the
clock. Six-thirty. Not bad for a Christmas morning. Jason
used to get Gerry and her up at five.

Once Christmas was over, Sarah planned to take a few
days just to relax, work on the new quilt, and enjoy being
cooped up inside her snug home. There had been too many
restless nights last week, not to mention she hadn't gotten
home until after midnight last night.

After meeting Chief Webber and turning over the ornaments to him for transport to Pittsfield, she had headed for
the church. The snow had been falling heavily and Chester
headed for home in case the roads became impassable. She'd
driven to the church and caught the last fifteen minutes of
the special Christmas Eve service, sneaking into the pew in

the back where Jason and his family sat. Jason had scolded her for getting mixed up with the police on Christmas Eve, but he couldn't manage to hold his stern look on his face. Maggie teased him that he was secretly proud of his detective mother.

Feet pounded on the stairs, interrupting Sarah's memory of the night before, and a moment later the door to the kitchen burst open. "Merry Christmas, Grandma!" Audrey and Amy shouted. They gave her a hug and ran for the parlor, nearly knocking over their mother who had entered the kitchen right behind them.

Maggie shuffled into the kitchen wrapped in a fuzzy pink bathrobe. "When you said you'd be here early and make a little something, I didn't expect this."

"I hope I haven't imposed. I just wanted to share a tradition from the Hart side of the family." She held up the platter of cinnamon rolls. "There's fresh fruit and coffee. I have a quiche in the oven too."

Maggie snagged a roll and bit into it. "Yum! You won't hear me complaining. These are delicious. Let's take the rolls to the living room. The girls are going to burst if they have to wait much longer to open gifts."

Sarah grabbed a couple of mugs of coffee and followed. Jason sat in a chair in his blue-striped bathrobe. His hair was mussed and his eyes glazed with sleep. Sarah waved a mug under his nose, and he perked up enough to take it. He'd spent most of Sunday evening in consultation with the families of the girls who had shoplifted. They'd struck a deal with the store owners. Brita and Pam would work off the cost of the items they'd stolen, and they'd meet with a police counselor who'd take them on a tour of a juvenile detention center to see where they could've ended up.

Sarah sighed with contentment as she watched her family open gifts. Audrey squealed over her new clothes. Amy loved the gloves Sarah had given her and the ski suit from her parents. She couldn't wait to try them outdoors in the piles of snow that had fallen overnight. Two new sleds waited on the porch to be tried out. Jason had woken up enough to try on his new slippers when the doorbell rang.

"Who could that be so early in the morning?" Maggie asked as Jason opened the door. Belle stood on the threshold, looking forlorn. He asked her to come in.

"I'm sorry to interrupt," she said, "but I was wondering if I could talk to Sarah. I ran by the house, but no one was home. I figured she might be here."

Sarah hurried to the entryway. "Belle, are you okay?"

"I'm really tired," Belle said, her face pale and still smudged with dried mud. "They didn't let me out of the police station until an hour ago." She glanced around the room. The twins stared wide-eyed at her. "Oh, I'm so sorry I've interrupted your Christmas with your family. I should just go home." Tears threatened to spill onto her cheeks.

Sarah wrapped her arms around Belle. "Oh, sweetheart, everything's fine. Don't you worry. I'm so happy to have you back. We'll just go in the kitchen for a minute. Maggie, is that okay?"

"Of course, and Belle, please help yourself to breakfast. There's plenty to eat."

Sarah made Belle a plate of cinnamon rolls and melon and cut her a slice of quiche. The girl tore into the food like she hadn't eaten in days.

After a long gulp of coffee, Belle looked up. "Sorry. I was starving. Mr. Warthorne's goons didn't bother to feed us much."

"How's Ben?"

"I think he's going to be okay. They're still holding him for more questioning, but I don't think he's going to be charged. Mr. Warthorne's prints were on that ornament you found in his office. The lady on the fund-raising committee confirmed that she'd told Ben he could have the ornaments used for the decorations. She'd taken a liking to Ben and wanted him to have a nice Christmas."

"That's excellent news!"

Belle nodded. "Mr. Warthorne must've switched the royal ornaments earlier in the day when they were setting up, and then planned on getting them from the storage room the next day. Of course Ben was already gone with the real ornaments when Mr. Warthorne went to retrieve them, so he sent those guys after Ben and then me. I'm so sorry I brought you into this. I panicked. Ben called and said a guy was on his way over. I knew I had about forty minutes, and I wanted to make it look like I'd moved out so they'd look elsewhere."

She rubbed her hands over her face. "I couldn't think. I didn't want the ornaments to be found in case they caught up with me, so I stuck them in one of the presents under the tree. I know it was stupid and it didn't work. They went to your house anyway."

"I think they thought the ornaments on my tree may have been the real ones. When they discovered they weren't, they started looking through the gifts. It was fortunate I had already taken that box over to the nursing home," Sarah said. "So how did your suitcase end up in the cellar?"

"I was going to take it with me, but those guys showed up at the house and started looking in the windows. I went through the cellar and out the bulkhead. I got scared and dropped the suitcase somewhere."

"Was one of them skinny and had freckles?"

"Yeah. How did you know?"

"He was here the night of the home tour searching your room."

Belle held her head in her hands. "I'm so sorry for all this, but Ben has really been the only close family I have," she said in a trembling voice. "Although I got a chance to talk to my dad last night—he's coming to the States for a while."

"I'm glad. He was worried about you," Sarah said. She'd left a message for Dr. Silver when Ben and Belle were found, but she hadn't heard back.

Belle nodded, a tear rolling down her cheek. "I have one other thing I have to tell you...."

"About my quilt?"

She looked at Sarah. "Yeah. It was an accident. I went up to the attic to look for something to use at Mrs. Nelson's house for the treasure hunt. I took my smoothie up there with me and set it on one of the boxes. When I opened the trunk, I accidentally spilled the cup. I didn't even realize the quilt was in there until it was too late. It had a huge blueberry stain on it. I wanted to get it cleaned before you saw it. I was rushing to the cleaners when Ben showed up with the ornaments, so I never got there."

Sarah felt a surge of hope. "Well maybe I can repair it. Where is the quilt now?"

"That's the awful part. After those men caught us, one of them took off with my car. I have no idea what he did with it. They joked about setting my car on fire. The quilt was still in the backseat the last time I saw it."

Sarah sat still for a few seconds. "You know what? Much as I cherished that quilt, you're more important. You're back safe, and you and your brother get a fresh start."

Belle sniffed. "I'll move out if you want. I know what I did was terrible."

Sarah took Belle's hands in hers. "Look at me. It's okay. Go home and get some rest."

"Really?"

"Really. And if you want to talk later, I'll be home this afternoon after I visit my father."

She walked Belle to the backdoor, and then tidied the kitchen as she waited for her emotions to settle. Losing the Hart quilt still twisted her insides, but if Gerry were here, he'd tell her to move on. Make a fresh start.

Sarah opened her tote bag and took out the package she'd wrapped for Maggie in the wee hours of the morning. She took it to the parlor where her daughter-in-law lounged on the couch.

"Everyone went up to get dressed," Maggie said. "I was just enjoying the fire. Did Belle leave?"

"Yes, she went back to the house. She's exhausted." Sarah held out the package.

"What? Another gift? I already love the wind chimes you gave me." Maggie unwrapped the package and lifted out the green and red starburst Sarah had finished piecing the night before. "Sarah, it's gorgeous."

"I'm sorry it's not finished. Give me a couple more weeks."

Tears filled Maggie's eyes. "This is just like your Christmas quilt. Did you get it back?"

Sarah shook her head, swallowing the lump in her throat. "I started this one because I couldn't bear the thought of losing Gerry's family's quilt. But as I worked on this new one, I started remembering all the good times as well as the sad. I realize now that memories and traditions are things to cherish, but they shouldn't be more important than the present."

"Well, this moment will be one of my cherished memories." Maggie squeezed Sarah's hand. "This means so much to me."

Sarah smiled. "When I finish the quilt, you can decide if you want to carry on the embroidery tradition or not."

Maggie's face lit up. "This is going to be so fun. I love that family tradition. Someday I'm going to pass this quilt down to— Oh! How do I choose?"

"Maybe we need to make two quilts," Sarah said and laughed with Maggie.

"Dad, Mom, it's Aunt Jenna on the phone," Audrey called.

Maggie popped up. "Oh, I hope they got my packages on time. I'll be right back, and I'll bring the other phone so you can talk."

Sarah leaned back on the couch and gazed around the room at the beautiful Christmas clutter of wrapping paper, ribbon, and gift boxes. In the distance she could hear the happy chatter of her family. The smells of freshly baked bread and cinnamon wafted through the air, her own symbols of continuity and lasting love.

Later, she'd make Gerry's mother's famous cranberry-orange bread and take it over to the nursing home to share. She also needed to call Chester to wish him a Merry Christmas and thank him for all his help the previous night. He'd be happy to know she'd chosen the topic for her next column. She was going to tell the story of the Hart family Christmas quilt and how she made a new one. The title of the article would be: *Making New Traditions.*

The racket of pounding feet sounded on the stairs. Audrey shouted. "Hey, that's my new brush. Give it back."

"It is not!" Amy landed in the entryway and spun to run toward the kitchen, her socks slipping on the hardwood floor. Audrey plowed into her, and they went down in a tumble, sliding to a stop on the parlor rug.

Sarah jumped to her feet. "Are you all right?"

Giggles erupted as the girls untangled themselves. Sarah chuckled. This was truly a Christmas to remember.

About the Author

From her first introduction to the beginner readers with Dick and Jane, award-winning author Kelly Ann Riley has wanted to be a writer. She started penning stories at an early age, and received special recognition for her short stories. Later, she became a reporter and the editor for her high school newspaper.

Now Kelly Ann enjoys writing romantic suspense and cozy mysteries. Her past hobbies of quilting, cross-stitching, and crocheting make the *Patchwork Mysteries* particularly fun to write. She loves watching fabric, string, and yarn transform into art.

She is a member of American Christian Fiction Writers and Romance Writers of America, and lives in Alabama with her family. You can contact her through her Web site at www.KellyAnnRiley.com

HERE'S A SNEAK PEEK AT THE NEXT
PATCHWORK MYSTERIES BOOK!

PIECES OF THE PAST

BY SUSAN PAGE DAVIS

 CHAPTER ONE

Sarah Hart got out of her silver Grand Prix and pulled a large bundle wrapped in a plastic trash bag from the backseat. The Bradford Manor Nursing Home grounds were blanketed in shimmering snow, but the parking lot and driveway had been plowed down to the bare pavement. The distant Berkshire Mountains glistened white, with purple and gray shadows on their snowy slopes and swaths of dark evergreens among the bare hardwood trees. The view satisfied something in Sarah's artistic soul, as her breath formed white vapor clouds in the air. She hefted the soft package and shoved the car door shut.

She entered the lobby, stopping briefly at the front desk to say hello to Grace, one of the nurses. A moment later, she tapped softly on her father's half-open door. From inside his room, she heard him talking with another man.

"We had an awful time in Italy," her father said. "I was at Salerno."

"That was a tough battle."

"Sure was—Fiats zooming in low over us and strafing the ground. I thought we'd never get out of there."

"I hear ya. The fight in the Pacific was half a world away from Italy, but there was more than once when I thought we'd never get out of that jungle."

"Hello, Dad!" Sarah entered the sunny room and smiled at him and the man he regaled with his battle tales. "Hello. I'm William's daughter, Sarah."

The gray-haired man in the wheelchair quickly tucked something into his pocket and looked up at her. He nodded and smiled, his brown eyes sweeping her face. "Vern Pickett. I'm down the hall. William and I were just swapping war stories."

William had served in the European theater in the 1940s.

"Those Italians were lousy shots, or I wouldn't be here," William said.

He didn't talk about it often. In fact, he didn't talk so passionately about much of anything these days. She laid the garbage bag she carried on her father's bed.

"Are you a veteran, Mr. Pickett?" she asked as she unzipped her down parka.

"Yes, ma'am. I joined my state National Guard infantry unit in 1942, but we became part of the American Division, in the Pacific, under Major General Alexander Patch."

William squinted at Vern. "What did you say your name was again?"

"Vern Pickett."

William nodded, though he might not remember the name five minutes from now. His eyelids drifted shut, and Sarah stepped closer to his chair.

"Dad, I brought your present over. I'm sorry I didn't have it quite finished on your birthday yesterday."

"What?" He blinked and focused on her. "What's that?"

"I brought the quilt I made you. It's finished now." She turned and slipped the garbage bag off the gift and took the quilt in her arms. She unfolded one end and draped it over her father's lap. "There, see? I finished the stitching last night. Would you like me to put it on the bed for you?"

William nodded and ran his fingertips over one of the squares. His lips curved into a slight smile. She and Jason and Maggie and the twins had come on his birthday to tell him how much they loved him.

"You made that?" Vern asked. "That's some fine work. Looks nice and warm."

Sarah unfolded more of the quilt. She placed one edge in his hand. "Thank you. I hoped it would help since Dad gets cold, even when the heat's up. I used a few of his old flannel shirts to make most of the squares for this."

"That's a great idea." Vern fingered the soft plaid material. "I'm sure he'll use that all the time."

"I hope it gives him good memories and pleasant dreams," Sarah said.

Vern looked over at William. "So, you just had a birthday, eh?"

But William was silent, his hands caressing the edges of the quilt.

Sarah and Vern exchanged a knowing look.

"How old is he?" Vern asked.

"Ninety-seven."

Vern whistled softly. "He seemed pretty alert today."

"I'm glad you caught him at a good time."

Vern nodded. "Well, I suppose I'd better head on down the hall. Nice to meet you." He groped for the brakes on his wheelchair's side, then bent over the armrest, trying to see it.

"Let me help you."

As Sarah stepped to his side, Vern shifted and a small square photograph fell from his shirt pocket, landing face up on the carpet. Sarah picked it up.

She glanced at it as she held it out to him. A young woman smiled softly at whomever had taken the picture, the life in her eyes shining clearly from the black-and-white wallet-size picture.

"Oh, thanks." Vern took it and stuck it into his pocket.

Sarah released the brake on his wheelchair. "She's striking. It that a picture of your wife?"

He hesitated, not meeting her gaze. "No. She ... her name was Alice."

"She's very pretty. That picture looks as though you've been hanging on to it for a while."

"Oh, yes." He smiled then. "Been carrying that for a long time. It went to Guadalcanal with me."

"She must be special."

"Well … yes."

Sarah remained silent and waited. Something about the yellowed picture made Vern uncomfortable.

He gave a halfhearted shrug. "I haven't spoken with her in years."

"You lost touch?" Sarah asked.

"Something like that. After the war, I tried to find her, but … well, some things just don't work out."

"Do you want to tell me about it?"

He squeezed up his lips for a moment. "Not much to tell now. It's been over sixty years."

"Have you tried looking for her recently? You know, on the Internet, a lot of people have success in locating old friends."

"I tried a little bit, but I'm not exactly a whiz with those computers."

Sarah nodded.

A tall young man in jeans and a Red Sox sweatshirt appeared in the doorway. "Hey, Grandpa! I've been looking for you. Thought you were AWOL."

Vern chuckled and looked at Sarah. "My grandson Scott." He began to turn his wheelchair toward the door. "I met one of my neighbors and got talking. You know how that goes."

Scott stepped into the room and smiled at Sarah. "Hi." His warm brown eyes matched Vern's, but Scott's held a friendly twinkle his grandfather seemed to have lost.

"Hello." Sarah stood. "I'm Sarah Hart, William's daughter."

Her father opened his eyes and blinked. "Who's that young man?"

"He's Vern's grandson, Dad."

"Who?"

She drew his attention to Vern. "Your friend Vern's grandson."

"Is that right? How are you, son?"

Scott nodded at him. "Just came to find Grandpa for a game of checkers."

"You should see what Mrs. Hart made for her dad." Vern said to him.

"Oh?"

Sarah stood and gestured to her father's bed. "He's talking about this quilt. I made it for my father's birthday."

Scott surveyed the quilt, which Sarah had refolded and placed at the foot of the bed. "That's really nice. My wife likes to sew, too, but she hasn't done much lately."

"Sarah's always sewing something," William said. "Quilts are a specialty of hers."

"Know what's extraspecial about it?" Vern asked.

Scott looked down at him, a ready smile playing at his lips. "Why don't you tell me?"

"She made it out of William's old shirts."

Scott blinked and glanced at Sarah. "Really? That is interesting."

Sarah laughed. "Dad had several older flannel shirts that he liked, but they were getting thin on the elbows. I decided to put pieces of them into the quilt top. He can enjoy their colors, and they'll still keep him nice and warm."

Scott stepped over to the bed and fingered one of the red plaid squares that still held a pocket with a buttoned flap. "That's a very thoughtful gift."

"Thank you."

Scott positioned himself behind Vern's chair. "You ready to go down to the lounge and get beat at checkers?"

"Ha! We'll see about that." Vern lifted a hand in farewell. "Nice talking to you, William. And nice to meet you, Mrs. Hart."

"It's Sarah."

Sarah smiled as she watched them leave. Scott guided the wheelchair carefully through the doorway, all the time keeping up a cheerful interplay with his grandfather.

"Nice young man." She swung around toward her father again.

"You could help him find her," he said.

"Oh, you heard all that? I don't know, Dad."

"It's a terrible thing to lose someone you care about."

William's mother had disappeared when he was a young boy. He knew what it was like to lose someone close. He'd lived his whole life that way.

Sarah spread the flannel quilt on her father's bed and smoothed it down. When she'd finished, she looked over at him. He sat leaning back in his recliner, his eyes closed, and he gave a soft snore. Zipping her parka, she walked into the hall and closed the door.

As she entered the sitting room at the front of the nursing home, Scott Pickett was crossing the room carrying some packets of sugar. On a small table over near the aviary, Vern was setting up a checkerboard next to two large mugs that sat on the table.

Scott paused when he saw her. "Mrs. Hart, it was nice to meet you and your father. Thanks for talking to my grandpa."

"I enjoyed it. Sometimes my dad is a little fuzzy on conversation, but your grandfather seems sharp as a tack."

"Oh, he is. He's only here because he took a fall a few weeks ago."

"I'm sorry to hear that. Was he injured badly?"

"Cracked his tibia. That's why he's in the wheelchair. His shoulder was kind of messed up, too, and he had a lot of bruises. He stayed in the hospital a few days, then went to rehab for two weeks, but he was still weak. The doctor felt he ought to go into a skilled care home, where he could have supervision and therapy."

Sarah nodded. "Sometimes that's best, especially for older people who live alone."

Scott hesitated for a moment. "That quilt you made your father—Grandpa's right. It's very special."

"Thanks. I think he'll enjoy it."

"I wondered . . . do you sew for other people?"

"I've been known to make quilts for folks outside the family." She thought she knew what was coming.

"My wife McKenna doesn't sew much since she had our little boy. He keeps her hopping. But... well, I wondered how much it would cost for a quilt like that for Grandpa. He's got a closet full of shirts like that, and he only wears a few now. He seemed to really like the quilt, and it would mean a lot to him. Like you said, it's useful, but at the same time, it's..."

"Full of memories?" Sarah suggested.

"Exactly."

She nodded. "I like you, Scott, and I like your grandfather. I'd be happy to work on a quilt for him. My father's is all machine stitched, so it didn't take all that long."

His sunny grin broke out. "Terrific. I'll pay you, of course."

Sarah patted his arm. "Just bring me a few of his old flannel shirts." She opened her purse. "Let me give you a card with my address on it. Do you live here in Maple Hill?"

"Yes, ma'am."

She handed him one of her business cards. "You give me a call when you're ready to bring them over. I have some scraps left from Dad's in case I need to fill in a little."

"Don't you need more than that?"

She shrugged. "I'll pick up some batting and a flannel sheet for the backing, but I'll wait until I see what colors you bring me before I think about that."

"Thank you very much." Scott slipped the card into his pocket.

He walked with her to the door and reached to open it for her.

Another thought popped into Sarah's mind. "Scott..."

He paused with his hand on the doorknob. "Yeah?"

"That picture your grandfather carries around with him—the woman named Alice. Has he ever shown that to you before?"

"Many times." Scott sighed. "Don't tell me he dragged that out and made you look at it."

"No, it was accidental. It fell on the floor and... I just wondered who she is."

Scott shrugged. "We'd never heard of her until after Grandma died a couple of years ago. But since then, it's come up a lot. Alice. Apparently she was his girl before the war."

"He said he couldn't find her after the war ended."

"I'm not sure how hard he looked. I mean, he and Grandma were married in 1947, and they were very happy together, so he couldn't have been too heartbroken, could he?"

Sarah considered that. It certainly was easy to become nostalgic as time passed. To be sure after her husband Gerry passed away, she had spent many hours thinking about "the good old days."

Scott glanced over to where Vern waited, watching them across the large, sunny room. "Hey, I'd better get over there. It just bothers me a little that he talks about Alice Ward more now than he does Grandma." He flashed a smile. "Anyway, thanks for talking to him. I'm sure he gets lonesome."

"It was my pleasure. And you bring me those shirts, all right?" Sarah touched his sleeve. "Keep taking good care of your grandfather. I know how stressful that can be, especially when they drift off into the past. I'll enjoy making the quilt for him."

Sarah went out into the cold air. The sun was setting behind the hills to the west. She got into the car and headed for town, thinking about her family and Scott's. She hadn't thought she'd wind up this way—widowed, and with her father spending his last years in a nursing home. She'd always thought she and her husband Gerry would age together and enjoy this part of their lives as a couple. But Gerry had been gone five years now. She had her children and grandchildren, and she had dear friends and interests that kept her busy, but she missed Gerry terribly.

Her father knew what it was like. "It's a terrible thing to lose someone you care about." Sarah could reunite two people torn apart by war over fifty years ago. It was worth a shot.

A NOTE FROM THE EDITORS

Guideposts, a nonprofit organization, touches millions of lives every day through products and services that inspire, encourage and uplift. Our magazines, books, prayer network and outreach programs help people connect their faith-filled values to their daily lives. To learn more, visit www.guideposts. com or www.guidepostsfoundation.org.